"Dearly beloved…"

The minister's gaze swept the onlookers, then focused on Chloe and J.T., a small smile curving his lips. "We are gathered together to join this man and this woman in the state of holy matrimony."

"Who giveth this woman…?" the minister began, and before the words could be fully spoken Chloe's brother muttered the appropriate response and pressed her hand into J.T.'s palm. And then she was caught up in the beauty of words and phrases that promised to change her life forever.

She spoke her responses in a voice that barely trembled, heard J.T.'s own vows offered in dark, husky tones, and felt the cool circle of gold surround her ring finger as he placed it there. His kiss was circumspect, brief, but warm against her mouth. His lips touched her cheek and then whispered words against her ear.

"You won't be sorry. I promise…."

Reading and writing have always been major interests in **Carolyn Davidson**'s life. Even during her years of raising children and working in a full-time job she found time to read voraciously. However, her writing consisted of letters and an occasional piece of poetry. Now that the nest is empty she has turned to writing as a full-time occupation. She has been married for many years to a man who gives her total support and an abundance of love to draw on for inspiration.

Recent titles by the same author:

THE FOREVER MAN
THE MIDWIFE
THE BACHELOR TAX*
TANNER STAKES HIS CLAIM*
WISH UPON A STAR
  (short story in *One Christmas Wish*)
THE WEDDING PROMISE
MAGGIE'S BEAU

Edgewood, Texas mini-series

A MARRIAGE BY CHANCE

Carolyn Davidson

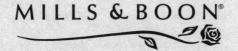

MILLS & BOON®

All the characters in this book have no existence outside the imagination of the author, and have no relation whatsoever to anyone bearing the same name or names. They are not even distantly inspired by any individual known or unknown to the author, and all the incidents are pure invention.

First published in Great Britain 2004
Harlequin Mills & Boon Limited,
Eton House, 18-24 Paradise Road, Richmond, Surrey TW9 1SR

© Carolyn Davidson 2002

ISBN 0 263 83955 9

Set in Times Roman 10½ on 11½ pt.
04-0304-88265

*Printed and bound in Spain
by Litografia Rosés S.A., Barcelona*

Prologue

Silver City, Nevada
March, 1894

Three queens and a pair of deuces appeared before him, and Peter Biddleton all but licked his lips as his eyes flickered to the mound of cash in the middle of the table. It was a cinch, he decided. He had bet first on the three ladies, tossing in his other two cards, and watching as the dealer slid two more in his direction. Now he felt the thundering of his heart as the pair dealt him nestled beside the aloof trio of royal blood.

"Reckon I can bet," he drawled, pushing in his last gold piece, watching as it rested against several more just like it, there where bits and pieces of cash lured him.

The dark-featured man across the table watched from beneath hooded eyelids, silent as he considered the cards he held. And then he placed them facedown on the table and nudged three gold coins toward the pot. "Got something you're proud of, sonny?" he asked mildly. "It'll cost you to stay in."

Peter aimed a futile glare at the man who spoke. Tall, dressed in the well-worn garb of a cowhand, the stranger had walked with an arrogant stride across the floor of Molly's Saloon only two hours before. He'd watched for long moments, then joined in the game already in progress. Now his dark, flat gaze focused on his lone opponent, the rest of the men surrounding the table watching with eager eyes the silent battle between the two men.

"That's the last of my money," Peter said reluctantly, glancing down again at the full house he was certain was a winner. *It felt right.* The cards were warm in his hand, the queens looking triumphant, the deuces paired beside them.

"Are you out?" the stranger asked, unmoving except for the lifting of his eyelids as he bent his attention on Peter's face.

"I've got a half interest in a ranch in Wyoming," Peter blurted. "Worth more than the whole pile," he muttered, his free hand gesturing at the seductive kitty in the middle of the table.

"Call me or fold." Lazily spoken, the words were a challenge, one Peter could not ignore.

"I'll bet the ranch," he said, making up his mind quickly, before the image of Chloe could force him away from the table and out the saloon door.

"Let's see your deed."

"I don't have it," Peter admitted. "But I'll handwrite a letter of ownership."

"Is there a lawyer in Silver City?" The dark eyes lifted to sort through the gathering crowd.

"I'm a lawyer." Stout and well dressed, a middle-aged man stepped forward, then directed his attention to Peter. "You sure you want to do this, son?"

Peter nodded, his jaw set, his hands sweating.

"Where's the ranch?" the lawyer asked, drawing a small notebook from his pocket. His pencil moved quickly across the page as Peter spoke, describing the location and size of the Double B Ranch, his father's legacy, and then he placed notebook and pencil on the table. ''Sign here,'' he said, watching as Peter's trembling fingers grasped the pencil.

Torn from the notebook, the single page fluttered in the air, settling with a whisper of sound atop the pile.

A long index finger nudged the brim of his black hat as the man across the table leaned forward, fanning four jacks across the battered tabletop.

''Let's see what you've got, boy.''

Chapter One

Ripsaw Creek, Wyoming
April, 1894

"Of all the stupid idiots in the world, why did my brother have to be at the top of the list?" Chloe Biddleton's hand clutched a single sheet of paper, the scrawled letters a tangible threat to everything she held dear. "Damn you, Peter," she snarled, glaring up at the shimmering sky as though her brother might be visible there among the clouds. And then she repeated the words, softly, in a barely heard whisper, as hot tears filled her eyes.

"Let me see it." Calm and patient, Hogan held out his hand. "Let me have the letter, Chloe." Reins in hand, her ranch foreman stood before her, and Chloe placed the missive she'd all but clenched into a wrinkled ball in his palm. Hogan spread it carefully, reading the blotted words and phrases slowly, and his face took on a deadly cast.

"Sold you out, didn't he?" He read it again, muttering phrases aloud. "A damn poker game. Boy never could hold five cards without losing his shirt." And then his voice deepened. "Jasper Thomas Flannery. Sounds like a city slicker to me, Chloe. And he's on his way to stake his claim."

"If Peter ever shows up here again, I swear I'll kill him." Chloe's anger knew no bounds as her gaze encompassed the house and barns surrounding her. "He lost half of my ranch to some dude, cleaned out our bank account, and I'm supposed to *understand*." Her shoulders slumped as Hogan placed a callused hand on her arm.

"He never loved the place the way you do, Chloe."

Her head lifted abruptly and her eyes glittered. "And that's supposed to make it all right? He loved spending the money Pa left. I'll bet he's having a good time going through every cent of our inheritance."

"Wouldn't be surprised," Hogan agreed mildly. "Don't get your drawers in a twist, boss. Maybe this fella will take a gander and decide to be a silent partner. Could be he's not interested in running a ranch."

"Yeah, and could be, with my luck, he'll want to run the whole show." She'd known early on that the day was headed for disaster. Losing a prized colt to colic in the early hours of the morning had been more of a heartbreak than a financial disaster, but that loss had set the tone of the whole livelong day.

She'd wished more than once for Aunt Tilly's comforting presence during the long hours. From mending a jagged barbed wire cut on a cowhand's arm to the burning of six loaves of bread, forgotten in the oven as she sewed up the injury, one thing after another had fallen into place, equaling total disaster. The sewing of torn flesh was bothersome, but she'd done it before. When it came to baking, the presence of Aunt Tilly was almost a necessity. And it would be several weeks before she returned for the summer months.

Now Hogan stood before her, weary from the long ride to town, where he'd picked up the mail and done the banking chores on her behalf. Wisely, she'd kept extra cash, both for minor emergencies and for the mortgage payment, beneath the mattress in her bedroom, away from Peter's grasping hands. At least the ranch was safe for the next six months.

Hogan cleared his throat and she looked up at him. *Don't kill the messenger.* The old adage held new meaning as she silently berated the man for the letter he'd carried.

"Don't get mad at me, Chloe," he told her, accurately reading the anger she tossed in his direction.

She wilted, accepting the letter from his hand, folding it carefully, almost feeling like she needed to preserve the latest threat to her welfare. "I'm not. Not really, Hogan. I'm just worn-out. I knew better than to count on Peter for any help. I guess I just didn't think he'd be such a hindrance." Her lips curved in a rueful smile, a gesture of apology to the man standing before her who worked so hard for so little recompense.

"Things'll get better," he said staunchly. "The herd looks good this spring, and you've got pret' near two dozen mares already dropped their foals. There's more calves out there than I can count—"

"And not enough hay to see us through to the first cutting," she reminded him glumly. "We need a good spring rain to green up the pastures. At least the river's running good, and we don't have to tote water."

"I arranged for a load of hay from Hale Winters on my way to town," Hogan told her. "He'll deliver it tomorrow."

Chloe sighed and turned from him to walk up the porch steps. "Maybe Jasper Thomas Flannery will be old and fat and not long for this world. Do you suppose he'll be willing to spring for a load of hay?" She laughed, a harsh sound unlike her usual cheerful demeanor. "Maybe when he discovers he hasn't won a gold mine, I won't have to put up with him for long."

"Yeah, and maybe those hogs out in the pen will take

off flyin' any minute now.'' Hogan lifted his gaze to a puff of dust in the distance. ''Either we got company comin', or that's a dust devil whirlin' up the road.''

Chloe turned back to follow his pointing finger, and then turned to meet his gaze. ''Jasper Thomas, himself. How much do you want to bet?''

His horse was trail-weary, his saddlebags nearly empty, and his stomach in need of a good home-cooked meal. The bank in Ripsaw Creek was richer for the deposit he'd just made, and unless he missed his guess, the woman standing in front of the white ranch house a hundred yards ahead was his new partner.

A firm believer in fate, he'd sat in on the poker game on a hunch. Weary of wandering, his spirit yearning for a place to call his own. Now, at thirty-two, he'd decided to sink his funds into a homestead, settle down and think about a future. One that didn't include a deck of cards. California was calling, a nebulous dream of home, and maybe even a family, luring him.

Four jacks. Four pieces of heavy, well-worn paper, had put the Double B Ranch in his pocket. Only half of it, he reminded himself. But with a woman as his partner, he'd still be in charge. Another look at the female watching him diluted the strength of that assumption.

J. T. Flannery touched his hat brim, lowering it a bit, the better to shade his eyes, and stiffened his spine. Trouble. He could smell it three hundred feet, dead ahead. The boy had been a soft touch, a weakling of the first water, a traitor to his family's heritage.

The sister looked to be another story altogether.

She was short, but sturdy, with a neat compact body tucked into a pair of trousers and a dark shirt, and from her stance, he'd say she was halfway to being in a temper. Not that he could blame her any. He'd warrant she was expecting him, given the fact that the man pointed out as her foreman had collected the mail in town, and J.T. was dead certain Peter's letter was contained in the batch. Generally, a barkeep knew everyone in the area, and the one J.T. had quizzed was free with information.

He'd watched as the lean cowhand rode from the bank to the general store, where the post office occupied one corner, noted the scowl on his face as the man examined the outside of the single envelope among the various catalogues and periodicals he held in his hand. An hour seemed like a reasonable length of time to dally along the way, assuring the letter would be read before they rolled out the welcome mat at the ranch. And at that thought he'd grinned privately, before lifting his considerable length into the saddle, and set off for the ranch.

"What do you want, stranger?" The woman asked as J.T. rode within six feet of her, refusing to back off as the big stallion snorted and stretched out his long neck to check her scent. She was brave, he'd give her that much.

"J. T. Flannery, ma'am, coming to claim my winnings."

From the look in her eyes, it might not have been the brightest opening he could have come up with. She looked as though she were wishing for a shotgun to aim in his direction, and he tried in vain to restrain the satisfied grin that curved his lips. "I take it you're not happy to see me," he continued smoothly. And then he answered his own query with a slow shake of his head.

"Naw, I didn't think you would be." Watching her, he wondered at his own lack of caution. She wasn't armed, but the man behind her wore a gun and she looked capable of snatching it from the holster and aiming it in his direction.

"You thought right, mister."

Her voice was calmer now, but no less threatening for all its softness. He'd met more women than he could shake a stick at, but this one was in a niche of her own. No fussy ruffles for Peter Biddleton's sister. No curls adorned her head. No paint or powder covered the freckles that thrived on her cheeks and across her nose. She was pure female, all right, but didn't bother to dress up the packaging. Her long, dark hair was braided, the thick plait wound around her head, and her eyes were the icy blue of a winter sky.

She stuck her palms into the back pockets of her trousers and he almost grinned again at the picture she presented. If she only realized how her stance emphasized the lush lines of her bosom, how her neat little figure was revealed by the pose she'd taken, she'd no doubt shoot his eyes out for the liberties they took.

"So you're the rotten bastard who cheated my brother out of his inheritance," she said, her gaze narrowing as she took his measure. "And I suppose you think I'm going to welcome you and show you around, don't you?"

He shifted in the saddle, and in a swift movement slid to the ground, facing her head-on. His jaw set, he fisted his hands against his hips, the better to control the sudden urge for battle her remark had brought to the surface. "Number one, ma'am—" his hesitation was just a bit longer than a heartbeat "—my mother and father were duly married when I was born. I take it as an insult to the lady who changed my drawers to be named illegitimate."

He caught a glimpse of regret in her eyes, and then it vanished as quickly as it had come to be, and he softened his stance. "As to the other, no, I don't expect a welcome. But—" this pause was longer, and he included the man beside her in his lingering look "—but I do expect to have full access to every single speck of property I own a half share of. That includes the house, the outbuildings, and every living creature in the barns and out of them."

She inhaled sharply, and her face was white beneath the freckles now. "I'll be seeing a lawyer in town as soon as I can make arrangements, Mr. Flannery. If your claim is valid—''

"It is, ma'am. I assure you the transfer of deed was accomplished by a genuine attorney in Silver City, Nevada."

"Was that where you met my brother?" she asked tightly.

He nodded. "He was in a poker game in Molly's Saloon, and I sat in on the action. Trust me, lady. If it hadn't been me, he'd have lost the ranch to someone else. He was headed for disaster when I walked in, and I just sat there and waited for it to happen."

"I told you the boy couldn't play poker for crap," the tall ranch hand said harshly.

"You the head man here?" J.T. asked, and was rewarded by a glare from the woman before him.

"I'm head of the place," she said. "Hogan's my foreman."

J.T. held out his hand, fixing his gaze on the husky rancher. Hogan's hesitation was brief, and his callused palm gave as good as it got as the two hands clasped with a show of force. "You any good at your job?" J.T. asked quietly, assessing the man with a glance. Well put together, wearing his work clothes like a second skin, he stood tall and straight, his eyes wary as he lent silent support to the woman.

"I like to think so."

"He's the best there is," his employer stated firmly. "I'm Chloe Biddleton," she said grudgingly. She slid her hands from their moorings and fished the letter from her front pocket. "According to this, your name is Jasper Thomas—"

"J.T." Firm and harsh, his voice spoke the abbreviated title, and her chin lifted as she nodded.

"J.T. it is, then."

"You want to come out to the barn and take a look around?" Hogan asked, and J.T. wondered if the man sought to lessen the pressure on Chloe. She looked like a good strong wind would blow her over right now, her faith in her brother in shambles and faced, out of the blue, with a new partner.

"Might as well," he answered. "My horse could use a rubdown and some feed." He nodded at Chloe, feeling a twinge of regret. Her head high, her lips compressed, she looked like a woman about to burst into tears, if he was any judge, and he'd just as soon not be in the same vicinity if that happened. A crying woman was about his least favorite thing to deal with, right alongside a cornered rattler or a drunk with a gun in his hand.

The two men led their horses toward the big barn, where a lone cowhand lingered near the doorway. Chloe watched in silence as they ambled across the yard, halting next to the horse trough for the big stallion to drop his muzzle into the water. J. T. Flannery glanced back at her, a quick summary from narrowed eyes, and she felt a flush warm her cheeks. The man was arrogant. Not only that, he was equipped with a tall, rangy body, and an intelligence she could not mistake, gleaming from dark eyes that had viewed her with an appraisal which left her aware of her imperfections.

She knew her limitations as a woman, had looked in her mirror enough times to recognize her lack of beauty. Her fair skin invited freckles, and though her hair was thick and long, she thought sometimes it was more trouble than it was worth. Too short to be impressive, and too well-rounded to be chic, she'd found it handy to have a man she could rely on when it came to running the ranch. Her dependence on Hogan was a trust he'd lived up to.

After Pa died two years ago, she'd taken hold, and in the past year, she'd managed to keep afloat. Until the discovery six months ago that her bank account was bone dry, and Peter had left town with every red cent she'd counted on to buy supplies and coast into the summer. The ability to make the payment on the mortgage was a blessing, but without spare cash, she was faced with the delivery of hay tomorrow and the pride-crushing task of asking for credit from her neighbor.

Thankfully, the general store would keep her on the books until she could round up a few yearling steers and sell them. But at spring weight, it would be for a price less than their worth. She sighed as she climbed the two steps to the porch, then shivered as the wind sought her in the shelter of the back door.

The sadness that overwhelmed her couldn't be helped. Peter had stolen more than the money Pa had left. He'd made his departure with her youthful optimism in his pocket.

Now, she faced a struggle for survival, and a rusty laugh accompanied the first hot tear that streaked down her cheek. At least she had a partner to share the process.

The choice of sleeping beneath a tree or in the bunkhouse with six men who had no reason to enjoy his presence among them was a toss-up, J.T. decided. If he'd had another alternative such as sleeping in the house, he'd have joyfully embraced it, but somehow he didn't expect Chloe to offer him a bedroom right off the bat. She'd decided to wait until morning to take the trip to Ripsaw Creek, once Hogan murmured an admonition in an undertone. And then she'd looked up at J.T. with defiance.

"The barn or the bunkhouse, mister. Or beneath a tree in the orchard if you like."

He left her the remnants of her pride, nodding and sliding his bedroll beneath his arm as he sauntered toward the orchard. The barn was too enclosed, and he was a stranger there. Better to be on the outskirts, with a view of house and bunkhouse. He'd slept in worse situations, and the bedroll was warm. Traveling light meant he only had one more clean shirt, and unless he headed to town on a shopping trip, he'd better beg the use of a scrub board from his partner.

The moon was new, a thin sliver against a cloudless sky. Stars filled the horizon, providing a canopy of silver sequins overhead, visible through branches only beginning to show signs of leafing out. At least it didn't look like rain, he decided, and leaned against the tree trunk he'd chosen, wrapped in wool, his gun at hand. The house was dark, all but a single window on the second floor. White curtains floated from the open pane, and he thought of the woman who slept with fresh air as her companion.

Chloe couldn't be more than—what? Twenty-one, maybe a year or so older. Too young to be faced with the burden of running a ranch, especially with a lack of cash, if what he'd overheard at the bank was to be believed. A clerk, in an undertone that carried to J.T.'s hearing, spoke of Peter Biddleton's perfidy to a townsman, shaking his head as he told the tale. The rascal had walked off with the contents of their joint bank account, leaving Chloe empty-handed and in desperate need of funds.

As J.T. watched, a figure clothed in white passed the window. Probably a nightgown, he decided, his eyes focusing on the movement of curtains and the hand that brushed a filmy panel to one side as its owner looked out upon the yard and toward the barn. Decently covered, she was still a temptation, he decided. A couple of the men sleeping in the bunkhouse might look with greedy eyes upon that slender form. His gaze became thoughtful.

If she were his, he'd— But she wasn't, he reminded himself. And stood no chance of belonging to him. Nevertheless, she was his partner, unwilling or not. He owed her his protection. His mother had taught him a few things before the fire that cost him the lives of both his parents. One was the sanctity of womanhood. It seemed that he'd taken on the task of keeping Chloe Biddleton safe, along with the responsibility of keeping the ranch afloat.

Breakfast was a simple affair. Tea and toasted bread usually. Today was doomed to be different. Chloe watched as her new partner approached the porch, his bedroll once more tucked beneath his arm, his hat pulled low, hiding his expression from view.

"I don't suppose you've got coffee in there," he began from the other side of the screened door. His voice was early-morning husky, and she rued, for just a moment, the urge that had sent him to the orchard to sleep. It wouldn't have been any trouble to toss a set of sheets on Peter's bed or offer him the parlor sofa to sleep on.

And so her tones were moderate as she waved him into the kitchen. "I have tea made. Does that suit you?"

His nose twitched and a glum expression turned his mouth down. "I can just about stomach it. Coffee's better." He cast a look at the stove. "I know how to make it, if you have the fixings."

"In the pantry," she answered, and then her upbringing had her on her feet. "I'll get it. Sit down." In moments, she'd rinsed the pot, filled it halfway and added coffee. The stove was freshly stoked, and she placed the blue-speckled pot on the hottest area. "It won't take long. Would you like some bread? It got neglected yesterday when I had an emergency to tend to."

He eyed the scorched loaves she'd rescued from the oven and nodded. "I'll cut off the worst of it, if you'll tell me where the knives are."

Chloe waved at the shelf over the stove and he reached for the longest utensil, then busied himself with sawing off the darkest parts from the loaf she'd already cut into. "I heard from Hogan that you sewed up a man's arm. That your emergency?'' he asked, opening the oven door to place two thick slices of bread on the rack.

''Yes. It wasn't pretty, but I managed to do the job. Eight stitches.''

''You've got a strong stomach,'' he said, turning his head, his eyes fastening on her hands as she tore a piece of toasted bread into small bits.

''It comes with the job,'' she said. Her appetite was gone, what little there'd been to start with. The ride to town was a necessity, although probably futile. Peter's signature was strong and familiar on the paper she'd looked at yesterday. No doubt existed in her mind; yet, if there was any slight chance, any hope at all, she must pursue this to its end result.

''I'll be leaving for town in half an hour,'' she told him, watching as he opened the oven door to check on his bread.

He speared it with the knife and held it before him as he turned to face her. Chloe waved at the buffet where a stack of plates waited, and he followed her silent instructions. Plate in hand, he sat down across from her and she shoved the saucer of butter closer, offering her own knife for his use.

''Thanks,'' he said, absorbed with spreading a thick layer of her butter on the crusty surface. ''I didn't eat supper last night. This smells good.''

''Why didn't you go to the bunkhouse? They had a whole pot of chili.''

His shrug was telling, and she felt a pang of guilt. Courtesy called for a meal to any stranger coming down the road. And she'd sat in here eating her soup while J.T. went hungry. ''I wasn't sure how welcome I'd be, to tell you the truth,'' he said after a moment. ''Figured I'd wait till today, once you found out that my claim is on the up-and-up before I tackled your ranch hands.''

"Tackled?" She held her cup of tea midair, her eyes pinned to him as she considered his choice of words.

His look was level as he nodded. "They'll have to decide if they can follow my orders or not, before I decide if they still have a job here."

"Before you decide—" she caught her breath and almost choked on the bread she'd just begun to chew "—I hired most of those men, and if they cause a problem, I'll do the firing. That's not your problem."

His head tilted a bit as he considered her. "Maybe that's a matter of viewpoint," he said. "They'll take orders from me, or I'll show them the road, ma'am. I'm half owner, remember? I mean to begin as I plan to go on with this arrangement."

And she'd felt guilty for leaving him in the orchard overnight, and for not feeding him any soup. The tea was bitter on her tongue and the bread was a mass of gluten in her mouth. "That remains to be seen, Mr. Flannery," she muttered, rising and wishing she could spit out the sodden mouthful that muffled her words.

From the stove the scent of coffee met her nostrils, and she snatched up the coffeepot with a folded dish towel, dumping it in the sink. It splattered her trousers and sprayed across the front of her shirt, coffee grounds scattering the floor at her feet.

"Burn yourself?" he drawled, his eyes watchful. And yet, there was an underlying note of concern she thought as she shook her head. Not for the world would she admit to the stinging sensation on the tender flesh above her waist. With a glare he seemed to ignore, she left the kitchen, stomping up the stairs to her room where she slammed the door with a flip of her wrist.

The shirt hit the floor and she strode to the long mirror, peering at herself, one finger tracing the pink skin where the damp fabric had left its mark. Her washcloth was handy and she rinsed it in the pitcher, then wrung it out and placed it over the area, her hand trembling as she held it in place. Not from the pain, for there was little to bear, but from the chagrin of looking a fool before the man in her kitchen.

She loosened her belt and dropped the trousers to the floor, stepping out of them readily as she levered off her low shoes. Stocking-footed, she walked to the bureau and pulled open a drawer, seesawing it a bit as she worked one-handed to find fresh clothing. There wasn't much choice, her daily wardrobe consisting of a variety of shirts and several pair of nondescript trousers.

Back before the mirror, she removed the damp cloth and examined her skin. It wouldn't blister, she decided, only be touchy for a day or so. And that she could live with. Easier than she could tolerate the arrogant cowboy who'd come to play squatter on her ranch.

He was still there when she stalked into the kitchen minutes later. "You all right?" he asked, holding a cup before himself.

"Are you drinking my tea?" she asked, fury chilling her words.

"Not yours, ma'am. I found my own cup and poured from the potful you made. I thought you might like fresh, so I poured yours out."

He'd cleaned the floor, too, she noted, and wrung out the rag, placing it on the edge of the sink. Somehow, that small act cooled her anger and she only nodded as she refilled her cup and leaned against the buffet to drink it.

"I'll ride along with you, if you don't mind," he said.

"I don't need company," she told him. "Just give me the paper Peter signed and I'll take it to town to show the lawyer."

He shook his head. "You may not need company, but that paper proves my claim. It doesn't leave my pocket till you hear the verdict for yourself. And then I'll deposit it in the bank vault for safekeeping. I've already spoken to the bank president.''

She felt a flush rise, and swallowed hot words of anger. ''You discussed this with Mr. Webster? You told him that my brother gambled away half my ranch?''

He nodded. ''I also told him it was worth his hide if that information went any further. As far as anyone else knows, I bought it from your brother. I told Hogan to let your hands know they'd be facing trouble if they let the cat out of the bag.''

Her shoulders slumped and she placed her cup on the buffet. ''I'll saddle a horse and be ready to leave in five minutes.'' Unable to meet his knowing gaze, she tugged on her boots that sat by the back door, then snatched a jacket from a hook and jammed her arms into the sleeves. ''I'd suggest you do the same. And bring your damn piece of paper along with you.''

Chapter Two

"The whole thing looks legal to me, Chloe. Are you certain that's Peter's signature?" Paul Taylor returned the letter she'd offered for his inspection. Then, while awaiting her reply, he picked up the document J.T. had offered as proof of his claim.

Chloe looked for a final time at the wrinkled letter and felt the hand of fate clutch at her heart. "Yes, I'm about as sure as I can be, without watching him write it. He has a distinctive hand." Not neat, but certainly no one else she knew scrawled quite so boldly as Peter when he set pen to paper. "Can I do anything at all about it?" she asked quietly, ignoring J.T.'s presence at her side.

"Hmm—no, I doubt it," Paul said, shaking his head as he finished reading the simple note the lawyer in Silver City had written up. "He's tied it up neat and tidy, I'd say. Peter signed away his interest in your ranch, sure enough." He glanced up at J.T. and his eyes were glacial. "Took advantage of the young man, didn't you?"

J.T. returned the icy stare. Then, as Chloe shifted beside him, he stifled the harsh words that sprang to mind and softened his stance. "No, not really," he murmured. "The boy was set on gambling away everything he owned, it seemed, and I figured it was worth my while to spend a couple of hours helping him along. I gave him a stake when the game broke up, and advised him to go home and face the music.''

He looked down at Chloe's upturned face and shrugged. ''Apparently, he decided against it, and wrote his sister a letter instead.''

Paul watched the byplay in silence, then held out the document to J.T. and nodded, a curt movement of his head. ''You're in the clear, as far as I can tell. Enjoy your winnings, mister.''

His tone gentled as he turned his gaze on Chloe. ''Can I do anything else to help?''

''No.'' She shook her head, not willing to encourage him in any way, shape or form. Paul Taylor had more than once expressed a desire to keep company with her; and though he was a nice man, she wasn't interested in pursuing a courtship with him. ''I think you've covered it all,'' she said quietly, and turned to leave Paul's office.

The door closed behind her and J.T. caught up with her rapid pace as she headed for her horse. ''Slow down, lady,'' he said smoothly. ''Let me drop this off at the bank and I'll ride back with you.''

''I don't need your company,'' she told him sharply. ''And I don't intend to be seen waltzing around town with you.'' Leading her mount to the edge of the boardwalk, she stepped into the stirrup and onto the saddle.

J.T. watched, and his chuckle galled her to the core. ''You need to carry a mounting block around with you, ma'am. Either that, or get a shorter horse.''

She swung the black mare around and faced the man. ''I've got shorter horses, but this is the one I prefer. Keep your advice to yourself, Mr. Flannery. I'm sure you'll find good use for all your knowledge when you start working the ranch.''

He rocked back on his heels, hands thrust into his pockets, and his grin was cheeky, she decided. "Never said I had a lot of experience at ranching, Chloe. But I'm more than willing to learn the details from you."

"And here I thought you were already making decisions about changing my way of doing things," she taunted, holding a tight rein on her horse. The black pranced sideways, fighting the bit, and J.T. reached out a hand to grip the reins beneath the horse's jaw.

"Now, here, I'm qualified to give a little advice, ma'am. The first thing you need to do is let up on those reins," he said quietly. "Don't let your temper spill over onto the animal you're riding. You'll have her all lathered up before you leave town." The mare tossed her head and J.T. released his hold. He reached to tilt his hat brim a bit, then watched as Chloe turned the horse in a tight half circle and loosened the reins.

Her mount broke into a quick trot, and J.T.'s eyes lit with appreciation. The woman could ride, sitting the saddle like she'd been born there. Her head high, nodding at several passersby, Chloe rode quickly toward the edge of town, and J.T. headed for the bank. In moments he'd placed his proof of ownership into an envelope and watched as Mr. Webster deposited it in the big vault.

His next stop was at the general store, where he chose pants and shirts to fill in his sparse wardrobe, adding socks and drawers to the pile before he nodded to the woman who'd gathered the assortment together for him. "How much?" he asked.

"Let me see," she told him, obviously adding the total in her head. "That'll come to four dollars, even." She took his money and hesitated. "You stayin' at the Double B Ranch?"

"Word gets around fast, doesn't it?" he said with a grin.

"Yeah, I'm the fella that bought out Pete Biddleton's share. Just arrived yesterday."

"That boy's a scamp," the woman said, shaking her head in judgment. "Never figured he'd amount to much, even before his pa passed on. Since then he's been pretty predictable, leavin' everything up to his sister to tend to."

"She seems pretty capable to me," J.T. allowed mildly.

"And it's a good thing she is," the woman snapped. "That boy spent more time shufflin' cards than he did workin' the ranch. His pa was ready to disown him, according to Mr. Webster, then the old man died real sudden like, and the boy inherited half of everything. Doesn't seem fair to Chloe, if you ask me."

"Well, you never know how things will work out, do you?" J.T. said, picking up his package. "I assure you I'll do my share of work at the ranch. She may be better off with me there, than with the last partner she had."

"She's been the backbone of the place since she was sixteen, when her mama took sick and died. Folks around here think a lot of Chloe," the woman said, her eyes scanning J.T. as if she issued a warning.

"I'm sure they do," he said agreeably. "She seems like a fine woman." He headed for the door, aware of listening ears, grinning to himself as he thought of the discussion he would miss once the door closed behind him. He'd given the town a brand-new topic of gossip today and hadn't offered much for them to base their speculation on.

The ride back to the ranch was long, spanning almost two hours, and he wondered how often Chloe made the trek. Between them, they probably should have picked up supplies, but buying groceries was no doubt the last thing on her mind right now. She'd gone home empty-handed today, with only her frustration and anger for company. By the time she got to the ranch, she'd probably be in a stew, ready to make his life a misery.

He'd have to watch his step, especially when he announced his intention to move into the house. His new partner might be small, but he'd be willing to bet she knew how to handle a gun. And getting a load of buckshot aimed in his direction would certainly put a damper on his day.

"You're gonna do what?" Hogan's exasperated query was met by a shrug.

"I'm going to fix up a room for Mr. Flannery to sleep in," Chloe said quietly. "He owns half the ranch, and that gives him the right to Peter's bedroom, I'd say."

"When did you decide to be so easygoin'?" Hogan asked. "Last I talked to you, you were hell-bent on makin' the man's life a misery. I thought sure you'd make him stay in the barn or the bunkhouse."

"I know," she said. "I thought so, too, but he gave Peter a stake after the poker game and advised him to come back home. At least that's what he told Paul Taylor. I guess he doesn't have any reason to lie about it." She looked toward the town road where the big stallion would shortly appear, and decided she'd pretty well gotten over her mad. Fair was fair, and if J.T. had tried to do right by Peter, he deserved at least the treatment she would offer anyone else.

Hogan was silent for a minute, as he digested J.T.'s generosity. "He seems a good enough man to me," he said finally. "So long as he doesn't start throwin' his weight around, we'll get along all right, I expect."

"Don't count on that," Chloe told him, remembering J.T.'s remarks. "He may be trying to run roughshod over all of us before he's done." She sighed, thinking of the tasks awaiting her in the house. "Once Aunt Tilly shows up, I'll be free to work with you on roundup."

"And I'll feel better about having Flannery in the house with you," Hogan said bluntly. "I don't like to think about folks making remarks, with you and your new partner sharing the house. If you're giving him Peter's room do you need to be moving furniture or anything?'' he asked. ''I can send one of the boys up to give you a hand.''

Chloe shook her head. ''No, he'll get Peter's room just as it is. Clean sheets is about as far as I'll go to get it ready for him. And as far as propriety's concerned, I've been doing a man's job for a lot of years already, Hogan. Folks quit talking about me a long time ago. I don't think half of them even consider me a woman. I'm just a rancher. And that suits me just fine.''

Hogan shook his head. ''Maybe. Maybe not, Chloe. This might be a good thing for you, set you to thinking about woman stuff, instead of pushin' yourself so hard. And another thing. You gonna be doing the cooking for Flannery, or send him out to the bunkhouse for his grub?''

She hesitated and then, casting another long look at the town road, made her decision. ''I'll feed him in the house. If it was Peter, I'd cook for him. The man is half owner, no matter whether I like it or not. And once Aunt Tilly gets here, she'll be cooking for everyone anyway.''

''Chloe?'' From the bottom step of the long, curved stairway, J.T. called her name, then listened as light footsteps moved overhead. A door opened and closed and he watched as Chloe hesitated at the top of the stairs. ''Hogan said you were fixing up a room for me.''

''Did he?'' Her foot touched the top step, and she grasped the banister as she made her way toward him. Pausing two steps above him, she hesitated, looking down at his upturned face. ''I'd begun to think your hat was a permanent part of you,'' she said idly, her gaze lifting to where dark waves cascaded almost to his collar.

''I take it off every once in a while,'' he told her. ''When I eat and sleep anyway.'' Refusing to give way, he watched her patiently, waiting for her response, and then nudged her with another query.

"What changed your mind?"

"About the room?" Her shrug lifted one shoulder. "You own half the house. The least I could do was let you have one room to sleep in."

He stepped back, allowing her passage past him, and then followed as she moved down the wide hallway to the kitchen. Leaning his shoulder on the doorjamb, he watched as she snatched an apron from a hook near the pantry, halting at the sink to wash her hands.

"I'm heating up chicken soup from last night, if you'd like to have a bowl," she told him. "I'll cook supper after a while, but this ought to hold you over for now."

"I appreciate that." For some reason she'd changed her tune, and he searched her profile for a clue to her mood. Women were usually a puzzle, and this one was no exception. "Some reason why you've decided to allow me in the house?" he asked, noting the subtle hesitation in her movements at his words. She paused in the pantry door, cans of fruit in her hands.

"I already explained that." The cans hit the table with a thump. "You own half of it," she said simply. "Or at least half of the part that isn't mortgaged."

J.T. ambled toward the round table in the middle of the room. "I didn't know there was a mortgage on it. Peter didn't tell me that." He shot her a sidelong glance as he pulled a chair from beneath the oilcloth-draped table, then hesitated. An offer of help might be appreciated. "You want me to get out the dishes?"

"All right." She pulled a kettle from the back of the stove, lifting the lid to inspect the contents. "This is almost ready. We'll have shortcake with it. I made biscuits." The tinned peaches sat on the buffet and she pulled out a can opener from a drawer, offering it in his direction. "You know how to use one of these?"

"I reckon I can figure it out," he said, tossing the utensil in the air and catching it by the handle. "I've kept one in my saddlebag ever since I discovered all the different things I could do with it."

"Those saddlebags looked pretty flat to me," she said, lifting an eyebrow as she glanced again in his direction. "You travel light."

"Doesn't pay to haul too much around with you, I've found," he said, working at the cans of peaches. "Where do you want these?"

Chloe pointed at a blue bowl on the buffet. "Pour them in there. Soup bowls are in the left hand door, spoons are on the table in the jar." She picked up a ladle and lifted the lid of the kettle, watching as the steam rose. "Why don't you hand me the bowls?"

Abandoning the peaches for a moment, J.T. did as she asked, reaching to accept the hot vessel from her hand. Beneath his callused fingers, the back of her hand was soft, and he thought she slid it from his touch with haste. But not rapidly enough to dispel the effect of warm skin and the faint scent of soap wafting from her hair.

He placed the bowl on the table with care, reflecting on the woman behind him. This wasn't in the plan, this sudden awareness of her as a female. He'd assessed her yesterday, viewed her with an eye to getting in her good graces, hoping to ease into the running of this operation without any amount of hassle. That alone had been a futile thought, he decided, recalling her eyes spitting fury in his direction.

Taking a liking to the woman was a far cry from being attracted to the female element. And why that was a fact was beyond his reckoning right now. He only knew that for a moment, there'd been a recognition of that subtle warming within him that signaled desire.

"I'll get the biscuits from the oven," Chloe said from behind him, and he turned, grasping the second bowl, only to find she'd slid her hand from contact with his, her eyes avoiding him. Her movements were brisk as she retrieved the biscuits, as if she were more than familiar with the kitchen and the tasks inherent in providing meals. Yet, who had she cooked for, he wondered. The boy had taken his leave months before, apparently.

Chloe had been alone. Alone with a handful of ranch hands, and the awesome responsibility of turning a profit from a ranch that was struggling along without a bank account to dip into. *Damn.* Peter Biddleton had a lot to answer for.

"Who's Aunt Tilly?" he asked idly, picking a spoon from the jar in the center of the table.

"My father's sister," Chloe told him. "Where did you hear about her?"

"Hogan told me she'd be here soon." He grinned. "That was when he told me there'd be a chaperon to keep me in line."

Chloe turned a sharp look in his direction. "You'll mind your manners or end up in the bunkhouse, Aunt Tilly or no." She picked up her spoon and dipped it into the fragrant soup. "She came to us after Pa died, pitched in and took care of things. I ended up working the ranch, taking Pa's place. When cold weather came that year, she took a train south to her daughter's place for the winter. Did the same thing before the first snowfall back before Christmas. I got a letter from her last week, saying she'd be back as soon as the weather broke, probably within two weeks."

"Did you ever think of offering her a permanent job here?"

Chloe looked up at him as she buttered a biscuit. "She may decide to stick around, once she sees you here. She's a real stickler when it comes to respectability, and she won't like the idea of our sharing the house.''

"I pretty much expected a battle over that," he said quietly. "You surprised me, Chloe."

"I've learned there's some things you've just got to live with," she said. "It seems you're on *my* list, J. T. Flannery."

The youth named Willie was cocky. There was no other word to describe the toss of his head and the arrogant look he offered as Chloe entered the barn. "Ma'am?" His single word caught her attention and she turned at his bidding. "You need anything?" he asked, his gaze sweeping her length.

"No," she answered sharply. "I'm just looking for Hogan."

"He's out back, talking to Lowery."

J.T. watched, noting the appraising look the boy cast on Chloe's backside, bristled as the grin reappeared once she was out of sight and inhaled sharply. His fist clenched as he stepped noiselessly from the tack room. Willie glanced in his direction, and the grin vanished. "You need me, J.T.?" he asked smoothly. "I was just fixin' to clean the stalls."

"Sounds like a good job for you," J.T. answered. He watched as Willie snatched a pitchfork from the wall and turned to the closest stall. "I'd suggest you remember your place, young'un. I've watched you for three days."

Willie looked back over his shoulder. "And what's that supposed to mean?" Defiance edged his words.

"Miss Chloe is the owner of this spread. She's way out of your class."

A sly grin curved one corner of Willie's mouth. "Can't help it if I admire a good-looking female, can I?"

"You make any move toward my partner, son, and you'll be in more trouble than you can imagine."

"Kinda slick, the way you rode in here and took over, mister," Willie said, leaning indolently on the pitchfork.

"I'm legally half owner of the place. You want to challenge my authority here?" J.T.'s voice deepened, and his clenched fist opened against his thigh. Poised, he ached for the younger man to dispute his words. But it was not to be. The boy's gaze wavered and he shook his head, sliding the pitchfork beneath a section of soggy straw.

A nearby wheelbarrow received the load, and Willie turned back to his chore.

J.T. strode past him, catching a glimpse of Chloe's checkered shirt beyond the far doorway. Two men stood before her, arguing heatedly, and J.T. grinned, surmising the dispute in progress.

"Hell, I've worked with worse than this," the redheaded cowhand thundered, waving a bandaged forearm in the air.

"Not for me, you haven't," Hogan countered, his jaw thrusting forward.

"How about some light duty?" J.T. asked, approaching the trio.

Chloe's mouth closed with a snap, and her eyebrows lowered. "I can handle this."

J.T. shrugged negligently. "I imagine so, ma'am. Just thought I'd mention that the tack room needs some attention. Enough work to keep a man busy for a couple of days, I'd say."

"I earn my keep," Lowery said, pale beneath his freckles. Frustration rode each syllable, and J.T. nodded agreeably.

"I've heard that," he said, a bold-faced lie, to be sure, but one he didn't think either Chloe or Hogan would dispute. "Nobody's saying otherwise, Lowery. Just makes sense to me to let the thing heal properly, give the cut a chance to mend." He tilted his hat back and faced the man head-on. "Every job on a ranch is of equal value, far as I can see. It takes well-tended tack to work with horses, and clean stalls to keep them healthy."

His shrug was offered to Chloe. "What do you say, partner?"

Her eyes still glittered with subdued indignation, but she stifled it, earning a grin. "I won't argue with that," she replied, then turned back to Hogan. "Are you picking up more hay from the Winters' place today?"

His glance encountered J.T.'s as he hesitated. "Thought maybe you might want to talk to him. If you take the wagon, he'll have his men load it for you."

"Why don't I go with you?" J.T. asked smoothly, taking her arm and leading her back toward the barn. "Do we pay cash on the barrel, or wait till the next trip into town?" It seemed not a subject to discuss in front of hired hands, even though Hogan was obviously privy to financial dealings.

"He'll wait," Chloe said quietly, snatching her arm from his grasp. "I don't care if you go along. You might's well know the bottom line, anyway." She turned to face him, and a glance over her shoulder told him that Willie stood just inside the door.

"Let's take a walk," J.T. said, his glare sending Willie into motion.

"All right." Chloe set the pace and they headed for the corral fence, climbing in unison to perch on the top rail. Before them, three young steers moved aimlessly within the confined area. "How much you think they're worth?" Chloe asked as J.T. settled beside her.

"How much do you need?" he countered, placing his hand careful inches from hers.

"Right now, enough for a couple loads of hay. I can sell these three in town."

"That's not good business," he said flatly.

"Maybe not," she agreed. "But I won't take advantage of a neighbor."

J.T. nodded, judging the weight of the animals Hogan had penned. He looked down, considering his options, his fingers gripping the rail he perched on. His quick gaze noted the hand beside his own, and measured the contrast, hers narrow, tanned, yet feminine, his own broad and scarred from numerous encounters. One slash, from a broken bottle swung in his direction, had merited a line of stitches. Another pale nick told of a knife blade that he'd barely escaped.

She lifted her hand, and her index finger lightly traced the raised scar, its ragged edges pale against his bronzed skin. "You've been pretty battered in your time, haven't you, cowboy?"

"Never had anybody like you around to mend my bruises," he said with a grin. "Old Lowery doesn't know how lucky he is." And then his mouth firmed. "I'm not a cowboy. Maybe a sometimes gambler, and I've spent my share of time on the range, riding herd when I needed a grubstake. But never a *cowboy*." Spoken aloud, he gave the word a distasteful sound.

"Didn't mean to insult you," she said. "I just figured you've been riding for someone, somewhere, to come up with the usual assortment of scars a man collects."

His look was long, and she glanced aside. "How much do you need?" he repeated.

"I told you. Enough for a couple loads of hay." Her hand lifted to rest atop her thigh, and he mourned its absence. He'd enjoyed its presence, basked in the warmth of soft flesh against his callused skin, there for a moment.

"Seems like a pity to sell off a steer that doesn't have enough weight on him to bring a good price."

"Think I don't know that?" Her words were sharp-spoken. "We all do what we have to, Flannery."

"Well, you don't have to raise money that way, Chloe.
I'll spring for the hay, and we'll settle up later. I've got a
bit of cash on hand."

Her lips compressed as she concentrated on the young
beef cattle before her. "I'll set up a page in my record
book," she answered grudgingly. "I won't cheat you."

He nodded. "Another thing, Chloe." Silently, he waited
for her to respond.

She sighed and turned her head, offering him a patient
look from blue eyes. "What now?"

"I'm not real fond of Willie-boy."

"He's all right," she said after a moment. "Young and
a little arrogant, but his mama needs the money his pay
brings in."

"He'll either stop looking you over like you're on display
for his benefit, or he'll be looking for another place to
work."

"He doesn't mean anything by it."

His laugh was harsh. "Either you're more innocent than
I thought, or—"

"I'm not a child, Flannery. I can handle Willie." She
eased down from the fence and tugged her pant legs in place
over her boots. "If that's all for now, I've got a meal to put
together before I hitch the wagon and pick up my hay."

"You get the meal together and I'll hitch the wagon,"
he countered smoothly. "If I'm paying for the hay, I want
to see it first." She stalked away and he watched her, ad-
mired the rounding of her hips beneath the denim pants, and
privately agreed with Willie that she was, indeed, a good-
looking female.

"I've been thinking," Chloe said, watching as J.T. picked
up the reins. The horses moved out at his bidding and she
half turned to face him. "Maybe we need to hammer out
an agreement."

"Thought we'd already made some progress at that," he said, lifting one booted foot to rest against the frame of the wagon. His trousers were snug, outlining his thigh, and Chloe tore her gaze from the sight.

"Hogan's a good man. I want you to leave him in charge."

He nodded. "All right. Up to a point."

"A point?" she repeated. "What does that mean?"

"He'll carry out my orders, and see that the men do as they're told."

"What about my orders?" she wanted to know. "I'm in the habit of meeting with Hogan every day, keeping up with things. Lots of days I ride with the men, work alongside them."

"Not anymore," he said shortly. "You've branded your last calf, lady. I caught sight of a scar on your hand that shouldn't be there."

She turned her hand over and examined it briefly. "I've got several. It comes with the job." She outlined one that formed a neatly imprinted *B* on her palm. "I did this when I was sixteen. The first time Pa let me help in spring roundup."

"You won't wear another brand like that," he said harshly. "You're a woman, not a cowhand."

"I'm a ranch owner," she reminded him. "I won't be treated like a fragile flower, Flannery. I can get banged up just as easily in the kitchen." Her hand lifted to press against her stomach, and his eyes followed the gesture.

"Did you blister?" he asked quietly. "I didn't think the coffee had drenched your shirt. Was I wrong?"

Chloe shook her head. "Just left a red spot. Nothing to talk about." She rolled her fingers into a fist and rested it on her knee. "When Aunt Tilly comes back, I'll be free to work outside all day, instead of just piecemeal."

His jaw tightened as she watched. "There's some of the

work I'd rather you didn't tackle," he said. "I expect you're good at training horses, and that's one thing. Now, roping steers is another thing altogether."

"I'll bet you've got in mind letting me keep the books, haven't you?" Her words oozed sarcasm as she thought about being penned up in the big office, adding and subtracting lines of numbers and, more often than not, coming out short. At least, that had been the situation for the past months.

"Maybe," he said easily, ignoring her tone. "We'll go over them together," he told her. "Then decide from there."

"There's not much to decide on, right now," she admitted unwillingly. "You might as well know the whole story, *partner*. There aren't any funds available. My brother cleaned out the bank account when he left town. We'll be operating on the cuff until fall roundup."

"I figured as much," he said, lifting the reins to crack them with a sharp sound, sending the team into a quick trot. The harness jangled and the wagon wheels rode roughly over the rutted town road. Chloe grabbed the side of the seat, holding herself in place.

"Peter's young," she said quietly. "Maybe too young for the pressure I put him under, trying to make him into a man."

"How old is he?" He turned a harsh look in her direction. "I'd thought you were pretty close in age."

"We're twins," she said shortly. "Twenty-two our last birthday."

"And he's young, but you're not?" Skepticism coated the words.

"He didn't take well to responsibility," Chloe said quietly. "Ranching wasn't his first choice."

"What was?"

She was silent, weighing her words. And then she

laughed, a humorless sound. "Let's just say that anything involving hard work didn't come easily to Peter. He might have done well if Pa had sent him East to school and he'd been able to learn a profession."

"Bankers and lawyers work hard, Chloe," J.T. reminded her. "There isn't a job in the world that doesn't take some elbow grease of one kind or another to accomplish. I think you've been protecting Pete long enough. You need to take a long look at him and recognize his faults."

"His name is Peter. And I'm aware of his faults, thank you." She sat upright, forsaking her relaxed stance on the seat.

"A man his age should have outgrown a boy's name. When he turns into Pete and makes his own way in the world, I'll be able to respect him."

"Well, there's not much chance you'll be running into him again, is there? I'll warrant he's nowhere near Ripsaw Creek."

"He'll be back one day, mark my words," J.T. growled. "When his grubstake runs out, he'll show up like a bad penny." His eyes flashed darkly as he glanced at her. "There'll be hell to pay when that happens, Chloe. He lost his share of the ranch in a fair game, in front of witnesses. And you're not giving him another slice of the pot."

"Damn!" She shot the word in his direction, and ground her teeth together lest another follow in its wake. "You don't have Boss Man printed across your forehead, Flannery. And being my partner doesn't mean you control my share of the ranch."

"We're gonna butt heads over this, aren't we?" His look was measuring as he drew the wagon to a stop in the middle of the road.

"What did you expect?" she asked. "That I'd sit here and have you tell me what to do? I don't think so, Flannery. You can just take your orders and put 'em—"

He grabbed her arms, stepping on the reins with one boot, lest the horses take it in mind to move. His grip was firm and unmoving, long fingers sliding up to wrap around her shoulders. Then he drew her closer and she lost her balance, falling against him. His nostrils flared and his eyes narrowed as his glittering gaze scanned her startled face.

"Don't say it," he warned, his voice low, rasping against her hearing. "Don't say one more word. Just keep your mouth shut."

"Damn you!" The curse dared him, spurting in his direction from between clenched teeth, and he inhaled sharply, reaching further, his gaze on her full, lush lips.

"I said not another word," he whispered, the sound seeming more hostile than a shout. And then his head bent, and she felt her eyes widen as he pressed his lips against hers. His mouth was hard, his lips firm, and she heard a low moan deep in her throat, an anguished cry that protested his touch.

"Hush," he whispered, allowing her breathing space for a fraction of time that was barely long enough for her to inhale. And then his mouth was there again, softer this time, persuading her to his purpose, his lips warm and damp against hers.

His hands slid from their firm grip to encircle her back, and she was drawn across the seat, to lie precariously against his chest. Her fingers clutched for purchase, gripping handfuls of his shirt, and she fought for balance, aware that only his strength kept her from sliding to the floor beneath the seat.

"Haven't you ever been kissed?" he asked quietly, easing his mouth from hers, his dark eyes surveying her.

She shook her head, aware of the flush that rose from her throat to cover her cheeks. Her heart thumped within her breast, an uneven rhythm that caught her attention. His hands held her in place, and she felt the heat of his body, even through the layers of clothing separating them.

"I'll do better next time, Chloe. I'd hate to have you think this was the best I can manage." His touch softened and he lifted her, settling her on the wagon seat, straightening the collar of her shirt with gentle hands.

Next time? She shivered. If this was any example of the man's skill, she'd do well to steer clear of another demonstration.

"I expect you want an apology," he said, his mouth twitching at one corner.

"I doubt if I'll get one, will I?" Her lips tingled, her vision was blurred with a mist of tears and her hands were trembling as she clenched them into fists. And then as she caught a shuddering breath she heard the apology she'd not expected.

"I'm sorry I upset you," he said. "But I can't say I'm sorry I kissed you, Chloe. I'm just wishing it had been for another reason than to get you calmed down and settled."

Well, he'd certainly failed at that. Calm? And settled? She'd never felt so discombobulated in her life.

Chapter Three

For a week she steered clear of him. Keeping the books was a daily task, one she found more to her liking when being in the black seemed more of a possibility. But discovering a bill of sale tucked inside the cavern of her ledger brought her out of the desk chair with all flags flying.

"Damn, damn, damn," she muttered beneath her breath, setting off for the barn.

"What happened to being partners?" Chloe asked. Her anger held on a short leash, she faced J.T. down in the central aisle of the big barn. Lowery was in and out of the tack room, and if she knew anything about it, he was listening for all he was worth. Apparently J.T. shared the thought, for he only glared at her for a moment, then gripped her elbow and shuffled her toward the double doors.

"We're not going to argue in front of the men," he muttered between gritted teeth. "If you've got something to say, I'll listen to it out here, without an audience."

"If?" The single word was all she could manage for a moment, and she inhaled deeply. "You know damn well I've got something to say." Her hand was fisted around a yellow slip of paper, and she released it, allowing it to flutter to the ground at his feet. "Would you like to explain just

how you figured we could afford a new stallion right now? And what we needed one for, anyway?''

"I didn't ask you to put out one red cent," J.T. said calmly. "I bought him."

"And I'm supposed to write that amount on your side of the ledger book, I suppose," she hissed. "Which gives you the edge, having invested your own money."

"Chloe, you've got mares dropping foals out there that aren't going to amount to a hill of beans. They're only good for pulling a buggy or carrying kids back and forth to school. Wait till you see this stud. You need new blood, or your herd is never going to be worth anything."

"What's wrong with using the stallion you rode in here with?" That his words were true wasn't the issue. Her father's stud was old, and he'd been interbreeding over the past several years. But buying a new stallion was a major investment, and now J.T. viewed the news of the horse's imminent arrival as if Christmas were coming at the end of a lead line.

"I told you already. His bloodlines aren't what we need. We'll use him, too, but this new stallion is almost guaranteed to give us a herd of horses that will make some real money a couple of years down the road."

"You planning on being here that long?" she asked tartly.

His jaw clenched, as did his hands, and she wondered for a moment if she might not have pushed him a bit too far. "Are you bein' obnoxious on purpose?" he asked, "or is it just your natural disposition?" His hands were hard, callused and strong, and when he used one of them to propel her toward the house, she had no choice but to march beside him. He turned her around when they reached the back porch and deposited her on the top step.

"I don't like being manhandled," she told him, snatching her arm from his grasp and sitting down. "There's not a

man big enough to push me around and get away with it.''
And yet it seemed he had. For the moment at least.

J.T.'s mouth thinned and twisted, his eyes sending sparks
that should have warned her off. He stood tall before her,
anger oozing from every square inch of his being. "I'm not
pushing you around, and I didn't leave a mark on you, Miss
High-and-Mighty." Bending a bit, he peered into her face.
"But I'll tell you one thing right now. You won't give me
orders when it comes to spending my own hard-earned
money."

"You had no right to—"

"I had every right," he boomed. "The damn horse was
on the auction block. If I hadn't bid on him and bought him
outright, I'd have missed the chance to get a stud like that.
And like it or not, he's exactly what your herd needs."

"And what's he going to do for my mares? Put thor-
oughbred fillies and colts in their bellies?"

J.T. shook his head. "Better than that, lady. We'll have
a pasture full of paints within five years, horses that'll be
known throughout the state once we get them trained. Do
you know that any cowhand worth his salt will pay fifty
dollars more for a paint than a solid-colored horse?"

A glimmer of interest nudged her as his words made in-
roads on her aggravation. "Why?" she asked bluntly.

"Because a well-trained paint is the best cow pony you
can buy. The Comanches have been hunting buffalo with
them for years. We'll have buyers waiting in line." He
turned to sit beside her, enthusiasm vanquishing his anger,
and she listened intently, excitement growing as he spoke.

"We'll use the best of your mares for breeding, and concentrate on selling off the stock we don't need. There's always a buyer around for everyday mounts, and by the time
we weed out the bottom of your herd, we'll have a crop of
foals dropping next spring that'll really put a shine in those
blue eyes of yours."

"And when do we get to begin this breeding program you've come up with?" she asked. "I assume the horse is being delivered?"

"Hogan is bringing him home later today."

"Hogan went along with it?"

J.T. had the grace to look chagrined, and long fingers raked through his hair. It fell in place, dark and wavy, touching his collar, catching her attention so that his words took moments to penetrate. "He told me you'd have a fit, and I'd better come home and get you softened up before he arrived."

She stiffened at his words, her cheeks warming with a flush of anger. "And do I look properly *softened?*" Dark, assessing eyes measured her as his gaze swept her form, finally focusing on her face, and the silence was long, as though he contemplated several words before choosing to speak.

"You look soft in all the right places, Chloe, but I think you're still madder than a wet hen." His head tilted to one side and he allowed a grin to play about the corners of his mouth. "I can't say as I blame you. I suspect I knew you'd have a hissy. I just didn't think you'd cause a fuss in front of your hired hands."

"I didn't," she protested, raking her mind. They'd been alone in the barn, all but for Lowery, coming in and out.

Apparently J.T. had the same thought. "Lowery was in the tack room, and Willie was right outside the back door," he said quietly. "It won't do to air our differences in front of them, and I couldn't let you raise Cain with me that way. Not without having a knockdown battle right there in the barn."

"They listen to you," she said harshly, looking aside, unwilling to allow her hurt to show.

"I'm a man," he said simply. "Men always respond better to another man. Except in some things," he added softly.

She turned quickly, her mind snagging on his words. "Like what?"

"Like…" He hesitated, and she wondered at his loss for words. J.T. never thought twice before he spoke, as if the phrases he wanted were ready and available at the tip of his tongue. Now, he watched her warily, and she felt the rosy flush of anger recede, only to be replaced with a warmth generated by his slow appraisal.

"Like the way I react to you," he said finally, and his mouth twisted wryly, as if he rued the words he spoke. "There's something about you that brings me to attention." He shook his head. "And isn't that a fine thing to be telling my partner."

"I bring you to attention? Well, whatever that means, I'd say there's nothing about me that suits you," she told him tartly. "And you aggravate *me* beyond belief. No matter what I do, you've got to have the last word. You'd think I didn't know how this place operates." Again she felt the threat of angry tears behind her eyelids and blinked them away, unwilling to waver before him as she defended herself. "What do you suppose I did before you got here?"

"Got along the best way you could," he answered amiably. "And did a decent job of it. Hogan's a good man, and you're lucky to have him."

He took the wind out of her sails. Just when she was working up to a good mad, he managed to be agreeable and she was left to bluster.

"By the way, I gave him a raise in pay," J.T. said, eyeing her for a response.

"Well, twice what he's getting this month is just about zero," she said with an angry laugh. "I told you there's no money for wages, or anything else, till we get some income. I barely paid the new men their wages the past three months. And I'm at rock bottom right now."

J.T. watched her, invigorated by the quick-witted responses she gave, the sharp working of her mind. She'd only get mad again, but he might as well have it over with, he decided. "I put money in your account."

She was pale beneath the freckles, and her jaw flexed as though she gritted her teeth against angry words. And then she spoke, and her voice held more than a trace of the frustration she battled. "You're putting me in a hole, J.T. What if I can't get out? What'll you do next? Just take over the whole place?"

He reached for her hand, enclosing it within his palm, reaching out for her understanding in the small intimacy of flesh against flesh. "I knew you'd take it that way, Chloe. And that's not what I intend. I figured we can't expect these men to stay on here much longer if we don't pay them. It's not fair, and you don't want to take a chance on losing Hogan, or Lowery or Shorty, either, for that matter. The others you could replace if you had to, but not those three."

She nodded, accepting the warmth of his fingers enclosing hers. There seemed little to say. No doubt he was right, but her independence was threatened more each day, simply because he was there, with his influence reaching to every area of her life.

Including her awareness of herself as a woman. And at that thought she felt a nudge of apprehension. He'd kissed her once, a week ago, and then as if it had never taken place, ignored the episode, not in any way referring to it again.

Until now. She retrieved her hand from his, clenching it in her lap as her mind replayed the words he'd spoken in that dark, rasping tone. *You look soft in all the right places, Chloe.... There's something about you that brings me to attention.* He'd bewitched her with his flattery. That was all there was to it, she decided. Pure and simple flattery, designed to throw her off guard. She clenched her jaw as he spoke again.

"Chloe? Are you going to give me a hassle over this?

Can we just agree to let things ride for a while, at least until we sort through the herd and decide which animals you want to sell off?''

"What?" His query caught her unaware. Her mind had traveled far from the discussion over wages and hired hands, and for a moment she faltered, willing herself to concentrate on his words. He was making plans, while she was still dithering over his foolish talk.

"I'm not trying to push you," he said quietly. And perhaps he wasn't, she thought. Yet, to her discerning eye, he was poised for action, impatiently absorbed in his plans, and she knew a sense of disquiet. For one thing, she was ignorant when it came to a breeding program such as the one he spoke of.

One hand lifted, as if to assure him of her compliance, and she gathered her wits. "I'd rather talk about this later. Maybe after supper tonight." To give in so readily was against her nature, but he'd boxed her into a corner and the need to regroup was foremost in her mind.

A look of pure relief erased the frown lines he wore, and his mouth curved slowly. "Whatever you want," he said agreeably. "Hogan should be here right soon, and I've got to get a stall fitted up for the stud. We'll keep him in the corral for a day or so, till we decide which mares we want him to cover, and then go on from there."

Excitement filled his voice, and Chloe nodded, his exuberance contagious. "I want to come out with you."

"All right. There's not much for you to do, but you need to take a look at him anyway."

Perhaps she'd expected a creature of majestic size, or at least an animal more impressive than the painted horse that followed behind Hogan's gelding an hour later. "He's not very big, is he?"

"Big isn't always better, not when it comes to a good cow pony," J.T. said, intent on passing his hands over the side and flank of the black-and-white spotted stallion. He lifted one hoof after another, and Chloe watched as shivers rippled the smooth coat, the stud sidestepping from J.T.'s touch.

"He looks all right," he told Hogan. "Give you any trouble?"

"Not on the end of a rope," Hogan answered. "I'm waiting for the chance to get on his back. Fella at the auction said this one's the best cutting horse he's ever seen."

J.T.'s eyes lit with satisfaction. "You'll get your chance, come tomorrow morning. I thought we'd just handle him for now, feed him good and let him settle in."

Chloe could barely hide her disappointment. Having reconciled herself to the plan, she was filled with misgivings now. She watched as Hogan led the horse into the barn, and then, as she turned away, she heard the shrill sound of his trumpeting. From the near pasture a mare returned the challenge, and she spun around in time to see Hogan gripping the lead line, even as he dodged the stallion's tossing head.

Tail swishing and hind legs bent, the stud seemed intent on freeing himself from the man holding him, and J.T. moved quickly. His laugh rang out as he came from the far side to grasp the horse's halter. His considerable weight pulled the stallion's head to meet his chest, and then J.T.'s voice became soothing, his words soft as he strove to quiet the animal.

"Well, he seems to know what he's here for, don't he?" Hogan asked, breathless from his efforts. His grin flashed in Chloe's direction, and then as though he reconsidered his words, he turned his head aside. "Sorry, ma'am," he murmured politely, but Chloe heard the amusement beneath the muttered apology.

Unused to such blatant masculine emotions, whether they be from man or beast, she felt a quickening as she thought of what would take place here in the next weeks. The process of breeding had always been confined to the pastures, at the discretion of both mares and stallion, and with no set purpose, only the intention of new life each spring.

Now it seemed there would be a scheduling of those events, and as she turned from the barn and headed with haste toward the house, the realization of change became a fact. J. T. Flannery was about to set out upon a path that would make mockery of her father's haphazard operation. And she had given him the go-ahead to do just that.

The table was set for three when J.T. entered the kitchen hours later, and he tossed Chloe a quizzical look. "You expecting company?"

"Not really. Just Aunt Tilly. She arrived an hour ago. Howie Henderson brought her out from town and dropped her off." Chloe opened the oven door and pulled a roasting pan from its depths. "She's upstairs, settling in." Her grin was quick as she glanced his way. "She asked about you."

"Me?" He pulled his chair from beneath the table and eased himself onto the seat. Muscles well used over the past couple of weeks were protesting, and getting dumped in the dust of the corral by a half-broke horse hadn't helped any. "How'd she know about me?"

"Howie gave her all the details about my new partner on the trip out from town," Chloe said.

J.T. watched her as she dealt with the contents of the roasting pan. The woman was adept at more than just riding and tending to ranch business. The pot roast, surrounded by potatoes and carrots, was a tempting sight, and he hoped fervently that Aunt Tilly was at least as handy in the kitchen as Chloe.

"And does she approve of your new partner?" he asked, aware of footsteps approaching from the front hallway. The scent of lilac preceded the woman as did her voice, its tones sharp, her words cautious.

"If he turns out to be a scalawag like the last one, I've got a shotgun that'll guarantee he won't last long." Iron-gray hair, curled and crimped into an abundant mass, topped the sturdy figure in the doorway. Eyes the startling color of a bluebird's back scanned him thoroughly, as if she sought out every possible defect and scar on his miserable hide. From where he sat, Tilly looked to be nearly six feet tall, altogether a woman to be aware of. A brilliantly flowered house dress covered her ample frame, and sturdy black-laced oxfords, surely made to fit a man, carried her toward him.

J.T. rose, bowing his head just a trifle in greeting. "Ma'am?" he said politely. "I'm the fella you'll be gunning for, should I not come up to snuff." It took all his control not to smile at the picture she presented, but he managed to subdue his humor.

Aunt Tilly halted several feet from him, and he waited as she scanned him from top to bottom. A flash of approval from brilliant blue eyes, and an abrupt nod that barely disturbed her curls, told him she'd completed her appraisal, and he moved to pull a chair from beneath the table.

"Won't you sit down, ma'am?" he asked politely.

She shook her head. "I'll give Chloe a hand first."

"I've got everything ready," Chloe said quickly. "Just sit, Aunt Tilly." The platter centered the table, steam rising from its contents, and beside it were bowls of applesauce and some sort of greens J.T. didn't recognize. "I just need to pour the coffee."

Tilly sat down, allowing J.T. to play the gentleman, and he held her chair with a flourish, earning a sharp look as he smoothly seated her.

"Where you from, boy?" she asked bluntly. "You're pretty slick with the manners, seems to me."

"My mama raised me to be polite," he said, allowing a smile to appear. "I know enough not to wipe my mouth on my sleeve, and I learned how to ask nicely when I want a favor.''

"Well, that says something for you," she answered, watching as Chloe sat down across the table. "You make biscuits, girl?"

"No, but there's bread from yesterday," Chloe told her.

"You can get some out after we bless the food," Tilly said, and immediately bowed her head, booming words of thanks to the Almighty for the supper Chloe had prepared.

J.T. leaned back in his chair, amused by Chloe's quick movements as she unwrapped a fresh loaf of bread from its dish towel and quickly wielded the knife. Four slices were deposited on a plate and she brought it to the table. "There's fresh butter, Aunt Tilly," she said, uncovering the glass dish.

It was easy to see who was in control here, J.T. decided. The kitchen was suddenly Aunt Tilly's domain, and Chloe bent to her will in a way he hadn't expected. And then the older woman paused midway in the process of buttering her slice of bread to cast her eyes on her niece.

"You've taken off a few pounds, girl. Been working too hard, I'll warrant."

Chloe laughed aloud. "I could take off a few more, Aunt Tilly. And once I get you back in charge here, I probably will. I need to be out with the men, working with the new foals. Hogan says we've got a dandy crop of calves already." Her enthusiasm seemed to be generated by the thought of being relieved of kitchen duty, J.T. decided.

"You're turning out to be a good cook," Tilly decreed, tasting the beef roast and savoring the flavor. "You use bay leaf in this?"

Chloe nodded meekly, though her eyes glittered with good humor. "Just like you told me, ma'am. And I picked the dandelion greens early this morning while the dew was still on them."

J.T. stopped chewing, his mouthful of greens suddenly losing their appeal. "Dandelions?" he asked dubiously. "I'm eating dandelions?"

"Just the greens," Chloe said patiently. "They're good for you."

"Whatever happened to turnip greens or collards?"

Chloe turned patient eyes on him. "It's too early for them." She waved her fork in the direction of his plate. "That's good spring tonic. Even the Indians eat them."

"I'm not sure I need a spring tonic, whatever that is," he told her, forking up another mouthful. "My mama used to give me a dose of castor oil when the trees started leafing out." He chewed a moment, then swallowed the greens dutifully. "But only one dose, mind you." His fork stirred the green mass on his plate. "Do I get to eat these every day?"

"I could probably locate a bottle of castor oil, if you'd rather," Tilly said helpfully, obviously amused at his dislike for Chloe's chosen vegetable for this meal.

"Thank you, ma'am," he said politely. "I'm a big boy now. I'll do just fine without."

"That you are," she agreed. "Came from south of here, didn't you?"

He hesitated. Giving details about his background was something he steered clear of usually. "Yeah, I guess you could say that."

Tilly nodded. "When I arrived on a wagon train from Saint Louis and met my husband for the first time, he said he'd always wanted a Southern belle to grace his table." Her laughter rang out. "He was looking for a dainty little creature with curls and a sunbonnet to keep her skin all nice and pale. Instead he got me, with my Georgia tan and a body almost six feet tall."

"I'll bet he wasn't disappointed," J.T. ventured, enjoying the tale she wove.

"Not after a week or so," Tilly admitted with a grin.

''Bless his heart, he decided I was a lot of woman, just what he needed. And he gave me three handsome boys and a pretty baby girl, about half my size, once she got to be full grown.'' She eyed J.T. intently. ''If you don't have specks of *y'all* hidden under that nice Western drawl of yours, I'll eat my hat.''

''You may be right,'' he conceded. ''My mama was a Southern lady.''

Chloe perked up at this bit of news. This was the first time she'd heard one word about his background. He'd insidiously wormed detail after detail from her about the running of the ranch, about Peter's affinity for poker and about the sudden attack that had brought her father to his knees.

She'd relived that afternoon with barely concealed tears as she spoke of John Biddleton's death. She'd told of his gasping for air as his skin took on a bluish cast and his breathing became tortured, and J.T. had halted her before she reached the final part of her story. Reaching to place long fingers on her forearm, he'd squeezed gently to get her attention, then shook his head to halt her words, seeming to understand her pain.

And now, from that silent, closemouthed man, Aunt Tilly had managed, with blunt queries and canny insight, to learn more in two minutes than Chloe had gotten from him in almost two weeks. She leaned toward him. ''Where do your parents live?'' she asked. ''Still in the South?''

His eyes met hers and she felt his withdrawal even as she finished her question. ''They're buried on the home place,'' he said shortly. ''The house caught fire and neither of them got out.'' He picked up his cup and drank deeply of the hot coffee, seemingly immune to the scalding heat.

''How old were you?'' she asked quietly.

''Old enough to be on my own,'' he answered. ''It was a long time ago. No sense in raking up the past, to my way of thinking. I've traveled a long way from that life.''

And that was probably all she'd ever hear about it, Chloe thought, totaling up her scant store of knowledge. The man was a gambler, and he knew horseflesh. Beyond that, and the small addition of facts he'd just offered, he was a puzzle. His dark eyes held secrets, and his long, lean body bore muscled strength. Sharp featured and equally sharp spoken, he was arrogance in its finest form, she thought ruefully.

And more of a man than she'd ever come across in all her twenty-two years of living. The thought of his hands against her skin, or his mouth touching hers, was enough to bring her to a level of anticipation she refused to consider. Even during the dark hours before midnight, when she tossed restlessly in her bed, reliving the single kiss that burned in her memory, she'd been aware of the insidious attraction of his presence.

Foolishness on her part. He was her partner. And didn't seem inclined, as far as she could tell, to press her into a more intimate situation.

"You ever been married?" Aunt Tilly's words caught Chloe unaware and she stiffened, certain that J.T. would take umbrage at the bold query.

Instead he grinned, an expression that totally changed the stern lines of his face. "A man who keeps on the move doesn't need to tote a woman along with him."

"You're not on the move anymore," Tilly pointed out. "Seems like a fella who owns half a ranch ought to be thinking about putting down roots and looking to the future."

Chloe choked on a half-chewed piece of beef and pushed her chair back from the table. Coughing and gasping, she headed for the back door, aware of J.T.'s chair scraping across the floor. She bent over the porch railing, catching her breath and felt his warm hand against her back.

"You all right?" he asked, concern mixed with amusement as he bent to peer into her face. "I think your aunt kinda threw you there, didn't she?"

"I can't believe she was so brazen," Chloe managed to gasp. "The next thing you know, she'll be arranging a wedding for you."

"Nah," he said, drawling the word in a teasing tone. "When I decide to tie the knot, I'll do my own arranging, partner." His hand slid up her back to rest against her shoulder, and he squeezed lightly. "And trust me, Miss Chloe, you'll be the first to know."

Chapter Four

"There's a dozen or so cattle missing, boss." Shorty Kendrick swung down from his horse and stood before J.T., his fists clenched, one still holding his reins. Aware that Shorty still considered him an unknown quantity, and unwilling to spew his anger on the unwitting messenger, J.T. received the news with barely a show of emotion, only gritting his teeth against the fury that welled up within him.

"From the range beyond the far pasture?" he asked tersely. "You sure of the count?" Not that Shorty couldn't be depended upon. He was probably the best all-round cowhand on the ranch. Hogan and Lowery's talents leaned toward the training of horses, but when it came to cattle, Shorty was tops.

"Pretty much so. We've been keepin' a good eye on them, what with calves droppin' right and left." His shoulders lifted in a shrug. "I left Tom and Corky out there last night at the shack, but they said they didn't hear anything."

"How reliable are they?" J.T. asked, wishing he'd made it his business to know the answer to that question sooner.

Shorty's mouth twisted as he shrugged again. "About as reliable as any other two roving cowboys. They've only been here for the winter. Chloe took them on when the weather got bad, and they've been workin' for keep and five dollars a month.''

"Hardly enough to make it worth their while." *And maybe incentive enough to steal a few head of cattle, figuring they had the right.*

"Winter wages are always low. And Chloe's fair. They didn't complain none, but then, they knew she'd up the ante once work picked up."

Obviously the men, other than Hogan, weren't aware of Chloe's dearth of funds. From what the foreman had had to say, there was but a scant supply of money beneath her mattress. She'd probably scraped up their five dollars a month from there.

"I'll take a ride out and look things over," J.T. said. "We'll need to be culling the herd anyway. Might as well start right now."

"You plannin' on doing something with that stud today?" Shorty asked, his eyes flickering to the corral where the new stallion was pacing the barriers to his freedom.

"You're a cattle man," J.T. said with a grin, his mind captured for a moment by thoughts of the horse. "What do you care about my new stallion?"

"He's gonna throw some dandy colts, I'll bet," Shorty said with enthusiasm. "I'm plannin' on being around to ride one of them. I've heard some tall tales about paint ponies. One fella said they can turn on a button and be headin' back in the other direction before you can bat your eyes. I'd sure like to see that critter in action."

"Why don't you saddle my horse and we'll take a look at the herd first," J.T. said, "and then we'll decide about the stud."

"What's going on?" The crisp tones of Chloe in a snit echoed from the open doorway, and J.T. turned to face her.

"Got a problem beyond the far pasture. Shorty says there's a few head missing."

She frowned, and J.T. saw her eyes take on a calculating gleam. Depend on the woman to be subtracting dollars from her profit, right off the bat. "How many?" she asked briskly, heading for the tack room.

Probably lifting her saddle down right now, he decided, following in her wake. "I'll handle it, Chloe," he said quietly, closing the door behind himself as she turned to face him, setting the big saddle on end in front of her.

"They're my cattle. I'll ride along," she said, tilting her chin in a defiant gesture.

"No need," he said easily. "I'm going to check the fence line for breaks and talk to the two men who spent the night at the shack, see what they might have heard or seen."

"Who's out there? Tom?" She reached for a bridle and he grinned.

"You're a determined woman, aren't you, partner?"

"It's my ranch, and if we've got cattle missing, it's hurting my profit, pure and simple," she said harshly.

Her gaze clashed with his, and he watched as blue eyes took on an icy gleam. Color streaked her cheeks, and he considered its source. The woman was mad, feeling betrayed or invaded, or both, and he couldn't blame her. And yet, should there be trouble with the two men he planned to confront, he didn't want her in the vicinity.

"Why don't you let me handle this?" he asked, tempering his need for action with soft words meant to pacify her.

"I'm not a child, J.T.," she said curtly. "I know how to use a gun, and I can ride as well as a man. If there's a problem on my ranch, I need to be on top of it."

He reached out for her, and silently cursed the saddle standing between them. "I know," he said, one hand touching her cheek. "But I don't want you getting in the middle of a fuss." His other hand gripped her shoulder and she flinched from his callused fingertips.

"Don't treat me like the bad guy, Chloe," he told her,

dropping the offending hand to circle her other shoulder. "I just don't want you hurt." His fingers tightened, and with a surge of strength, he lifted her away from the restricting presence of the saddle.

Her eyes widened and her mouth opened as she was settled, with a lack of ceremony, in his embrace. Encircling her, his arms were bonds she stood no chance of breaking, and as if she understood that fact, she was immobile in his grasp. Small, yet defiant, she looked up at him, her eyes narrowed and challenging.

"Let me go, you big bully. The only man around here who'd dare put his hands on me is right in front of me," she muttered, lips taut with anger, yet trembling.

"I'd never put a bruise on you," he said quietly. Yet his fingers loosened their hold as he considered his grip. She was soft, her skin smooth beneath the cotton shirt she wore, but the muscles were there, beneath his hands, making their presence known as she wrenched from his grasp. And somehow, that feminine strength drew him, attracting him more than did her flashing blue eyes or the shapely form he'd held against himself.

Chloe backed away awkwardly, and stumbled. With one long step he was on her, taking hold anew, this time his arms circling her back, as he succumbed to temptation. His head bent low, seeking the soft, lush fullness of her mouth. She murmured beneath her breath as he found his mark, and he inhaled a hint of sweet tea.

"Don't fight me, honey." His voice was a rasping, grating sound he barely recognized, and his heart pounded forcefully as he felt soft curves brush against his chest. His tongue touched the tender surface of lips that moved tentatively against his, and a groan of satisfaction echoed from deep in his chest.

As if that sound triggered opposition to his will, her teeth clenched, refusing his entry, and she was, at once, a taut bundle of female resistance in his arms. With the tip of his tongue, he traced the firm outline of her mouth, and for now that was enough, he decided. Her flavor was delicate and he savored it as he inhaled the scent of woman that rose from her small, compact body.

Chloe tempted him mightily, but he'd been a fool to begin this in the middle of the tack room, with no time to spend wooing her to his cause. His lips gentled, soothing her as he suckled carefully at her lower lip.

She murmured then, relaxing against him, softening in his embrace, her hands lifting to press against his chest, fingers widespread. A soft hiccup of sound broke her breathing and he relented, his lips pressing once more against hers, tenderly easing from the intimacy he'd assumed without her consent.

"You're not fair," she said, her whisper harsh. "You know I can't fight your strength." Her eyes opened and the defiance was gone, tear-drenched lashes blinking as if she would conceal the emotion he'd brought to life. "I don't have anything to compare this with," she told him in a trembling voice, "but I'd say you've had a lot of experience at it."

"At kissing?" he asked, tasting her flavor on his mouth. "A little, here and there. Not as much as most men, probably. I'm kinda fussy about women."

"And you've decided I'm worth your attention?" She'd regained her composure now and her hands slid from his chest as he allowed his arms to lower, until his hands were at the small of her back. He held her in an easy embrace, and when she edged back, released her from his hold.

"I let you know the other night I was more than interested in you, Chloe. Having Tilly make such a blatant remark didn't bother me nearly as much as it did you." He stepped back from her, lifting her saddle easily with one hand.

"You're a good-lookin' woman, and why you're not already married is beyond me."

"I'm not giving up my share of the ranch to anybody," she said defiantly, her mouth taut as she vowed her independence. "Marriage would turn me into a mealymouthed creature fit only for having babies and keeping up a house."

He laughed, unwilling to insult her, yet amused by the thought of Chloe being anything but what she was. "You'll never be a mealymouthed woman, no matter what," he said. "You've got too much spunk to let a man run roughshod over you."

"Maybe so, but I'm smart enough to know I'd have a battle on my hands. I wouldn't have a leg to stand on, once I signed a marriage certificate," she said sharply. "The law says that a man owns the property, and pretty much the woman who comes along with it. I'm not handing over my inheritance in exchange for a wedding ring."

"Well, I guess I've got my work cut out for me, don't I?" He turned to the door, opening it and stepping across the threshold before she could form a reply. Better to keep her off guard, he decided.

Marriage hadn't been in his plans, at least not for the next few years. But the idea of hauling a preacher out from town and putting a halter on Miss Chloe was starting to sound like a winner. Without half trying, she'd managed to get a grip on him that was becoming downright uncomfortable these days. Two kisses had only whet his appetite for another taste of her mouth, and she was spending more and more time at the back of his mind, keeping him on edge during the day and invading his dreams at night.

When he spoke again, he nonchalantly asked, "Which horse you planning on riding, Partner?"

"You're not going to make a fuss about this?" she asked, hurrying to reach his side, the bridle and reins caught up in her hands.

"Not worth it," he announced, as she halted before the stall where her tall, black mare was tied. "I need to be on my way, and short of tying you to a post, I don't know of any way to persuade you to let me handle it on my own."

"I wouldn't try it if I were you," she snapped, obviously fit for battle once more.

His hand sought out the currycomb hanging from the wall, and with a few strong, sweeping strokes, he cleaned the area where Chloe's saddle would rest. "You got a blanket handy?" he asked, and watched as she snatched a heavy woolen square from a sawhorse. She snapped it sharply to remove the dust, then handed it to him. In moments it was in place and he swung her saddle atop the horse, looping the stirrup over the horn. His movements were quick, strong and practiced as he tightened the cinch and then backed the horse from its stall.

Chloe slid the bit in place, and the mare obligingly ducked her head as the bridle replaced her halter. J.T. followed her to where his stallion stood, tossing his head impatiently at the restriction of his reins tied to the handle of the barn door. The blood bay switched his tail, as if aware of the attention he drew. The mare passed him by and he whinnied, a shrill, sharp sound that drew little response from the black, but a quick grin from Chloe.

She mounted quickly, stepping up onto a block of wood apparently kept there for the purpose, and gathered her reins, turning the mare. Waiting as J.T. attempted to quiet his horse, her grin turned to a smile as the stallion defied his efforts. "Sure you don't want to use him for breeding?" she asked. "He's not going to be happy to lose a chance at my mares."

"He'll live through it," J.T. snarled, grasping a handful of mane as he swung into his saddle. "Damned horse is spoiled rotten. I should have gotten rid of him a long time ago, traded him in for a good gelding.'' He glanced up at Chloe's stifled laughter.

"You'd never do that and you know it," she said. "You're a windbag, Flannery."

"He'd behave better if he knew how close he is to getting sold," J.T. growled, drawing up the reins, until the stallion's nose was pressed close to his chest. "Let's move out and let him run some of it off."

"How many head am I missing?" she asked, turning her mare to join him as he allowed the stallion to break into a sharp trot.

He turned his dark gaze on her and Chloe thought for a moment that there was a definite resemblance between man and horse. Both were magnificent specimens, J.T. with his lean, long-legged, yet muscular body, the blood bay sporting black stockings that emphasized the sinewy, narrow lines of his legs and led to the heavy haunches that provided barely leashed power.

"A dozen or so, from what Shorty said," J.T. answered shortly. He rode, she thought, like a centaur, as though he were a part of the splendid creature between his thighs. And now, his look was impatient as he lowered the brim of his hat with a jerk and nodded at her to take the lead.

They crossed the meadow, and he bent low to open a gate in the pasture fence, allowing her to ride through and waiting to close it behind himself. He caught up to her in moments, the stallion unwilling to be left bringing up the rear. "There's only one shack, isn't there?" he asked, and she nodded.

"Never needed more than one. Not with the size of herd I run. We don't use it much, just during branding and roundup usually."

They rode the length of the big pasture, and again he opened, then closed, a gate. Now the wide-open range of the northernmost part of the ranch was before them, only the farthest boundaries enclosed by barbed wire. It would be an easy thing, she decided, to clip the wire and run a dozen head of cattle through the opening. The task now was to find the gap in her fence line, and make quick repairs before more of the herd wandered off to Hale Winters's neighboring ranch.

J.T. loosened his reins, allowing his horse to stretch long, dark legs in a gallop, and Chloe's black mare followed suit, eager to spend some of her pent-up energy. The chill of spring made her thankful for the coat she wore, and she buttoned the top button with her free hand, tugging her hat lower to protect her from the wind. There was a simple joy in the rolling gallop of her mare, a pleasure that ignored the purpose of this ride.

And it seemed that J.T. shared her thoughts as he turned his head to offer her a look of satisfaction. His gaze narrowed on her face, and he slowed the pace of his mount, motioning with an uplifted hand for her to follow suit. They settled into a easy lope and he rode beside her in silence for a moment, his jaw set, as if he pondered over words he was hesitant to speak.

"We'd make a good team, Chloe. I'd make sure you held your portion of the ranch with no strings attached." His words were rough-edged, his eyes penetrating, as he turned his gaze in her direction, referring apparently to the sparring they'd done in the tack room.

"We are a team, whether we like it or not, Flannery," she answered coolly. "And I'll hold my share of the ranch without your help."

"I've never done this before," he said, his jaw clenching. "I didn't make myself clear, apparently."

"If you're talking about a wedding, you can forget it," Chloe said, sudden realization making her aware of his line of thought. She pressed her heels against the mare's sides, and the horse delivered a spurt of speed. "Besides," she called, over her shoulder, "we've got more important things to be concerned about right now."

J.T. caught up with her and passed her by, his stallion's long legs stretching, nostrils flaring as he left the black mare behind. Chloe let her horse run, aware that she was certain to be viewing the bay's wide haunches. If she wasn't mistaken, she'd just turned down a backhanded proposal, and damn if it didn't feel good to get the best of J. T. Flannery.

The wire had indeed been cut, and if the language coming from Tom's mouth was anything to go by, it had not been an easy task to repair the damage. He and Corky had strained mightily to draw the ends together, winding each cut strand with pliers, their work hampered by the heavy, leather gloves they wore. And still they each bore small gashes, one leaving a dark stain on Tom's shirt, another on Corky's cheek still oozing blood.

"You didn't hear anything?" J.T. asked for the second time, and was given an impatient glare by the older of the two cowhands.

"If I had, you think I wouldn't have used my shotgun?" Tom asked, his anger obvious. "There wasn't any reason to stand guard, far as I could see. We'd worked hard all day, and we slept inside the shack."

Shod horses had crossed the boundary line, their riders cutting the fence and riding a half mile or so onto the Double B before the rustlers had made away with a portion of the herd bedded down by a southward winding, narrow creek. Wise enough to limit their take to a few head at a time, they'd evaded discovery. The tracks J.T. followed for less than a mile had cut across hard, rocky ground, leaving him little trail to follow, mixed in as they were with those of other cattle.

Corky offered a thick slab of beef, tucked between two

slices of bread, and J.T. took it gladly. "You get something to eat?" he asked Chloe.

She sat against the wall of the shack, out of the wind, the sun full on her face. Her hat resting on one knee, she looked pensive, he decided, and he stalked over to sit with her.

"Want some of this?" he offered, and was treated to a long look that disdained his crude sandwich.

"I get sick of beef," she said shortly. "And today, I'm totally fed up with everything attached to owning a cattle ranch."

"I gave her a biscuit left from breakfast," Corky said from his perch on a stump.

"Well, I guess you won't starve then," J.T. allowed, tucking into his makeshift meal. He wiped his mouth with his bandana and slanted a glance at her. "First time you've lost cattle to rustlers?"

"First and last, I hope," she told him. "It makes me angry to have something stolen that I've worked so hard to tend to."

"We'll have to bring the herd in closer and keep a weather eye out," he said, biting into his bread.

"Damn it, anyway. We shouldn't have to be looking over our shoulder." She glared at him as if it were somehow his responsibility that such a thing had come to pass. "If I had my way, I'd string the thieves up on the nearest tree," she said bitterly.

"That's been done before," he said agreeably, "but we'll have to catch them first. On top of that the constable would probably rather we let the law handle it."

"My pa always said his gun was the law on this ranch." Her gaze moved to the shotgun slung behind her saddle. "I think he may have had the right idea after all."

J.T. chewed slowly, then swallowed. "You didn't always agree with his theory?"

She shook her head. "No. I was all for law and order."

Her eyes flashed anger again and he recognized her frustration. "That was before it happened to me."

"Yeah, that does make a difference in viewpoint," he said obligingly. The last bite was gone, and he rose, a single, smooth movement that caught her eye. He offered his hand. "Come on, Chloe. Might as well head back home. There's not much we can do here. I'll send Willie and Shorty out this afternoon. Between the four of them, they should be able to round up the best part of the herd and head them toward the north pasture, closer to the house."

"All right." She took his hand and allowed him to tug her to her feet. He was beside her horse, tightening the cinch before she could tend to it herself, then circled to where his stallion was tied to a crude hitching rail.

She held the reins in her left hand, eyeing the stirrup that would require an awkward mount. And then he was behind her, and she was lifted, her waist gripped between wide hands as she grasped the pommel and slid her leg over the saddle. J.T. stood at her knee, tucking her boot into the stirrup.

"You need a shorter horse, ma'am," he said, his grin reminding her of the words he'd spoken in town.

"I can mount without help if I have to," she said defensively, and then softened. "There's something about this mare that appeals to me. She's a little bit ornery, but I know her well. Her mama died when she was born, and I raised her with a bottle till we could get another mare to accept her. Besides, Hogan trained her well for me. She's a good cow pony."

"A little bit ornery, huh?" J.T. mounted his stallion and his eyes surveyed the prancing mare and the woman who rode her. "I'd say you nailed that about right."

Micah Dawson wore a silver star pinned to his pocket, a star that hadn't been polished in a very long time, J.T. decided. But the man who'd pinned it there didn't appear to hold much with fancy fixings.

"We've hung more than one rustler in Ripsaw Creek, back in the old days," he said mildly, but the hard look he turned on J.T. was not that of a pushover. His gun looked to be well cared for, and his horse was sleek and well tended. The man who hoisted himself into the saddle knew what he was doing, if Flannery knew anything about men in general, and lawmen in particular.

"You find tracks?" Micah asked, his horse setting a quick pace as the two men headed from town toward the Double B.

"Not much to go on," J.T. said. "They cut across rocky ground, and by the time I got to the other side of the patch there were all sorts of prints. Hale Winters runs his cattle pretty close to the boundary line, same as Chloe and her father have for years."

"Wonder if Hale's missing any stock?" Micah's eyes scanned the horizon as they rode, his hat pulled low to shade his eyes from the afternoon sun. "You know this running around is makin' me miss my supper, don't you?" he asked, casting a glance at J.T. He cleared his throat and adjusted his seat in the saddle. "Heard that Tilly was back at the ranch. Suppose she's fixin' fried chicken tonight?"

J.T. grinned, and after a moment allowed it to turn into a chuckle. There wasn't any grass growing under the lawman's feet. "I take it you've had your feet plunked under Tilly's table more than once," he said. "And," he added, "as a matter of fact, I saw her killing two chickens this morning."

"She's a fine woman," Micah said. "I hope John Biddleton's resting easy in his grave, knowing that Tilly's lending a hand at the ranch."

"You've known her a long time?"

"She lived hereabouts when she was first married. Whole

family came in on a wagon train. And then after she got her a husband, she moved south a ways. Hated to hear she was a widow lady, but—'' his eyes warmed as he met J.T.'s gaze ''—I can't say I'm sorry she headed back this away.''

To the north, a rider appeared on the horizon, lifting a hand in greeting, and Micah muttered beneath his breath. ''That's Hale Winters now,'' he said. ''Something's goin' on. I'll lay money on it.''

Across the wide expanse of open country, the rider traveled at an angle, the paths of the three men converging as they neared the long lane leading to the Double B Ranch. ''Hey, Micah.'' Chloe's neighbor was a big man, hearty and good-natured, but if his scowl was any indication, his mood was anything but cheerful this afternoon.

''You got a problem?'' Micah asked, pulling his mount to a halt as Hale left the stubbled field to join the two men.

''Damn rustlers made away with nearly twenty of my best cattle, and it looks like they did it in broad daylight.'' He pulled his horse to a halt, and snatched his hat from his head, slapping it against his thigh. Beneath it his hair had matted against his skull, and he ran long fingers through its length. ''I about sweat up a storm, tryin' to chase them down. Lost them in the foothills, and I suspect they're holed up in a canyon. Would've been stupid to make a target outta myself, riding in there.''

Micah frowned. ''How'd you figure out what happened?''

''My men had 'em all rounded up, ready to cull 'em out and start in branding. Then some fool fired a gun and started 'em milling around and they scattered, some headin' for the river, and my boys split up six different ways, trying to get things back in order. By the time they got things settled down, somebody noticed the count was down.''

''How many head you got out there?'' J.T. asked.

''Couple hundred in that bunch, give or take. We already brought in the calves and yearlings. My breeding stock's dropped pretty near fifty calves already. What those crooks got was prime beef.''

''Hell, so much for fried chicken,'' Micah grumbled. ''We'd might as well go take a look up by the high country, see what we can find.'' He turned to J.T. ''You got a couple men to spare for the rest of the day?''

J.T. nodded. ''We'll ride on out to where Tom and Corky have been working. I'll send them along with you. You can take a look there, but I doubt there's much more to see than what I found.'' He urged his stallion into motion. ''I'll go to the house and let Tilly know to hold supper till we get back.''

''It'll be late,'' Micah said glumly, turning his mount to follow Hale back toward the north.

''She won't care. Go on ahead and I'll catch up.'' Without waiting for an answer, J.T. loosened the reins and his horse headed up the long lane that led to the ranch. He quickly caught up with Chloe and explained the situation.

''I want to go with you,'' Chloe said, her jaw set, her mouth firm. She was making a stand, J.T. figured, and sighed inwardly. Damn fool woman needed to learn how to soften up and let him handle the rough stuff. But apparently, this wasn't the day to convince her of that fact. Hands on hips, she watched from the porch as J.T. watered his horse at the trough.

''I won't stop you, Chloe,'' he said, only too aware of the picture she presented. That was about half his trouble these days, he admitted to himself. She fit her trousers to a tee, and every time he got a gander at that round bottom of hers, not to mention the narrow waist and the generous curves of her bosom, he found himself thinking deep, troublesome thoughts.

He'd probably be better off taking her along than worrying about her while he was gone. She'd taken it into her head to work with the green-broke horses over the past cou-

ple of days, and a vision of broken bones and bruises on
her smooth skin was riding his conscience.

Chloe watched as his expression softened. She was tired
of fighting him for every inch she gained. "Let me get my
coat," she said. "And have Willie saddle my horse."

He nodded as he led his stallion toward the barn, and she
reached inside the kitchen door to snatch her coat from the
hook. "We'll be late for supper," she told Tilly.

"I figured that already," her aunt replied. "Chicken
keeps, and I'll just hold everything else on the back of the
stove, once it gets ready." She eyed her niece with a re-
proving look. "You carrying a gun?"

Chloe nodded, picking up the shotgun that stood in the
corner. "We're talking about rustlers, Aunt Tilly. Trust me,
if we run across them, they'll all be armed."

The long gun settled in its leather sheath, she climbed
into her saddle and followed J.T. from the yard, past the
corral and across the pasture. There was a certain comfort,
she decided, in allowing him to take the lead, and at that
thought, she grumbled beneath her breath. *Allowing* probably wasn't the right word to use, when it came to her partner.

He rode tall and straight in the saddle, a strong man. And
yet, he'd been careful of her softer flesh, earlier today in the
tack room. His mouth had surprised her, gentle against her
own, persuasive against her refusal to allow him the intimacy he'd initiated. He'd held her firmly, but in all fairness,
she recognized the truth of his words.

I'd never put a bruise on you. And he hadn't. Instead,
he'd given her warmth and a brush with passion. A small
part of her she'd held inviolate had been summoned forth,
and the touch of J. T. Flannery's hands and lips had made
her aware of places deep within her woman's body. He'd
tempted her, and she'd rebelled against the urge to allow
him his way. Hell, he tempted her right now, she thought

ruefully. Riding before her with a cocky arrogance that should be off-putting, but only succeeded in drawing her gaze to his long, narrow-hipped form.

She should be concentrating on the loss of part of her herd, and instead she was focused on a man's body, still torn by the havoc he'd wreaked with a kiss and an embrace that should never have happened. He'd set loose a cauldron of heat she'd fought hard to control, and only his release of her and the rueful look he'd offered had halted her submission to his persuasion.

They were partners, and over that fact she had no control. But his assumption that they should become entangled in a partnership of greater proportion was out of the question. Marriage would put her at a disadvantage, and she reined in the temptation that yearned for more of what his touch promised.

She'd managed to evade several men in the area who'd invaded her territory, suggesting a courtship, or blatantly offering to take on her problems in exchange for a wedding ring. Well aware of the value of her ranch, she knew what lured them in her direction. She'd become adept at refusing their advances. She was no beauty, and looking in the mirror every morning made her aware of a freckled face and ordinary features. But she'd learned to live with *ordinary* and found satisfaction in life without a man's approval.

Until today, when she'd found herself in J.T. Flannery's arms. *You're a good-looking woman.* And wasn't that about the fanciest compliment she'd ever received? At least he'd been honest, and not tried to add any frills to his assessment. Matched with her stubborn streak, her ordinary looks and determination to run the ranch on her own terms, she probably didn't measure up to most men's idea of the perfect wife.

But then, J. T. Flannery wasn't *most men,* was he?

Chapter Five

By some miracle the chicken was still crisp on the outside and tender within, the potatoes creamy and the gravy hot and thick. Micah smacked his lips approvingly as he lifted his fork and savored his first bite of Tilly's efforts. "Sure appreciate the invite for supper," he said warmly. "Reckon I'll take it as my just due for chasin' up and down those canyons."

"I'd appreciate the efforts more if we'd come up with something beside a lot of tracks," J.T. said quietly. "Small ranchers can't afford to lose even a few head of cattle."

"I suspect that being small makes you more open to the rustlers," Micah surmised. "The big fellas have a lot more ranch hands to spread around." He shrugged as he reached for another piece of chicken. "When you've only got a handful of men, you have a hard time keepin' things covered.

"How do you feel about Tom and Corky?" Micah asked, casting an inquiring look at Chloe. "You think they're on the up-and-up?"

"As far as I know," she said. "They haven't been here long, but so far they've done their work and done it well."

"I get the feeling Tom's an old hand at the business,"

J.T. said, "and I think he keeps Corky in line." He hesitated. "I'd be more wary of Willie than the two of them."

"Willie's a neighbor," Chloe protested. "His folks are good people, and his mama works hard at taking care of things."

"Where's his pa?" J.T. asked.

"Al Harper got hurt a couple of years ago, and he's been flat on his back ever since," Micah answered. "His wife's been running herself ragged, just keeping things together."

"How come Willie works here instead of on his folk's place?" J.T. glanced from Micah to Chloe, his curiosity aroused.

"This brings in cash, and along with his mother's butter and egg business, it keeps his folks going. His ma tends what livestock they have left, and Willie takes up the slack when he gets home at the end of the week."

"Then you'd think he'd watch his step a little better," J.T. murmured, "seeing as how he needs this job."

"And what's that supposed to mean?" Tilly asked sharply, her glance turning to Chloe. "Has he been trying his hand again?"

"Willie's all right," Chloe answered, tossing an exasperated glare in J.T.'s direction. "He doesn't mean anything. He's just a child."

"That *child* has eyes for you, Chloe, and you need to understand the difference between a boy who hasn't learned self-control yet, and a man who knows how to keep his place." J.T.'s words were harsh, and she stared at him unbelievingly.

"And who are you describing?" she asked. "Should Willie take lessons from you, Flannery?"

Micah cleared his throat. "I'd take another helping of green beans, Tilly. You sure do know how to make them tasty."

Chloe felt a flush rise, and she ducked her head to her

plate, unwilling to meet J.T.'s gaze, wishing she'd kept her smart remarks to herself. Her defense of Willie was automatic, based solely on her admiration for his mother. More than aware that the boy had cast calf eyes in her direction for the past year, she'd also noted his increasing confidence as his looks grew bolder and his remarks began hovering on the edge between friendly and amorous.

"I'm just telling you that Willie's about put his job on the line lately, Chloe. I won't have a man working here who offers insulting looks at your body." J.T.'s accusation was quiet, but his voice was firm as he spoke his piece.

"That's a pretty harsh accusation," Micah said, his fork halfway to his mouth. "Maybe you misunderstood what you saw."

"Did I?" J.T.'s query was directed to Chloe and she met his gaze defiantly.

"I'm not afraid of Willie," she said quietly, "and I don't appreciate you bringing this up."

"As I recall, I don't think I did," he answered. "But so long as it *is* up for discussion, I think we might want to keep an eye on a young man who's as needy of money as our Willie appears to be. I'd hate to think he's got anything to do with losing those steers, but I'd say he bears watching."

"Then you just keep your eye on him, partner," Chloe said sharply. "And I'll tend to the important things around here." She rose and shoved her chair back, the sound of it scraping across the floor loud in the sudden silence. With a final glance at J.T., she sailed out onto the back porch, the door slamming in her wake. Only to be faced with a sharp wind from the north as she stood shivering on the edge of the porch, her hands clutching the railing.

"Here, put on your coat," he said from behind her, settling the warmth across her shoulders.

She slid her arms into the sleeves, thankful for the comfort of the fleece lining. J.T.'s big hands grasped her shoulders through the wool fabric, and their presence lent a feeling of security as she considered the quarrel they'd indulged in. That a man could be such a combination of comfort and confusion was more than she felt able to understand tonight. And yet, from the beginning, there'd been that basic element of conflict in their partnership.

"Thank you," she said, aware that the acknowledgment of his courtesy was moments overdue.

"You're welcome," he answered gravely, his hands sliding the length of her arms, only to wrap around her waist, capturing her effectively.

His head dipped and Chloe felt his breath against her hair, each strand seemingly sensitive to his warmth. She turned her head, and heard the murmur of her name spoken from lips that touched her temple. "I'm afraid I embarrassed Micah," she said quietly.

J.T. chuckled softly. "I doubt he cares, now that he's got a few minutes alone with Tilly. You didn't tell me he was soft on her."

Her anger melting to a puddle of regret, she relaxed against him. "Is that what you call it?"

"Where Micah's concerned it seems like a good name for his tender regard in her direction." His pause was long, and his arms tightened their grip. "Now, if we're talking about me, and the way I'm looking at you these days, I could come up with a better description, I think."

She wiggled beneath his embrace and he loosened his hold, allowing her to slide her arms up, then bringing his forearms higher beneath her breasts. She placed her own firmly against his and uttered a firm rebuke. A single word, yet it spoke her mind.

"Don't." Not that she didn't enjoy the support beneath the soft curves. Not that she felt threatened by the movement. But simply because the subtle caress spoke of his intentions. Intentions she'd been mulling over in her mind, even as they rode the length of canyons, finally filing it neatly in a mental pigeonhole labeled *Flannery,* as the sun settled against the western horizon.

His arms refused to shift their position. "I don't mean any insult to you, Chloe," he said quietly. "I don't know how many men you've kept company with, but I don't think there's a long list of them." And as she sputtered her way into a reply, he lifted one finger to press against her lips. "I don't want to know, honey. If there's anybody out there who's looking to stake a claim here, he'd might as well look in another direction."

She inhaled sharply as his silencing finger was removed and his hand found its place again against her midriff. "Does this have to do with you *staking a claim?*"

He was silent for a moment, and his mouth moved from her temple to her cheek, his breath warm against her skin as he whispered his reply. "Yeah, I guess you could say that." A soft chuckle escaped his lips as though he hesitated, groping for words. "I did mention the idea earlier, but now that I think about it, I came across sounding sorta…"

While he groped for a suitable word, Chloe grinned at his confusion. The man wasn't used to eating crow, she decided, and she wasn't about to make it any more palatable for him to digest.

"Are you laughing at me?" he asked abruptly, lifting his hands to her shoulders, turning her to face him. His frown was apparent in the moonlight, and she tried in vain to suppress the smile she wore. The light from the kitchen window exposed her face to his view, and then his head blotted the lamplight from her sight as he bent to touch his mouth to her forehead.

"Go ahead and laugh," he murmured. "I told you before, this is a first for me. I've never considered marriage, not until now."

''Well, you're getting practice at making the offer,'' she said lightly. ''By the time you find someone willing to take a gamble on you, you'll have it down pat.''

''You're not willing?'' he asked. ''I'm kinda fond of the idea myself.'' His mouth teased a path across her cheek, and she held her breath, aware now of his goal. ''I'm gonna kiss you, Chloe.''

It was risky, she knew. Yet the temptation he offered beckoned, and she felt a moment's resentment that these few stolen moments with J. T. Flannery might be all she'd ever have to tuck away into her memory box. Warm lips touched hers and pleasure welled within her, as she tilted her head to accept the caress he offered.

Warm, moist and knowing, his mouth opened a bit, his teeth sending a shiver to dwell at the base of her spine as they touched her lower lip and held it in a tender vise. His tongue dampened the soft flesh and measured its width, and then he suckled it carefully, only to release it as he fit their mouths together again in a gentle kiss.

Demanding nothing, seemingly willing to be satisfied with only the brushing of his lips against hers, he lifted his head to inhale sharply, his gaze seeking hers. ''Chloe? Will you think about it?''

Her body held upright by his strength, she leaned against him, her mouth cool as the breeze touched its moist surface. ''Think about it?'' Her mind focusing on the ability of a simple touching of lips to bring such delight, she could only repeat her query. ''Think about what?'' If only he'd lean just a bit, dip his head a few scant inches, that generous mouth would once more…

His quiet laughter brought her to her senses and she stiffened at his words. ''Don't you know you've been proposed to, for the second time in one day?''

''Really? I thought a genuine proposal included the words, *Will you marry me?*''

"I suspect you're right there," he said. "I'm not doing this well, am I?"

"Probably not, but it doesn't make a whole lot of difference," she told him. "I told you before, J.T., I'm not willing to get married, and much as I've enjoyed your kissing, it's not going to persuade me into a wedding." Her hands pressed firmly on his chest and his arms dropped to his sides.

"Would it help if I said the words nicely?" An element of teasing rode each syllable and she bristled at his nonchalant attitude.

"I don't know how to say it any more clearly," she said, her voice rising in increments as she spoke words she knew she would regret. And yet, no matter how the man appealed to her, no matter the lure of his touch and the kisses she'd reveled in, she would not allow him to sweet talk her into an alliance she couldn't afford. She'd lost half the ranch already, and risking what was left of her inheritance was out of the question.

"You'll probably make someone a wonderful husband," she told the man before her with exaggerated patience. "However, it isn't going to be me."

His eyes scanned her face slowly. "Don't count on that, sweetheart," he said softly, his hands lifting to cradle her face. "I'm not used to giving up so easily. Especially when I want something as badly as I want you."

Chloe grasped his wrists, tugging with little success. "Damn you, Flannery. I don't want *you*," she yelled, the lie almost sticking in her throat as she shoved him from her, catching him off guard. His back hit the wood siding with a thud, and, caught up in the momentum, she fell against him. "Is that so hard for you to believe?" she whispered.

The door opened with a bang. "Did you hear the lady?" Micah stood in the open doorway, and J.T. nodded a silent reply. His hands fell to his sides and Chloe closed her eyes, embarrassment sweeping over her like a tidal wave. She righted herself and stepped back, miserable, her heart aching with loss as she recognized the success of her denial.

"Chloe, you come on in the house." It was a command she could not ignore, given the respect she held for her aunt, and Chloe answered the summons, stepping past Micah and into Tilly's arms. Behind her the door closed, and Tilly pushed her into a chair.

"Now, you tell me what was going on out there, girl. I couldn't believe my ears when I heard the two of you carrying on thataway. Micah's about fit to be tied, and I'm not far behind him."

"J.T. wants me to marry him," she said dully, looking down at her hands. Fingers trembling, she clasped them together in her lap and counted the hot tears that fell to glisten in the lamplight against her skin.

Tilly laughed, a resounding cackle that brought Chloe's head up in surprise. "What did you expect, girl? The man's nearly besotted. Can't hardly keep his eyes off you. I saw this coming from the day I met him."

Tilly was a blurred vision as Chloe blinked away the tears, and looked directly into the older woman's eyes. "I can't risk losing my half of the ranch, Aunt Tilly. Once I marry, I'll lose any control I have over what happens here. When I think of what Peter's done to me, I could shake the stuffings out of him."

"Well, for heaven's sake, child. You can't blame Peter for making you so bull-headed. J.T.'s not after your share of the ranch. He just wants *you*. Is that so hard for you to understand?"

Chloe's jaw clenched as she considered Tilly's words, and then she shook her head in denial. "He thinks he can kiss me and make monkeyshines with me and I'll just give in, Aunt Tilly. He makes my head swim with all his foolishness."

"That's called *desire,* sweetie, for lack of a better word. And there's nothing wrong with having feelings and hankerin' after the man. He's wanting to make it legal, ain't he? He hasn't tried to get you between the sheets without a wedding, has he?"

Chloe shook her head vehemently. "Of course not. And I wouldn't anyway." Although, if she were absolutely honest, a few more minutes in his arms and she'd have considered it, had there been a feather tick right handy. What she'd have done, once she got there, was another thing to wonder at.

Breeding horses and cattle was a far cry from what went on between men and women. Even an ignoramus like her knew that.

Dinner the next day was a silent meal, and J.T. had left the table, leaving Chloe to her thoughts.

"Chloe, come take a gander at this." Aunt Tilly's tone was impatient and she turned from the window, holding aside the curtain, the better for her niece to look out across the yard. A rider sat atop his horse, shoulders hunched a little, his hat pulled low over his eyes, and the familiar silhouette of her brother brought a smothered gasp of surprise from Chloe's lips.

"I'll be—" she began, and then her voice trailed off. "Is it really Peter?" She opened the back door and stepped onto the porch, Tilly close behind her.

"Sure looks like it to me," Tilly said dryly. "I told you he'd turn up one day. How much you want to bet he's tryin' to sweet-talk J.T. into taking him on?"

"Why would he need to approach J.T.?" Chloe snapped, her boots striking the steps harshly. "He's family, and he doesn't have to kowtow to anyone. There's always a place for Peter here."

"Thought you were gonna shake the stuffings out of

him,'' Tilly said dryly. "Now you're ready to greet him like the prodigal son.''

Chloe came to a halt, then looked back at her aunt. "I'm still mad at him, but I'm sure glad to see he's all right. I'll wait till later to knock some sense into him.''

Her strides were long as she stalked across the yard, her boots kicking up small spurts of dust behind her, her gaze focused on the lean figure of her brother. "Peter?" A hint of apprehension tinged the syllables as she spoke his name and she watched as his shoulders stiffened, and then his head turned in her direction.

"Hey, Sis." The greeting was quiet, a bit defensive, she decided, as if he doubted his welcome. "I just sent Willie looking for your new boss man. Thought I might as well find out right off the bat how welcome I'm going to be.''

"You're always welcome when you come home," she said quietly. He looked young, she thought, unsure and utterly weary. "Aunt Tilly has a kettle of soup on the back of the stove," she offered. "Why don't you come on up and eat? J.T. can find you in the house just as easy as not.''

"I'd rather talk to him here.'' The tone was harsh, she decided, peering into the barn as J.T.'s tall figure appeared in the wide doorway.

"Why don't you let Tilly know your brother's here, Chloe?" J.T.'s eyes narrowed as he turned them on her, and she felt the chill of his anger, as if it were a viable thing.

It was a dismissal, and she stung from the lash of his words. "She knows already," Chloe said, standing her ground. "I'd like to hear what you have to say to Peter.''

"No, I don't think you would," J.T. told her. And to her surprise, Peter nodded glumly.

"Go on up to the house, Sis. If I'd wanted you to be in on this, I'd have come to the house first.''

It stung. The harsh message from J.T. was one she could handle; in fact this whole episode would serve to build a barrier between them, and that might be for the best. But to have her brother so easily shut her out delivered a hurtful blow, and she could only nod and turn away.

J.T.'s eyes noted her clenched jaw, and his gaze followed her as she walked back toward the porch. The pain of rejection gripped her, holding her stiffly erect, her head high. He ached for her, even as he acknowledged the need for privacy during these few moments with Peter Biddleton. His temper rode a fine edge as he turned back to the youth who sat astride his horse. Resentment was written on his young features, and stark hatred filled his gaze.

"You know why I'm here, I suspect," Peter said.

"Well, why don't you just tell me, and save me the guesswork," J.T. drawled. "I can't say I'd expected to see you hereabouts. Seems like you've given your sister enough grief without adding to it by coming around looking for a handout."

"I'm not looking for a handout. I expect to earn my way," Peter said staunchly.

"What's that supposed to mean? Spit it out, boy."

"I need a job," Peter told him. "Seems like there should be one here for me, seeing as how it's my own home."

J.T. shook his head. "That's where you're wrong, son. It's not your home. Not anymore. Remember? You gambled it away, as I recall, holding a full house against my four jacks."

"And I suppose you've had a field day, telling folks hereabouts how you got the best of the Biddletons, haven't you?" The words sounded petulant to J.T.'s ears and the accusation stung, unfair as it was.

"Matter of fact, I've told folks that you sold me your share of the ranch," he said mildly. "Take it or leave it, boy, that's the truth."

A look that might have been relief softened the anger in Peter's eyes and he shifted in his saddle. "Well, the truth is, I need a job for a while. I'm a good hand, Hogan can tell you that. Besides—'' his smile was faint, but taunting "—my sister'll be madder than a wet hen if you send me off without giving me a chance."

"Chloe doesn't tell me what to do when it comes to the hired hands," J.T. told him. "We have an understanding."

"Oh, I'll just bet you do," Peter said, his eyes measuring his opponent. "I suspect you figured Chloe for a soft touch, didn't you? A woman alone, trying to run this place. I'll warrant you fed her a line to get on her good side."

J.T.'s hands clenched, and he resisted the urge to haul Peter from his horse. Slamming him against the barn door would ease his aggravation, but it wouldn't do a hell of a lot for his tenuous relationship with Chloe. "Your sister doesn't enter into this," he said quietly. "If you're asking for a job, I'll have to tell you that the wages aren't much right now. You'd ought to remember how you emptied her bank account on your way out of town a few months ago. Your sister's been operating on borrowed funds."

"I only took what I had coming," Peter said harshly. "And if it hadn't been for you I'd still be in charge here."

"Now, how do you figure that?" J.T. widened his stance, his fists lifting to rest against his hips, even as he allowed a smile to curve his mouth. "I'd like to hear this, boy. You're saying I made you put your share of the ranch on the table in Silver City?"

Peter hesitated. "I'm saying you mighta had a little help with those four jacks, Flannery. Not that I have any solid proof, but it sure seems like the sun was shining on you that day."

"Well, sonny," J.T. drawled. "When the time comes that you want to make that accusation stick, you just let me know, and I'll be ready to take you on. In the meantime, you go on up to the house and let your sister pat you on the head and tell you how wonderful you are."

"While you decide if I'm to be allowed a place in the bunkhouse?" Peter's face colored as he jerked his reins. "I'm not sleeping in a bunk when I've got a room to call my own in the house, Flannery."

J.T. grinned, delighted with the revelation he was about to unload on the unwary youth. "I've got your old room, I'm afraid. If I decided to let you stay here, you'll just be one of the hired hands, *Pete,* not the prodigal son. And if that's not to your liking, you can head on down the road and find someone else's shoulder to cry on. I figure you've probably got Chloe all teary-eyed, but you don't impress me."

"You sonova—"

"Stop right there," J.T. interrupted. "One more word and you can forget the whole idea. Like it or not, that's the way it is. Hogan's the foreman here, and he answers to me. Anything you've got to say, you can spout out right here and now, but you won't be questioning my mama's virtue, not any day of the week."

Peter stepped down from his mount and raised one hand in greeting, looking over J.T.'s shoulder. "Hey, there, Willie. Come on out here and take my horse, will you? I'll be up at the house." His gaze flicked again to J.T., as he spoke with galling arrogance to the man who'd approached from within the barn.

"That's not the way it's gonna be," J.T. said quietly. "You'll tend your own horse, Pete."

"When I decide I need a nickname, I'll let you know." With a frustrated glare at J.T., Peter stalked past him, leading his mount into the barn.

J.T. turned to watch him go, and caught Willie's eye, a slight shake of his head sending a message the young man could not fail to understand. Willie's hands slid into his pockets as Peter approached, and then with a murmur, he headed for the back of the barn.

He watched Peter climb the porch steps to reach for and embrace Chloe's small, compact figure. And then she looked across the yard at J.T., her gaze piercing him like a lightning bolt, her head tossing in rejection as she opened the door and entered the house, Peter fast on her heels.

He'd known it would come to this one day. But now wasn't the time he'd have chosen for this confrontation, J.T. thought angrily. The boy was important to his sister, and she was going to lean in his direction. If a push came to a shove, Pete would win her affection, no matter how attracted she was to her new partner.

And that attraction was a given. He'd known since the first kiss that she could be wooed and won, and after the moments on the porch the other night, he'd tasted victory. The memory of her supple body and the recollection of her mouth, warm and welcoming beneath his, was solid. Chloe was a woman to be cherished.

She was exactly what he'd dreamed of in those long nights when he'd allowed his yearnings full rein, envisioning a place to call home and a wife to call his own. She was strong and capable, and had a backbone a mile long. She'd work beside him and give him sons. Partnership be damned.

She was worth whatever effort it took to persuade her to his bed.

"Is your brother going to stick around?" J.T. was a towering shadow in the moonlight. Chloe watched as he walked toward her, and her every sense was alert. For all her aggravation at the man, she could not fault his judgment when it came to Peter—or Pete, as the young man had mumbled at the supper table, in response to her speaking his name. And then he'd tossed a resentful look at J.T. as she repeated the diminutive.

His saddlebags in hand, he'd gone to the bunkhouse after

supper. Chloe's trip up the stairs had produced a fat feather pillow and one of her mother's quilts for Pete's use, along with a set of sheets for his bunk. She'd watched him, a strange sense of relief filling her. Hesitantly, she'd admitted to herself that J.T. was more able to handle her willful brother, lessening the load on her own shoulders.

Her father had despaired of his only son ever amounting to anything, and the admission had been painful for John Biddleton to come by. ''Your ma spoiled him rotten,'' he'd told Chloe, only days before his death. ''She always favored him, but you're the stronger one. I need to protect you, girl. I'll have Paul Taylor change things in my will one of these days, so you can run things here and keep Peter's hands out of things.''

But he hadn't. Perhaps it was the knowledge that her father would have done much the same as J.T., had he been here this afternoon, that made Chloe soften toward the man who stood before her now. ''Is he going to stay?'' he asked, repeating his query.

''I suspect so,'' she said quietly. ''He took his gear out to the bunkhouse. I'll get down his old clothes from the attic in the morning. I cleaned his closet and packed everything away when you arrived.'' She looked up at J.T. and tried to smile, but the effort failed. ''He didn't bring much with him, did he?''

He shook his head. ''No, not much. But then, neither did I.''

''You had cash to spend. Pete hasn't.''

''You've changed his name.'' J.T. sounded satisfied, and she nodded.

''He asked me to, remember? And I've a notion it was your doing.''

''Yeah, but I didn't know how you'd take to the idea.''

''You told me something once,'' she reminded him. ''You said one day he'd turn into Pete and become a man.

If he wants that to happen, I'll do everything I can to bring it about. Calling him Pete is easy enough for me to remember.''

"I hope he'll live up to your expectations," J.T. said bluntly. "I don't want to see you hurt, Clo."

She lifted her head, meeting his gaze without flinching. "It's happened before. It'll probably happen again."

"Not if I can help it." His words were insistent, and she felt a sense of comfort envelop her. A comfort she could not afford to embrace. His mere presence was a seduction of sorts, she realized, and too late she took a step back, easing from the scent of his shaving soap, the aroma of leather and clean clothes that were a part of the man.

He rarely approached her with the smell of cattle announcing his nearness, although she was not averse to the odor that sprang from barn and pasture alike. She'd been born here, raised with the animals that provided a living. But J.T. made it his business to be cleaned up for supper every night, and, not for the first time, she was aware of his efforts to please her.

Now he followed her hesitant retreat, and his hands reached to circle her waist. She wore a wrapper, donned after supper when she'd spent the better part of an hour in the tub. Beneath it she wore her undergarments, drawers and a vest. Her legs were bare of stockings, her feet uncovered, as she stood in the shadow of the porch. Her toes dug into the dust of the path, each of them curling in anticipation as J.T.'s palms lent warmth to her skin through the layers of fabric.

"We weren't going to do this anymore," she reminded him, unable to reject his advances, even as her mind put up barriers against his appeal.

"I never said that," he whispered. "You were the one who did all the hollering the other night. I told you I wouldn't give up easily, didn't I?" He tilted his head, allowing the moonlight to illumine her face. ''Matter of fact, you told me I'd make somebody a wonderful husband, Clo. I keep thinkin' that somebody oughta be you.''

Almost, she was persuaded by the whisper of her name, the single sound that was soft against her ear. But the rebellion welling within her prevailed and rallied against the temptation he offered. She shook her head, a slow, sad movement.

''No. Now that Pete's here, there's even more reason to hang on to my share of things. I can't afford to turn loose. Can't you see that? You've already got me in debt to you, what with the stallion and paying the wages out of your pocket. If I married you—''

''Stop it,'' he said harshly, silencing her with a brush of his mouth against hers. ''I've already told you—''

She twisted her head, escaping the seduction of his kiss. ''I know what you told me,'' she cried softly. ''But I can't risk it.''

''Not even if we put it in writing?'' he asked, his words harsh, as if her doubts were a personal affront to him. ''I told you I don't want your share, Chloe.''

She heard his voice speak the syllables of her name, and for a moment rued his rejection of the diminutive he'd chosen to whisper earlier.

''What do you want?'' she asked. ''Me in the kitchen and the bedroom, while you take over everything else?'' It went against the grain, the knowledge that he considered her unable to cope with the work she'd been obliged to handle for the past six years.

His smile was brief, overshadowed by the taut movement of his lips as he spoke words that took her breath. ''I want you. Pure and simple, I want *you,* Clo. In my bed, at my side, across the table in the morning and in my arms whenever I can manage it.''

''You want me.'' She heard her voice tremble as she repeated his statement, and she considered the words, acknowledging the absence of any emotion on his part except that of desire.

"That shouldn't be a surprise to you," he said quietly. "I've made it clear. You're what I've looked for in a woman over the past years."

"You didn't think so at first," she said, her words challenging his claim. "I saw the way you looked at me that first day. You wrote me off as a plain female with no chance of doing battle with a man like you."

"You really thought that?" he asked, and his grin was immediate. "And here I was admiring your pretty hair, all done up and wrapped around your head, and tryin' my best to count those freckles across your nose."

"I'm no fool," she told him harshly, yearning for his words to be true, yet unwilling to accept his blarney. "I look in the mirror every morning. I know what I look like, and that's all right. I've learned to live with being a plain woman with an ordinary face full of freckles, and a body that's about six inches too short."

"There's not a thing wrong with your body, sweetheart," he murmured. "You've got curves in all the right places, and I happen to like the freckles."

"I suppose you're going to tell me next that you fell in love with me at first sight," she scoffed.

He shook his head slowly. "No, ma'am. I won't lie to you. I'm not sure I know what 'fallin' in love' is. But I do know I'm willing to take you on as my wife and spend the rest of my life being a good husband to you."

"Well, that's all very charming," said Pete from the shadows at the side of the house, "but I'd appreciate it if you took your hands off my sister, Flannery. And I've got a gun in my hand, in case you need some persuading."

Chapter Six

"**I** don't think you want to aim that thing at me, boy."
J.T. eased Chloe from his grasp and turned to face the rifle
pointed in his direction. "And your sister's in the direct line
of fire, Pete. I didn't think you'd be so careless with your
weapon."

"Then why don't you just move away from her, big
man?" Pete waved the barrel upward as he spoke, and
Chloe found her voice.

"Put that gun down, you idiot. Pa would roll over in his
grave if he knew you were acting this way." She spun from
J.T.'s side and rounded the end of the porch, reaching for
the rifle. "I'm a big girl, Pete, and what I do is my own
business." The gun left his hands as she snatched it from
him, the barrel pointing toward the sky. "Now you get on
out in the bunkhouse and behave yourself. If you want a job
here, you'd better be up at daybreak and ready for some
long hours of hard work."

Pete's face fell, yet his jaw was taut with obvious anger
as he turned on his sister. "You're the one Pa would be
having a fit over, throwing yourself at a two-bit gambler,
and acting the fool right out in front of anybody wanting to
watch."

"Well, sonny," J.T. said, crossing the few feet between them, "I'd say that's none of your business. You'd do well to mind what your sister says and head for your bunk." He took the long gun from Chloe's hands and eased it into the crook of his elbow. "Where'd you get this anyway?" he asked.

"It was my pa's," Pete told him, his chin lifting defiantly. "And there's more where that one came from. I'd say I can claim any one of them I please."

"*I'd* say you'd do well to keep your hands off anything in the house," J.T. said quietly. "The guns belong to your sister. I thought I'd made it clear that you don't own one damn thing on this place, Pete. And if it wasn't clear enough the first time, I'll repeat it. You lost your share, fair and square. Take it or leave it."

Chloe stifled the words that begged to spill from her lips, aching to chide J.T., even as she yearned to comfort the boy who'd been her companion from birth. Good sense kept her silent, and she shoved her hands into the deep pockets of her wrapper, shivering from the emotions that gripped her.

Pete cast her a long look, and she lowered her head, unwilling to undermine the authority she'd just given J.T. by her silence. And yet there was alive in her breast the urge to offer comfort to her brother. She opened her mouth, forming her thoughts, only to hear the shuffle of feet as Pete made his way across the yard toward the lighted windows where the rest of the men were already settling down for the night.

The night promised to be chilly and a plume of smoke rose from the tin chimney, guaranteeing a warm fire in the woodstove. As Pete opened the door, a wave of laughter and the sound of Lowery's voice rose above the rest.

"What the hell do you think I told her?" he asked. "My mama didn't raise no fool. I just followed her right on up those stairs and—'' The door closed and Chloe shot a quick look at J.T.

"I don't think I was supposed to hear that, was I?"

"No, ma'am. I'd say that was man talk." Not so quick as she to forget Pete's angry words and hasty actions, he cradled the rifle in one arm and held out his other hand in her direction. "Let's go on in the house."

The coffeepot sat on the back of the stove, and Chloe poured two cups of the strong brew before she sat down at the table. A lamp glowed overhead, illuminating her as she sat within the circle of light. "You going to join me?" she asked quietly. From his post near the kitchen window, J.T. turned his head, his face in shadow.

"Are you wanting to talk about this?"

Chloe shrugged and drew her finger in a circle around the lip of her cup. "I guess we should. But I don't know what else there is to say." Her gaze rose to seek him out. "Pete was wrong, and he knew it. He's always had a problem with authority, from way back when we were coming up and Pa would get after him for not doing his chores. I don't see what else you could have done tonight," she admitted sadly, as though acknowledging her brother's flaws was painful.

Relief swept through him and J.T. approached the table, pulling a chair from beneath the checkered oilcloth and easing onto the seat. "I wasn't sure if you'd back me, Clo. I didn't want to hurt your feelings, but Pete's got to respect my authority here."

"I know that," she admitted softly, and her eyes were shiny with moisture as she allowed him access to the sorrow within her. She blinked, lifting her cup to sip from it, and tears made a path down each cheek, gleaming in the lamplight. The cup cradled in her palms, she peered into its depths as if the answer to all her problems lay beneath the dark surface.

"Pete's wrong about a lot of things," she said, "and if he can't start growing up now, I don't know what's going to happen to him."

"He was sure way off target when he accused you of throwing yourself at me," J.T. drawled. "Seems like the truth lays in the opposite direction. I'm following you around like a lost pup and you keep tossin' my proposals back in my face." He reached across the table, gripping the cup she held and lowering it to the table. And then his hands were on hers and he cradled them in his palms.

"I'm thinking that maybe it'll make Pete realize where things are heading if we get married, Clo. Once he knows that I'm here to stay, he might settle down."

"Either that or he'll blow up and head on out again," she surmised. Her mouth trembled as she spoke her fears aloud. "I'm afraid I'm losing him. And he's all I've got in this world."

His silence drew her attention more surely than as if he had quickly denounced her claim, and she looked up, unable to miss the stern line of his mouth, the darkness within him that wrapped him in stillness. He watched her, eyes hooded, his fingers brushing softly against the surface of her hand. And then finally spoke, his words measured.

"Are you sure he's *everything* to you, Clo? Don't I hold just a bit of your esteem? Is there any chance at all that you'll be able to come to me and let me share your life?" His pause was long as she considered his words, and then a smile hovered over his lips. "Guess I was whistling in a windstorm, wasn't I?"

He placed her hands together on the table with a gentle touch, then pushed back, rising from his chair quietly. "Good night, Chloe."

His boots touched the wooden boards of the hallway with care, as if he determined not to catch Tilly's attention as he headed for the stairway. With barely a sound he climbed to the second floor, only the creak on the fourth step giving away his location as he went.

Chloe sat beneath the warm lamp, with the stove at her back, listening to him make his way across the bedroom directly overhead and heard the quiet sounds of the bed as he sat on the mattress. One boot, then the other, hit the floor with a thump, and then the bed squeaked as he moved on its surface.

Bending her head, she focused intently on her clasped hands, drawing them toward her, until the tears she shed fell gently against her skin.

Outwardly, over the next two weeks, Chloe supported him, nodding when he gave orders, allowing his word to reign even when she differed with him over minor items, walking away rather than confronting him. And that very fact was irritating him beyond belief. Gone were the days when she argued ferociously over minor details, scrambling to maintain her hold on the running of the Double B.

Her eyes were sad as she watched the brother she loved, and J.T. could find no way to mend the fences that threatened to disrupt the peace he'd come to cherish within the walls of the ranch house. Meals were a silent battleground, the men taking their breakfast and supper in the house. With Tilly back, they no longer ate in the bunkhouse.

The work was heavy in late spring, and the hands labored for long hours. Several of them spent mornings training horses to be sold, riding them in the corral to the sound of shouts and laughter, and then taking turns with Chloe, cooling them down, pacing the length of the lane and back.

Her arms ached from using the currycomb and brushes on the sleek coats, and yet she thrived on the task. Handling the horses was an essential part of their training. Getting them accustomed to human touch was an ongoing process, one that involved more than just riding them. And she'd always loved the hours she spent grooming and whispering her hopes and dreams into ears that kept her secrets.

Today was no different, she supposed, except that her hopes for happiness in her future seemed farther away than ever before. She'd never set her sights on any man in particular, always wary that half her charm might be the Double B. As if she had any charm to begin with, she thought dourly, leading a sassy bay mare back to the pasture gate.

She slid the halter from its place and swatted the frisky creature as white stockings flashed past her, the slender legs carrying the mare swiftly toward the stream that dissected the grassy expanse. Trees sheltered a herd of horses halfway across the field, and Chloe closed the gate slowly, intent on the solid-colored assortment of animals.

J.T. had said a paint brought more money, and their new stud had been in use almost on a daily basis over the past weeks. She'd steered clear of the breeding area, leaving the job of tying mares in place and padding the hooves of the stallion to the men. Her father had simply turned his stallion loose in the field and let nature take its course. But J.T. had a different manner of doing things. Time would tell how well his method worked.

She fastened the gate and headed back to the barn, where Lowery was stripping the saddle from one of the young geldings. "You ready for me to walk him?" she asked, smiling as the frisky creature turned his head to nip at Lowery's sleeve.

"He's an ornery one, Miss Chloe. Keep a weather eye on him."

"Where's my brother working today, Lowery?" she asked idly. Pete was managing to disappear most days for hours at a time, and Chloe had a notion that J.T. was about ready to lay down the law.

"Can't say where he is, ma'am," Lowery said, evading her gaze. "J.T.'s got most of the men keepin' a good eye on the steers, and we've all been workin' on the young bulls, you know—'' He flushed as he cut off his words, and his shrug was eloquent.

"Yes," she said quickly. "I knew they were branding and taking care of the bulls. Maybe that's where Pete is today."

"Doubt it," Lowery said. "He was riding fences yesterday. Said he wasn't much on the dirty work." He grinned ruefully. "Your brother ain't much for ranch work, in any way, shape or form, is he?"

"No, he never was. You know that, Lowery."

"Well, here you go, ma'am." Sliding a halter on the gelding, Lowery fastened the buckle and attached a lead rope. "This one's all yours."

Chloe took the lead from his hand, and Lowery turned away, lifting the saddle and bridle as he headed for the tack room. She walked quickly from the barn, the horse butting at her shoulder playfully, jarring her from her doldrums. Caught off guard by his playful antics, she laughed aloud, and scolded him cheerfully.

"Don't hear that very often." The words were hushed, almost as if spoken beneath his breath, and Chloe's heart beat rapidly as J.T. stepped from beside the barn door to walk with her. "You don't laugh much lately," he said, reaching to brush back a lock of hair from her forehead.

She swallowed, aware of a lump in her throat, and recognized that its presence was familiar. For two weeks, she'd been on the verge of giving way to a bout of crying, only her intense work with the horses keeping her from wallowing in her slumping spirits. And now a plenteous supply of hot, salty tears appeared, as though called forth by his presence. She coughed and turned her head away, unwilling to reveal her weakness, but he would not be deterred.

"Clo?" His hand touched hers, there where her fingers

clutched the lead line, and enveloped her fingers in his. "Look at me, Chloe. Please."

"I can't," she whispered, blinking furiously at the salty drops trembling on her lower eyelids.

"Sure you can." His simple assurance coaxed her, even as his other hand brushed against her cheek.

The horse tugged at the lead, jarring the tenuous touch of his fingers, and J.T. growled a word beneath his breath. "Damn, Chloe. I want to talk to you."

"I'll see you at the supper table," she said, firming her voice, straightening her shoulders and jerking the lead line from his grip.

"Lowery!" J.T.'s voice rang out across the yard, and in seconds a reply came from inside the barn.

"I'm here, J.T. Something wrong?" The copper-haired cowhand hustled from the shadowed interior, a bridle in one hand, a lariat in the other. "I was just headin' out to the pasture to rope another one of the herd. Figured I had plenty of time…" His voice trailed off as he caught sight of J.T.'s face.

"Come take this horse and cool him off. Chloe and I have got something to take care of."

Lowery shrugged. "Sure, I can do that, boss. Give me a chance to work out some of the kinks." With a show of nonchalance, he took the lead line from Chloe's fingers, and with a cheerful whistle set off down the lane, the horse ambling along behind him.

J.T.'s hand was firm on her waist as he led Chloe toward the orchard. The leaves were fully unfurled, the blossoms falling to the ground in snowy splendor, and new grass grew beneath the widespread limbs. It offered a lush blanket and with little ceremony, he pulled her to the ground and sat beside her.

"Now," he began, "talk to me. Tell me what I can do to make things right with you." Lifting her hand to his knee, he held it firmly, his rough, callused fingers tracing the lines of her palm; then turning it, he brushed small bits of dust from her fingers. She was silent and he sighed, lifting her fingers to his lips.

She jerked away, but he refused to loosen his hold, and her eyes flashed as she met his gaze. "I told you once before about bullying me. You don't have to prove how strong you are, mister."

He reached to wipe a tear from her cheek, and she inhaled sharply. "Why the tears?" he asked quietly, ignoring her accusations.

"Something in my eye," she lied, her jaw taut as though she fought for control.

"You've got tears in your eyes, Chloe. Don't give me that stuff. And I want to know what's wrong with you." He was impatient now, his nights of broken sleep and days of long hours stealing his good nature.

"I swear I've done more crying in the past weeks since you showed up than I've done in my whole life. And on top of it all, I wish Pete had stayed away," she blurted out. "I feel so angry with him most of the time, and the rest of the time I yearn for things to be right between us." She lifted her free hand to swipe furiously at new trickles making their way down her cheek. "That'll never happen, J.T."

She tilted her head back and he noted circles beneath her eyes, apparent in the unforgiving glare of afternoon sun. "Damn!" she blurted out harshly. "He's not carrying his share of the load, and you're putting up with it, and you shouldn't have to."

"Maybe not, but he's your brother, Clo." And as if that were reason enough for his actions, he allowed his anger at Pete to fade. "I'll put up with him for a while, because I know he's mad at the world in general right now."

"He'll never make a rancher, will he?" Her fingers plucked at the grass beside her and she lifted her hand, allowing the fragile stems to float to the ground. "My father wanted so much for Pete to run the place, but he was never suited to the job. And they didn't hit it off, not from the time Pete was a kid."

"Did you get along with your pa?" J.T. asked.

"Always," Chloe told him. "We were on the same track, like our minds worked in harness. He'd stand on the back porch with me in the morning, and I almost knew what he was going to say before he opened his mouth. Pa was a good rancher, but he didn't have the ideas you do. It was simpler to let things go along and just tend to the calves and foals as they were born."

"Well, I'll agree with you there. He wasn't much of a breeder." J.T. looked at her, and she met his gaze.

"You've got him pegged," she said. "He never thought of improving the herd or bringing in new blood, the way you have."

He cleared his throat and reached for her hand once more. "I've been thinking about looking for a new bull, maybe next year. I'd like to get more bulk in the steers. If we breed the cows early on, as soon as they drop their calves, we'd have some dandy beef to sell in a couple of years."

"Sounds to me like you're sinking your money into this place hand over fist," Chloe said, allowing his fingers to grip hers. "You'll end up owning it, won't you?"

He shook his head. "No, I'm not planning on anything but a partnership with you. I don't mind investing my nest egg, Chloe. I've been handed the chance of a lifetime, with a base of stock that'll tide us over until the new blood makes a difference. Nothing is for sure, but if we're willing to work at it, I'd say we could have a thriving operation within three years."

"And how long do you think Pete will stick it out?" she asked.

He was silent, his callused fingers brushing across the

back of her hand. "Till he gets tired of taking orders, I expect. And I think he's about at that point right now, honey."

She nodded. "I wouldn't be surprised. He's managed to get lost in the shuffle most every day the past week. No one seems to know where he is or what he's doing. I keep waiting for you to nail him."

His laugh was harsh, and he took her hand between his. "You may not have to wait too long. He's about played out every inch of rope I've given him."

From the barn, raised voices caught their attention and Chloe turned her head, alert to the anger Hogan made no attempt to disguise.

"Damn it all, Pete. I sent you out to ride the fence line and catch up with any strays, and you came up empty-handed again. What the hell did you do all morning?"

"I don't answer to a ranch foreman," Pete snarled, his voice carrying to where J.T. and Chloe were scrambling to their feet. He looked in their direction, as though their movements caught his eye, and his eyes blazed scornfully.

"Why don't we ask my sister who I'm answering to around here these days?" he said. "Looks to me like her and her new partner are both taking the day off, sittin' under an apple tree, makin' monkeyshines."

J.T. stepped ahead of Chloe, and in less than five seconds was reaching for Pete's shirtfront, lifting him from the ground and shoving him against the side of the barn. "You'll show a little more respect to your sister," he muttered, his fist twisting in the dark fabric, his knuckles just beneath Pete's chin.

"J.T." Chloe moved to his side, and her hand was warm on J.T.'s upper arm, where the muscle bulged beneath her fingers. "Let him down," she said quietly, and with a glance in her direction, he did as she asked.

Pete's triumphant grin encompassed the watching ranch

hands, Lowery and Hogan standing in the barn door, their eyes apprehensive as they waited for J.T.'s response.

"You'll either do as Hogan tells you, or you'll pack your duds and be on your way," J.T. said quietly. "I won't have a man on the place who doesn't pull his weight."

"Is that so?" Pete asked, his hands cocked on his hips. His eyes narrowed as he turned to Chloe and his query was loaded with assurance. "What do you think, Sis? Are you letting the gamblin' man kick me off the ranch?"

Chloe was torn, unwilling to back from the stand she'd taken, yet aware that if Pete left, she would likely not see him again. "J.T.'s in charge of the ranch operation," she said finally. "You'll have to deal with him, Pete." Her heart ached as her brother turned away.

"Made up your mind, son?" J.T. asked mildly, and Pete stopped just inside the barn door.

"Yeah, I expect I have," he said. "Riding the fence line beats cuttin' bulls any day of the week." He led his horse from its stall and out into the sunshine. His face was stony, his jaw clenched as he mounted, and he tugged at his hat, shielding his eyes from view. "I'll be back for supper," he told Hogan. "And I'll drag all the lost strays with me. Hope that makes you happy, *little sister.*" His final words directed at Chloe, he turned his horse with a jerk of his reins and trotted past the corral into the near pasture.

"I thought for certain he'd bolt," Hogan said to J.T. as he watched the young man ride away. "He's never been one to take orders, even from the old man."

"So I've heard," J.T. answered. "I'd keep an eye out if I were you. Maybe one of the men can ride herd on him for a few days."

"We'll take a shot at it, but we don't have enough hands to play nursemaid," Lowery said harshly. "Pete's gonna go too far one of these days. You mind my words, he's headed for trouble."

* * *

Supper was a quiet affair, with Pete arriving late, after the first bowls of food had been passed among the men and emptied. Chloe stood at the stove, platter in hand as Tilly lifted pork chops from the big skillet. She turned as the door opened, and her heart lifted as Pete waved a greeting.

"Located a dozen strays for you, Sis," he said jauntily. "I put them in the pasture till they can be checked over." He settled at the table, drawing his plate closer as he prepared to heap it from the newly filled bowls of vegetables and gravy.

"See any sign of trouble?" Hogan asked, lifting his fork to his mouth as he bent over his plate. He watched Pete carefully as the young man buttered a thick slice of bread. "Any fence down, Pete?"

"Nah. There's nothing going on out there. Those rustlers are long gone. I'll bet they sold those steers before they went twenty miles."

"Not with the Double B brand on them, they didn't," Hogan said sharply. "There's not a man around who'd buy branded cattle. Not an honest man, anyway."

"Nothing to get all in a dither about anyway," Pete said sharply. "What's a few head of cattle when the range is full of stock?"

"You wouldn't be so generous with them if they were yours," J.T. said harshly. "I'd say you need to rearrange your thinking, boy."

Pete pushed his chair back from the table and stood. "I'm not a *boy*," he snarled. "I'm more entitled to this place than a penny-ante gambler any day of the week. Hiding that fourth jack up your sleeve might have made you a bigwig, Flannery, but you don't impress me."

"It didn't make me a *bigwig* to hold four jacks. It made me half owner of a ranch." J.T. stood, his chair moving soundlessly as he lifted it aside. "Now, if you'd like to go outside and talk about cheating at cards, I'll be glad to meet you behind the barn.''

Pete's eyes shifted from J.T. to his sister, and Chloe was breathless as she faced the choice she must make. ''Don't do it, Pete,'' she said quietly. ''Take back that absurd lie before you go too far.''

''You'd believe him instead of me?'' Pete's face flushed with anger as he turned to face his sister head-on. ''He's a gambler, a lousy four-flusher, Sis. He played me for a fool, and walked away with my share of the ranch.''

''I haven't any reason to think he's lying,'' she said, making the decision that might cost her the love of her brother, one she would rue, should that happen. Yet, maybe if she sided with J.T. in such a way that Pete could no longer play them against each other, things would be better. And at that thought, she made up her mind.

''I'm going to marry him,'' she said quietly, aware that J.T.'s hand fisted against his thigh, and his gaze was bent in her direction. She looked up into dark eyes that flared with satisfaction. ''We'll go into town and see the preacher tomorrow.''

''Well, it's about time,'' Tilly said sharply. ''You've dillydallied long enough, Chloe.''

J.T.'s lips twitched and a dark flush touched his cheekbones as he cut a glance in Tilly's direction. And then he aimed a hard look at Chloe. ''That'll suit me fine,'' he said, his voice husky, his nostrils flaring as if he sought her scent. And then he was against her side, his arm circling her waist.

''I wasn't sure you'd want to tell the men until the deed was done, honey,'' he drawled. ''But, anyway you want to handle it is all right with me. The sooner the better.''

Hogan grinned from his seat at the other end of the table, and Lowery chuckled, a low, satisfied sound. Willie rose from his chair and ducked his head. ''I'd better be getting out to the barn,'' he said harshly. ''Chores won't wait for this sort of foolish talk.''

''Well,'' J.T. said slowly, waving the boy on his way, ''I'd like to think it's far from foolish when a woman finally makes up her mind and decides to tie the knot. Matter of fact, I'd like to propose a toast to the new Mrs. Flannery.'' He lifted his cup of coffee from the table and held it high, and the men scrambled for their glasses and mugs.

Pete's chair fell to the floor, and the screen door slammed behind him as J.T. made his announcement. But it was no deterrent to Hogan's laughter as he pushed his chair back and stood before his place. ''Don't know much about proposing a toast,'' he said, ''but I'll drink to a wedding any day of the week. Chloe'll make you a good wife, boss man. And there's enough of us here to be sure you treat her right.'' He swallowed deeply of the dark brew, then wiped his mouth on the back of his hand.

''Now, I'm gonna finish my pork chop and have another helping of green beans, Tilly.'' With a satisfied grin, he settled down again, and the men laughed, jokes flying fast and furiously as they passed the food around the big table, apparently determined not to allow Pete's hasty exit to dim their excitement.

Chloe looked up at J.T. ''Will he be all right?'' Her words were spoken in an undertone, lest the others at the table overhear.

''Hard to say.'' His shrug was eloquent, admitting his inability to comprehend Pete's actions. ''But he'll have to make a choice, honey. Either he works at ranching or he'll have to leave. And you can't make up his mind for him.''

Her whisper was forlorn. ''He's angry with me.''

''You knew he would be.'' His grip on her waist tightened and he drew her toward the table. ''Come on and eat now. You can't do anything about Pete. He's a man full grown, and he'll have to live with his mistakes, just like we all do.''

Chloe acceded to his bidding and dropped into a chair beside his. In moments the men had passed bowls in her direction and their small talk seemed designed to lift her spirits.

"Haven't been to a wedding in years," Hogan said with a grin. "You gonna do it up brown, Chloe, with a dance and food enough for all the neighbors?"

"You bet," J.T. said quickly, his smile warm as he bent his attention on Chloe. "It's gonna be a real celebration."

"I didn't leave you an open door, did I?" Chloe leaned against the side of the house. Beside her, J.T. slanted a long look in her direction.

"Who said I wanted one? I've been steering you in this direction almost since I got here. I can't say I'm unhappy with the turn of events. Matter of fact, I think I owe your brother a word of thanks for bringing things to a head."

Chloe gazed across the side yard to where the orchard flourished, the pale blossoms that covered the grass shimmering in the moonlight. "I was afraid I'd put you on the spot, springing that announcement in front of the men."

"Did they look surprised?" His words held a cocky note. "They knew the direction I was heading, almost from the first, Chloe. I haven't made any attempt to hide the way I feel about you."

"And how do you feel?" she asked, bold in the darkness. Her heart fluttered as she waited, although a declaration of love wasn't likely in the works. Not from this man, who'd already made it clear that falling in love was not up his alley.

"I feel like I'm about to do the smartest thing I've ever done in my life," he said firmly. "You're smart and pretty and you hold your own, Chloe. You appeal to me more than any other woman I've ever come across, and if you're thinking it'll be a hardship to share a bed with you, you've got a big surprise coming.''

So much for a declaration of love, she thought, focusing on the orchard and the pasture beyond its boundaries. ''I'm not sure about sharing a bed, J.T.,'' she said quietly. ''I've always thought I'd have to love a man before I took his name or invited him to my bedroom.''

''I won't put any pressure on you, honey,'' he said quietly, but she thought his words held a touch of disappointment in their depths. ''I've never demanded anything from a woman in my life. I'm sure not going to start now.''

She turned her head to meet his gaze, peering into dark eyes that were shadowed by the wide brim of his hat. ''You're telling me you'd be willing to stay upstairs while I sleep down here alone in my parents' bedroom?''

He shook his head. ''I didn't say that. I told you I won't demand anything from you. I didn't say I wouldn't try to coax you a little.'' And then he smiled, and even in the shadows of night his eyes glittered with satisfaction. ''I'll share your bed, Chloe. I won't have it any other way, not with Tilly and six men watching every step I take. They'd know in a heartbeat if we said good night at the foot of the stairs and then went our separate ways every night.

''I'll be moving my things to your room, just as soon as we speak our vows.''

Chapter Seven

"What are you up to in here?" J.T. leaned against the doorjamb, watching as Chloe sorted through a stack of clothing. Dresser drawers were pulled out at odd angles and their contents strewn across the bed. As Chloe glanced his way, exasperation pulled her mouth into a pout.

"Making room for your things."

"I didn't know it would involve so much rearranging," J.T. said mildly, stepping warily into the room. "I just thought you'd clear out part of your dresser for my drawers and stockings and I could hang my shirts and pants on a nail on the wall."

"You're not pounding nails into my bedroom wall," Chloe said sharply. "I have a wardrobe you can hang your shirts in. Both of them," she said pointedly.

"I'm gonna get some new things next time I go to town," he assured her. "And I've got more than two shirts. You oughta know that." For some reason she was in a state this morning, and after last night, he'd thought things were well under control. He probed a bit further.

"Did you mean it about going to town today, making arrangements?"

She whirled on him. "That's what I said, isn't it?" Her

eyes were dark, stormy with an irritation he could not understand.

"When do you want to go?" Choosing the side of discretion, rather than pushing her into an argument, he watched guardedly as she folded the trousers she held. Her hands trembled and, as if she would hide them from his scrutiny, she buried her fingers in the denim fabric and turned away, facing the window.

Enough was enough, J.T. decided. Something was awry and he'd best make repairs right here and now. His strides were long as he circled the end of the bed and reached for her. Her shoulders seemed narrow in his hands, her head tucking beneath his chin as he drew her against his chest.

"What's wrong?" She jerked against his grip and he tightened his hold, refusing to allow her escape. "Changed your mind, sweetheart?" The words were husky, almost harsh, and she stiffened. "I won't let you, Chloe," he warned her. "We're gonna get married, and we're heading for town after dinner to make the arrangements. You're gonna have a new dress and I'm ready to spring for a suit, so I'll look worthy of you, all gussied up and pretty as a picture."

"I'll never be that," she whispered.

"I suspect you're entitled to your own viewpoint," he said quietly, "but I see things differently. And when we find you the right gown to wear and get me some Sunday go-to-meeting clothes, we'll set this town on its ear. You'll be the prettiest bride for miles around, Chloe."

"I have freckles," she said despondently. "They're not just on my face, J.T."

"And you think I care?" he asked, resisting the urge to grin at her confession. "I happen to like your sunspots." His voice lowered, and she tilted her head, as if she strained to hear his words. "I'm planning on kissing every one of them, come tomorrow night."

She jerked from him and spun to face him, her cheeks rosy, her eyes ablaze. "I thought I made it clear—"

His mouth found hers, and her words sputtered against his lips. Lips that claimed her decisively, branding her with the heat of his mouth, taking possession of flesh suddenly forming to his purpose. His arms circled her, drawing her against his hard body, and she was lifted from the floor, her feet left dangling as her hands sought for purchase, fingers clenching the fabric of his shirt.

He'd kissed her before. Kisses that had brought him to a state of arousal, yet he'd been careful not to press too far. He'd tasted her mouth, suckled on her lips, and heard sweet sounds of her passion. She'd shed some of her thorns, awakening to a knowledge of her own needs. Now she invited the intimacy of his touch as she moved against his needy frame.

His good sense began to surface as his hands lowered her to the floor. Unless he was careful, he'd have her across that wide bed, tasting the flesh that pressed against his chest, the warm, round breasts tempting his hands and mouth even now.

Right in front of an open bedroom door.

She stretched upward, and a murmur of protest escaped her lips, as though loath to call a halt to his foray. Her mouth was moist, opening beneath his, her lips flowering to accept his tongue, and he groaned, a sound of desire he could not repress. His common sense prevailed as once more the open bedroom door invaded his thoughts, and he turned his face from her seeking lips. "Chloe, I—"

"What the hell's goin' on in here?" Pete's voice, vehement in its censure, halted J.T.'s own attempt to withdraw from the woman he held. He felt her hands drop from his chest, heard the intake of her breath as she lifted dazed eyes to his. And then Pete was behind him, grasping rudely at J.T.'s shirt, muttering threats in an undertone.

"Enough." The single, harsh word was a censure even Pete was smart enough to take heed of, and as J.T. turned to face him, the younger man's hands dropped to his sides. "Don't ever interfere between your sister and me again. Do you hear me?"

Pete was grim-lipped, his gaze darting to Chloe who stood beside J.T. "It looked to me like you were taking advantage of her," he said tersely, stepping back a pace.

"What happens between us is none of your concern," J.T. said, his voice controlled, as though he had forced the words between gritted teeth. And perhaps he had, he thought, clutching at his anger as it would have exploded through his tightly clenched fists. "The next time you lay your hands on me, you won't know what hit you." It was a promise, and Pete's face colored darkly as he nodded.

"What do you want in here, Pete?" Chloe's query was hushed and she stepped past J.T. quickly, a living barrier between the two men whose hostility was tinder waiting to burst into the flame of open conflict. "Do you need to talk to me?" she asked, urging Pete toward the door. He obliged, giving way to her coaxing, and she shot a warning glance at J.T., her mouth still damp from his kiss, her hair ruffled from his touch.

He let her go, his body caught in the twin grip of anger and desire, and as she vanished from sight, he turned back to face the window. Self-control, that virtue he'd counted as one he owned, was on the verge of shattering. *Damn,* he'd come too close to forgetting everything else surrounding him, once Chloe's curving body was in his grasp. Letting any woman, even Chloe, rule his passions was not to be considered.

He looked around the room, where her clothing was scattered from bed to dresser, and he bent to pick up the trousers she'd been folding. He lifted them to his face, inhaling the scent of wind and laundry soap, with a faint residue of

Chloe's own aroma rising from the fabric. Folding them, he placed them on the bed.

Tomorrow he'd be here, in this room, his own things neatly arrayed where Chloe decreed they would be stored. And the door would be closed.

The mirror reflected her image, and yet it was that of a woman she'd never laid eyes on before. Her gaze wide and fearful, she touched a curl that dangled beside her ear, and watched as it wrapped around her finger. She turned to view her profile, twisting her head to note the clinging fabric that outlined her figure. Cheeks flushed and eyes shiny with anticipation, she looked almost pretty, she decided. And breathed a prayer of thankfulness that J.T. need not be ashamed of his bride.

From the doorway a snort of derision broke into her thoughts with the impact of an iron skillet hitting the floor. "I didn't think you'd go through with it. Matter of fact, I thought you were pulling my leg," Pete said bluntly.

She opened her eyes and watched him as he sauntered closer, his eyes scanning her form with a chill scrutiny. "If you're marrying that crook to keep me in line, don't bother. He's nothing but a big bully, and I'm not afraid of him."

That wasn't how it looked yesterday. Chloe lifted her chin in exasperation. "You don't know what you're talking about, Pete. J.T. has taken over here and relieved me of a whole slew of responsibility. He's put his money into stock and he works damn hard, right alongside the other men. If you'd been half as interested in the ranch as he is, I wouldn't be marrying anybody today. We'd have been partners and none of this would have come about."

Pete sneered, his angry gaze raking her lush form. "I see he got you into a dress for the occasion. I'd say the man has a powerful lot of influence over you, sister dear."

A flush warmed her face and throat as Chloe looked down

at her wedding gown, her joyous moments of pride vanquished by his words. ''I'm a woman, Pete. I wanted to look nice on my wedding day,'' she said in a strained whisper. Not that she would ever be a raving beauty, but the creamy silk dress J.T. had chosen from the single ladies' wear shop in Ripsaw Creek caressed her curves as though it had been made to fit each and every one of them.

Sylvia Madison, the local seamstress, had managed to take in the waist and let out the bust yesterday afternoon in a matter of two hours, ecstatic at being called upon to alter Chloe's gown. ''I declare,'' she'd said enthusiastically, ''I sure had high hopes for you getting yourself a decent man, girl, but this one is beyond first-rate. He's a choice specimen, if you ask me.''

And though she hadn't asked anyone's opinion of J.T., Chloe had preened as she listened to Sylvia's incessant chattering. Not that the woman was much of a judge of manhood, her own husband being short, squat and unappealing. But perhaps that made her more aware of a *choice specimen,* such as J. T. Flannery.

Sylvia's needle had flown as she stitched the last seam, and then shook out the yards of fabric, watching as the sunlight through the window brought to life the shimmering silk, the material rippling and flowing as though it were alive. ''All right, Chloe,'' she'd said, ''let's try this on for size.''

And Chloe had, struck dumb by the vision staring back from the mirror as she turned from one side to the other, admiring the softly draping fabric.

Now, she faced her brother, withdrawing almost visibly from the scornful look he tossed in her direction. ''I'm marrying J.T. because I want to, Pete. I want a family and a man to sit across the breakfast table from me every morning of my life. A partner who'll put me first and play fair with me.'' As he had yesterday in town, when they'd signed a final agreement of partnership under Paul Taylor's instruction.

Pete's lips tightened. "And you think Flannery's going to do that?" he asked disbelievingly. "More likely he'll sell off your stock and leave you empty-handed one of these days, once he's tired of playing mister nice guy."

"Oh? The way you did? Leaving me without one red cent between me and a stack of bills to pay?" The hurtful words sputtered from her mouth without ceasing as Pete's face turned crimson and his hands formed fists against his hips.

"I only took what was mine," he blurted defensively.

"You took it all, every last penny out of the bank," Chloe spat, "and if I hadn't hidden the mortgage money, you'd have had that too."

"Well, if I didn't feel needed here to keep an eye on things, and look out for you, I'd be down the road again," Pete said.

Chloe's eyes filled with tears as she listened to his words. "Why can't you just be my brother, Pete, the way you used to be when we were young? Just do your work, draw your pay, and get along with J.T. and try to make a go of it here."

Pete's feet shuffled against the braided rug as Chloe stepped closer, and his arms were reluctant as she drew him into an embrace. "Maybe I'll try, Sis," he allowed quietly. "I want you to be happy. I just don't think Flannery is the man for you."

Chloe lifted her chin and set her mouth firmly. "Well, this is the choice I've made, and I'd appreciate it if you'd accept the fact." Softening her ultimatum with a smile, she lifted on her toes to kiss his cheek. "Now, come on," she coaxed. "Remember? You're going to give me away."

His shrug was unenthusiastic, but he walked beside her down the staircase to the front hallway, offering his arm as they entered the parlor. The room was almost filled to overflowing with neighboring ranchers and their wives, plus an assortment of townsfolk from Ripsaw Creek. The minister stood before the open windows, small black book in hand as he watched brother and sister enter through the double doorway.

"Ah, here's the bride," he said in greeting. "And Mr. Flannery," he added, looking across the room to the dining room doorway where J.T. and Hogan stood, poised to step forward at the appropriate moment. The piano resounded with melodious strains providing a sedate march tempo and the minister lifted both hands as a signal. Keeping time with the music, Chloe paced across the parlor floor, noting the approach of her groom, with Hogan by his side. Tilly stepped forward from the front row of those watching the proceedings, to stand at Chloe's left side. The minister cleared his throat, opening his book and peering down at the words he sought.

"Dearly beloved..." His gaze swept the onlookers, then focused on Chloe and J.T., a small smile curving his lips. "We are gathered together to join this man, and this woman, in the state of holy matrimony."

Pete shuffled a bit, clearing his throat when the next words were spoken, offering him an opportunity to call a halt to the ceremony. Chloe glanced up at him in warning, and his mouth tightened as he looked at her searchingly.

"Who giveth this woman..." the minister began, and before the words could be fully spoken, Pete muttered the appropriate response and pressed Chloe's hand into J.T.'s palm. His resentment was a palpable thing as he stepped back. Chloe felt a pang of sorrow, a sense of foreboding filling her for a moment. And then, upon the next utterance to leave the minister's mouth, she was caught up in the beauty of words and phrases that promised to change her life forever.

She spoke her responses in a voice that barely trembled, heard J.T.'s own vows offered in dark, husky tones and felt the cool circle of gold surround her ring finger as he placed it there. His kiss was circumspect, brief, but warm against her mouth. His lips touched her cheek and then whispered words against her ear.

"You won't be sorry. I promise."

It was over then, and the guests descended upon them, congratulations being bestowed upon the bride and groom. As grown men slapped each other on the back and made an issue of saluting the bride with brief kisses, J.T. was deluged by the ladies of the community, their eager words welcoming him to the social circle of Ripsaw Creek.

Not that there was any great amount of entertainment offered in town, Chloe thought, watching as he was surrounded by young and old ladies alike. Only an occasional dance at the Grange Hall or a church ice cream social. And then, of course, the Fourth of July to-do, which involved a great number of children waving flags, towing bunting-draped wagons as they followed the band down the middle of Main Street.

And this year she would be among the ladies who sat and cheered their husbands on to victory as the men chose sides for the annual ball game in Robbie Wilson's pasture just outside of town. She envisioned herself sitting beneath a tree, surrounded by other wives as she watched J.T. hit the ball and then run the bases.

"Can you play baseball?" she asked, her voice a hoarse whisper as she lifted on tiptoe to breathe her query against his ear.

"Baseball?" he asked, surprise widening his eyes as he looked down at her. "Did you just ask me if I can play ball?" His own words were soft, as if he could not believe what he had heard from her lips.

She nodded impatiently. "You'll have to take part in the game after the Fourth of July parade. I just wondered…" Her words trailed off as J.T.'s smile exploded into laughter.

"And you didn't want to be ashamed of me in case I couldn't smack the ball a country mile, I suppose," he said with glee painting his features. "Are you afraid I'll make a display of myself, Mrs. Flannery? Strike out first time at bat?"

Her blush brought the gaze of several bystanders to her face, and Tilly bustled her way through the crowd, thrusting her jaw forward as she faced J.T. "Are you runnin' off at the mouth, making poor Chloe all red-faced here?"

"No, Tilly, he's not," Chloe said quickly. "I just spoke before I thought and it tickled his funny bone." And how her mind could have traveled so far afield on such an occasion was a wonder, she thought. But, she'd found herself placing J.T. in any number of situations during the past couple of days, imagining him sitting beside her in church, strolling down the street in town on a Saturday afternoon or evening. And even wondering how he would look in the big bed she slept in every night.

Especially picturing that, she thought, as the forbidden image invaded her mind again. She hadn't been able to visualize such a thing clearly, not until yesterday's kisses had given her a fuller glimpse of his passion. But in just a few hours the idea would become a reality. And she'd best be prepared.

Being prepared evidently required a great deal of cotton and lace in the form of a voluminous nightgown that Tilly offered as her contribution to the effort. And then there were the last-minute instructions from J.T. himself, his bold whisper requesting that she remove the pins and curls from her hair and allow it to flow freely. She felt the tension running through her body as she searched her mirror, her brush tangling in dark tresses as trembling fingers sought to bring order to hair suddenly prone to waving, no matter her attempts to bring it under control.

All due to Tilly's patient hands rolling and pinning in place a myriad assortment of curls, caught at Chloe's crown by a small wreath of wildflowers from which it cascaded to the middle of her back. And now she tried in vain to bring some sort of order to the tangled locks before J.T. said his last goodbyes to the men who lingered on.

Gone were the townsfolk, weary from three hours of dancing to the sound of Howie Henderson's fiddle, the echo of their goodbyes still ringing in her ears. Now, only the ranch hands remained, armed with a suspicious-looking gallon jug and an assortment of cups.

From the laughter beyond her window, Chloe felt safe in assuming it would be a while before her bridegroom showed up to claim his prize. And at that thought she dropped her brush and sat on the floor before the full length mirror, a rosy-faced creature amid a billowing cloud of fabric.

Some prize, she thought derisively, mocking her own ordinary looks with a scrunching up of eyes and drawing down of her expressive mouth. Beneath the all-enveloping nightgown she wore was the untried body of a woman who hadn't explored the idea of providing for the needs of a husband. Needs she hadn't planned on considering any time soon. Her idea of holding him at bay until she was ready for their marriage to truly begin seemed to have fallen apart.

He'd made his presence known last night, carrying his belongings down the stairs and tucking them away in the drawer she indicated. Hanging his new shirts in the wardrobe and placing new trousers in the drawer had only been the beginning. His small clothes, those items he wore next to his skin, shared space now with her own, and she recalled the moment he'd brushed his fingers over her drawers, handling the fine fabric of her shifts and touching the small bits of lace that trimmed her vests.

He would not take no for an answer. As surely as night

follows day, she knew that J. T. Flannery was not a man to be thwarted, especially on his wedding night.

And the man who stood in the doorway behind her lived up to that conclusion as she viewed his tall form in the mirror. Not hesitating one little bit, he crossed the threshold, closing the door firmly behind him as he entered his bride's domain.

"Chloe?" His voice was a husky drawl, and she heard her name murmured in syllables that drizzled desire, even as they fell from his lips.

She turned her head, and J.T. watched as her startled look dissolved into confusion. Sitting before the mirror, with an enormous amount of white cotton material surrounding her, she resembled a cloud with an angel perched in the center. And at that thought, his mouth twitched into a smile. Not an angel, not his Chloe. Perhaps a very young, very innocent woman, but he'd heard her ripe language too often to designate her as a heavenly being.

She rose quickly, smoothing down the yards of fabric she sat amidst, her face flushed as though she'd been interrupted in the midst of a private and personal perusal of herself. Her mouth was turned up at one corner, the smile trembling on her lips, and she clutched her hands before her, her knuckles white, her fingers tightly clasped together. And in her eyes was a shadow that might have been fear, if he hadn't known that Chloe feared no one and nothing on this ranch.

Except perhaps the unknown. She'd worried about Peter, wondering what he was up to, and had fretted about the purchase of the paint stallion until he'd set her mind at ease. Now she looked up with an expression of uncertainty that touched his heart. Chloe was afraid of what would happen, here in this room, between bride and groom.

And so J.T. grinned at her, sitting on the chair next to the door to pull his boots off. He tossed them in the direction of the wardrobe and watched as she hastened to sit them upright, side by side, as if any occupation that would fill her hands was better than waiting for her future to begin.

He pulled his stockings off and laid them next to his chair, his movements slow, his gaze flickering over her as she moved around the room. Her hairbrush lay on the floor and she stumbled over it, bending to pick it up, her cheeks flushing anew.

"I'm glad you left your hair down for me," he said quietly. "Would you like me to brush it for you?"

Her glance touched him and veered to one side, where the door was tightly closed. "It's all snarled," she said, absently picking at several strands of hair tangled in her brush.

"Go sit on the bed and I'll help you with it," he offered, rising and ambling toward the quilt-covered feather tick. His fingers casually slipping buttons from their moorings, he dropped his shirt on the floor before he sat down on the edge of the mattress to wait for her. She was slow in moving toward him, her feet brushing against the braided rug, her toes curling under as she reached his side.

"I'll tell you what, sweetheart," he said with an easy smile. "Just sit on the floor in front of me and I'll be able to reach it better."

She nodded, handing him the brush, and slid to sit between his feet. Her knees rose and she pulled the gown over them, enclosing herself in its folds, looking like a child buried in a snowbank. Yet this was no child he dealt with, but a young woman who had had no mother to speak with, whose father had treated her as a second son, and whose total experience with men probably consisted of the few kisses they had exchanged.

His fingers worked at unsnarling the mess she'd made, brushing out one curl after another, pulling the brush through the length of dark, silky waves, and his fingers ached to tug her head backward so that her face would be exposed to him, enabling him to scatter kisses over its surface. It would frighten her, he decided, but another time he would not hesitate to capture her to play the game of love in such a manner.

For several minutes he brushed, easy, smooth strokes that seemed to put her at ease, and then he tossed the brush aside and, easing his hands beneath her arms, he lifted her from the floor, catching her as she would have fallen. She groped for him as he swung her in his embrace, and together they sprawled across the width of the bed. Her face was rosy, her eyes wide, and her mouth was an invitation he could not refuse.

He brushed it with his own, then eased back to meet her gaze. "Sweetheart, are you afraid of me?" he asked quietly, and watched as her teeth pressed against her lower lip to stop its trembling.

"No, I don't think so," she whispered. "I just don't know what you expect of me, and I wasn't sure what we were going to do tonight."

"I'm not sure, either," he admitted. "I want to make love to my bride, but if you say no, I'll understand." *And probably die of frustration.*

"I thought maybe we were just going to share the bed, because you didn't want anyone to think…" Her voice trailed off and he rescued her with a quick nod.

"I care more about what *you* think, Clo. And if you're not ready for me to make you my wife, I'll wait." *But, damn! I sure don't want to.*

"I don't know if I'll ever be any more ready," she admitted. "When we talked the other day, I thought we could just share my room for a while, you know, maybe a couple of weeks or so, before we…before you…"

He'd be dead with this much temptation in front of him for a couple of weeks, he thought glumly. "I think you're ready,'' he said decisively, bending to kiss her again, teasing her with butterfly strokes that fell across her face.

She giggled. Chloe, who laughed aloud, who grinned joyously at times, actually giggled, and his heart twitched in his chest. Now, she'd done it. Invaded for sure the last citadel of his defenses, creeping past his intention of holding himself aloof and remaining in control. With one small, girlish giggle, she'd brought him to his knees, that gurgle of laughter magnifying her innocence.

''Chloe? Can I take off the rest of my clothes?'' And if the answer was no, his own needs would simply slip further into limbo. Whatever it took, he vowed silently to provide her with a wedding night to cherish.

She blinked at his query and solemnly nodded, then watched as he lifted from the bed and blew out the lamp she'd left burning on the table. In the darkness he heard her breath catch in her throat, and he spoke of nonsense, of the food eaten and the dances danced and the stack of gifts left on the parlor table. In moments he'd stripped to his drawers, and stood over her.

She was easy to spot, there in the middle of the bed, her nightgown white against the quilt, her face a pale oval, surrounded by dark hair. ''What do you want me to do?'' she asked, and he was humbled by her words.

He sat beside her and drew her up onto his lap, his palm pressing her head against his shoulder. ''I just want you to enjoy our time together,'' he said easily. ''Do you know anything about making love, Chloe?''

''No, I'm afraid not.'' It was a sad little whisper, as if she felt somehow lacking.

''Well, then this should be as easy as pie,'' he said cheerfully. ''You'll just do whatever I tell you, won't you?''

Her hesitation was brief, but her head nodded after a moment. ''All right.''

"Unbutton your nightgown, sweetheart," he said, his even tones belying the rapid beat of his heart.

Her fingers, normally agile, seemed to turn into an assortment of thumbs, as she fiddled with the buttons, finally reaching the bottom of the placket after much mumbling and muttering on her part. "There." As if some great accomplishment had taken place, she heaved a sigh.

He slid one hand beneath the white fabric and she jerked, a movement he hushed with kisses that took her attention. She lifted her face, the better to meet his lips, and his hand found the treasure it sought. Round, firm and possessed of a small, puckered nubbin at its peak, her breast filled his palm.

Glory be! A rush of exaltation filled him to the brim, and he kissed her more deeply, pressing her lips apart with the tip of his tongue. She responded quickly, opening for the gentle invasion, and her arm crept up to encircle his neck.

"You taste like hard likker," she whispered, gaining her breath as he pressed a series of kisses across her cheek.

"And how would you know what hard likker tastes like?" he asked with a chuckle, his thumb moving casually across the crest of her breast.

"I snuck a taste of Pa's once, but I didn't like it. It's not so bad secondhand though."

"Your mouth is sweet, like the wedding cake Tilly made for us," he told her. "Do you suppose this tastes the same?" His hand squeezed gently at its contents and she inhaled sharply.

"I never heard of such a thing. Why would you want to taste me *there?*"

It was going to be a long night, he decided, and about the only way he was going to make any progress was to strip Chloe of her covering. And then seduce her.

"You'll find out in just a few minutes," he said bluntly. "But I think we'll do better if we get you out of this bolt of yard goods first,'' he said, hoisting her against himself and tugging at her garment's hemline. It slid easily up the length of her legs and with a judicious amount of shifting and tickling and smothering her laughter with his mouth, he had it pulled over her head. In another moment he'd slid from his drawers and tossed them to the floor, then returned to her, pressing her against the feather tick and wishing fervently that he'd left the lamp glowing.

She was warm beneath him, her breasts against his chest, her legs held in place by his thigh. With an experimental wiggle she managed to lift one knee, and the solid weight of his thigh slid to be sandwiched between hers. Her breath caught, an audible sound, and he bent to whisper against her ear.

''Did I hurt you?''

''Oh, no. It just felt…kinda, sorta…odd.'' And as she spoke, she lifted her hips, enclosing his muscular leg more tightly in place.

''Odd? As in good or bad?'' His tone was amused as he waited patiently for her to absorb the movement of his thigh against her body.

''Oh…good, I think.'' She looked up at him, squinting in the dim light provided by the moon and stars outside the window. ''You're not teasing me, are you?''

''No, sweetheart. I just want this to be…'' He sought for a word, and murmured it with quiet certainty. ''Perfect, absolutely perfect.'' His head dropped to her breast and he brushed his nose across the plump surface. Beneath his mouth, the pebbled crest was a temptation he could not resist and he nuzzled it with his lips, aware of her stillness as she absorbed this new sensation.

He suckled gently, drawing his prize to be touched by the edges of his teeth and was rewarded by a murmur of pleasure. Chloe's hand swept to her mouth, stilling the moan, but he reached to remove her fingers.

"I want to know if you like what I'm doing, sweetheart. I can't hear you with your hand over your mouth."

"Oh, Jay." It was a gift he reveled in, the joyous whispering of a name she'd never spoken before, that only his mother had used in his childhood years. "Jay?" She repeated it, lifting her hand to touch his cheek, an unspoken message that told him she was willing to travel this road with him. And then her fingers made their way to the back of his head, tunneling through dark hair, gripping him with the strength of a woman whose hands were strong and agile.

And yet she was soft, rounded and purely female. His hand slid to span her belly, one finger circling the rim of her navel, before it probed gently within the small hollow. Shifting his weight from her he exposed her lower body, and his palm slid to her hip, the better to explore her silken skin. He lifted her leg higher, his fingers brushing the smooth flesh behind her knee and up the inside of her thigh, slowing his pace as she shivered and caught her breath again.

"Chloe?" Teasing the dark thicket of curls, he listened to her soft murmurs, his fingers careful as he discovered the flesh beneath. "Do you trust me?"

Her head nodded, a jerky movement, and her breathing was shallow and choppy, as if she hesitated on the brink of a cliff, torn between throwing herself on the mercy of what lay out of sight, or withdrawing into what was old and familiar.

J.T.'s mouth opened over her breast again as his fingers teased the exquisite, moist flesh that proclaimed her a woman. She twitched against his agile hand, then repeated the movement, a low whimper telling him she had discovered a new source of pleasure. One long finger traced through folds of flesh, searching for the place he yearned to make his own. His body throbbed with anticipation, his arousal even now pressed eagerly against her hip, and he eased himself with a careful movement.

Not yet. Not yet. His mind repeated the admonition and he gritted his teeth against the temptation to pierce that hidden place without further delay. *Not yet. Not yet.* He'd gained her trust, and to take his own satisfaction without bringing her to pleasure would undo everything he'd managed to accomplish.

There…he closed his eyes, willing his eagerness into abeyance, as his finger dipped within the constricting muscle. She whimpered against his ear, rising up beneath him to capture that errant member, and he moved it within her body, exultant as she met each thrust.

"Do you like that?" he asked softly, increasing the depth of his exploration by tiny increments. Until he reached the telltale barrier that proclaimed her a virgin.

"Do something," she whispered, her movements more urgent as he slid his finger from her body, and then back, once last time, to where her muscles clenched tightly.

"All right, sweetheart," he said, rising above her, lifting her legs higher to provide easier entry.

A shout from the yard, just outside the bedroom window, halted his movement and he turned to look unbelievingly through the window as men milled about the yard, mounted on horseback. And then another voice rose, calling his name.

Chapter Eight

Beneath him, Chloe stiffened, one hand grasping for the sheet, the other pressing against his chest. "Jay? What's wrong?"

"Hell, I don't know," he snarled. "But it better be a damn sight more important than what was goin' on here just now, or there'll be bloodshed out there."

His head dropped to rest against the side of her face, and his murmur was low. "I'm sorry, sweetheart." And then he was gone from her, rolling across the bed to snatch at his pants and shirt, his feet sliding into his boots as he fought with buttons and buttonholes.

Chloe watched from the bed, dazed by his speed, frightened by the sounds of the men in the yard. Gathering the sheet around her, she rose and scrambled to the window, standing to one side, lest she be seen. "They're bringing your horse out from the barn right now," she told J.T. and heard his grunt of acknowledgment as he tucked in his shirt.

"Stay right here, Chloe. If there's trouble, I don't want you in the middle of it."

He'd given her orders before, and she'd managed to coax her way past his reservations. But the tone of his voice warned her against any protest she might think to utter this time. "I mean it," he said harshly. "You stay in the house."

"All right." It was the least she could do, this simple accedence to his will. And then he was gone, making no attempt to muffle the sound of boots against the floors, allowing the back door to slam shut behind him.

She was dressed in moments, searching out her underwear which still lay on the chair where she'd dropped it prior to donning her nightgown. Snatching a pair of pants and a shirt from her drawer, she slid into them quickly. Should he change his mind, she'd be ready to ride with him.

Stumbling over the rug in the hallway, she clutched at her foot, hopping on the other as she made for the kitchen. Once at the back door, she watched through the screen as J.T. tightened his cinch. One of the men had hung a lantern in front of the barn, and the faces it exposed to light were stark and angry.

"How many head?" she heard J.T. ask as he mounted his stallion.

"Tom didn't know for certain. Said it looked like about fifty."

"Damn, we can't afford that," J.T. snarled. His glance back at the house was quick, and he spared a moment to ride toward the porch.

"Rustlers," he said, the single word holding a wealth of fury in its depth.

Chloe's gaze swept the mounted men. "Where's Pete?"

"That's what I'd like to know," J.T. said shortly, and then he was gone, the rest of the men riding out behind him. Six men heading toward the north, where the heart of the Double B's herd was in summer grazing land. There wouldn't be much they could do in the dark, and yet by morning's first light, they might find tracks. And Chloe knew that doing nothing in the meantime was not to be considered.

It was the way of a rancher to protect his holdings, and Chloe did not envy anyone J.T. warranted deserved his anger. Including Pete. Maybe especially Pete, given the fact that family loyalties should amount to something, and J.T. would be protecting Chloe's interests, first and foremost.

She closed her eyes, her mind scanning the events of the evening. Pete had been there after the ceremony, and even during the dancing. For a while, she'd watched him hover in the background, holding a plate and eating. Had he been among the dancers? She'd seen the ranch hands dancing with young women from town, all but Corky, who was with the herd.

And now that she scanned her memories, neither had Pete been among those who frolicked across the barn floor, their feet flying in time to the music and Howie's chanting of the calls.

"Where do you suppose that scallywag's gone to?" Behind her, Tilly's husky tones only added to Chloe's fears. "I knew he was stewin' about you marrying J.T., but I thought once the deed was done, he'd settle down. Guess I was wrong," she added glumly, tugging the belt of her wrapper tightly about her abundant waist.

"I don't even know him anymore," Chloe told her, turning from the doorway as Tilly stretched to light the lamp over the table. "Maybe he's left for good this time."

"Or maybe he's runnin' with the wrong crowd," Tilly predicted. Sniffing at the coffeepot, she grimaced and turned toward the sink. "This could use a fresh start," she said, rinsing it in the sink and measuring a handful of fresh grounds. In moments she'd held it beneath the kitchen pump, and filled the blue-speckled container with water.

It settled on the stove with a thump, and Chloe bent over the wood box, sorting out small chunks that would burn quickly. She turned with her hands full, and Tilly lifted the stove lid, watching as Chloe placed the wood atop the banked fire.

"You'd better tie back your hair, girl," Tilly advised, a crooked grin making her eyes crinkle at the edges. "Looks to me like you forgot to braid it before you crawled in bed."

Chloe's hands flew to the untamed waves on either side of her face. "J.T. asked me to leave it down," she muttered, pulling the dark length over her shoulder and plaiting it with practiced movements.

"Men are like that, as I recall," Tilly observed, and then her face softened and she lifted a roll of string from the buffet, cutting a length and handing it to Chloe. "Kinda ruined your wedding night, with all that upset out there."

Chloe twisted the string around the tail of her braid and tied it tightly. "I guess you could say that. But what there was of it was…" Her eyes flew to meet Tilly's knowing look. "I didn't know a woman could feel such things," she said quietly. "No one ever told me what to expect, and J.T. kinda had to play it by ear."

"I should've talked to you, I suppose," Tilly said with a sigh. "But, I kinda figured J.T. would take good care." Her gaze sharpened on Chloe's face and her words were harsh. "You're all right, aren't you?"

"I still don't know a whole lot about being married," Chloe admitted, "but if the rest of it's as—" She broke off, and felt a blush stain her cheeks. "I shouldn't be talking to you about this, should I?"

"I don't know why not," Tilly said amiably. "I'm probably as close to a mother as you're gonna get at this stage of the game." She turned back to the stove and lifted the lid to check the fire, then turned the damper a bit. "Might as well fix us a pan of cinnamon rolls for when those men come back," she decided. "They oughta have time to rise before dawn." Her eyes narrowed as she turned back to face Chloe.

"And then we're gonna sit down and talk a little bit."

* * *

Sunup found the cinnamon rolls fresh from the oven, their aroma filling the kitchen. Chloe tramped to the back door again, stepping out on the porch this time, peering toward the north where the men would most likely come from.

"You're not gonna get 'em here any sooner straining your eyes thataway," Tilly said from the kitchen table. "Come on in here and have a roll. It'll make you feel better." With an unmistakable sound, her chair was shoved across the kitchen floor, and Chloe turned to watch as her aunt slapped an enormous skillet atop the range.

"What are you doing?" she asked, casting one last look over her shoulder as she pulled open the screen door.

"Making a panful of sausage and gravy. Those men will be hungry when they show up here. Why don't you come on and mix up a batch of biscuits. Keep yourself busy."

Tilly was right, Chloe decided as she gently kneaded the biscuit dough, then patted it into a rectangle that covered the end of the table. With a table knife she quickly cut it into squares and transferred them to greased pans. She was better off venting her spleen on work than fretting and marching around the kitchen on her sore foot.

Already, her toes had begun to bruise from her episode with the rug in the hallway, and she could only hope her foot would slide into her boot. Opening the oven door, she slid the pans inside. "I hate not being in the middle of things, Aunt Tilly. I'm not sure telling God and everybody else that was here, right smack in the middle of that ceremony, that I'd obey J.T. was the smartest thing I could have done."

Tilly laughed at her grumbling, a hearty sound that must have reached through the open window and past the porch. Within seconds a voice boomed out, and even as Chloe watched, Tilly's cheeks bloomed with pink color.

"What's so funny in there? I've been called out of bed and hauled clear across the range to hunt down some low-life, and you women are havin' a party." A horse neighed loudly and Chloe bent to look out the side window, just in time to see Micah Dawson's form ride past.

"The town constable's here," she announced, and eyed Tilly's rosy complexion. "Not that you care."

"Always glad to have a man of the law drop by. Kinda like having a man of the cloth do the same," Tilly said jauntily. "Don't get sassy," she warned Chloe. "You always want to treat the constable nicely. You never know when you might need his help."

Micah stood before the screen door and peered into the kitchen. "You ladies must've been up since before breakfast," he surmised, "or else you hired a new housekeeper and she spent half the night bakin' cinnamon rolls." He grasped the doorknob and wiped his feet carelessly on the rug provided. "Don't suppose you've got coffee to go with those."

"Depends," Tilly answered with a grin. "You catch those rustlers?"

"Hell, no," Micah grunted. "They're probably headin' due south. They got a bunch from Hale Winters, too. He sent a man into town to get me. Woke me out of a sound sleep." He pulled a chair from the table and settled into it. "I think we've got somebody on the inside makin' it easy for this gang."

His quick look at Chloe apparently caught her gasp of surprise, and his brows lowered as he sought to reassure her. "Not your brother, honey. At least not from the beginning. I'm lookin' at Corky myself. But then, J.T. may have other ideas. But I've felt all along that that fella's too smooth talkin' for a cowhand. He just don't hit me right."

"You don't think that Pete was involved?" Her voice lifted hopefully as Chloe scooted a chair closer to Micah and perched on its edge. "We couldn't remember when he disappeared last night from the dancing. But I'm willing to bet my last dollar that J.T.'s convinced there's a connection."

Micah lifted a big hand to clasp Chloe's fingers. "Honey, your brother's not bright enough to set this sort of an operation in motion. Now, I'm not sayin' he's not a part of it, but I'll warrant these fellas are old hands at the snatch-and-run game."

He looked up as Tilly placed a mug of steaming coffee before him, and Chloe thought his eyes twinkled in a new way as he murmured his thanks. He bent to look past Tilly to where the pans of rolls rested on top of the warming ovens. "You don't suppose I could snitch one of those, do you?"

Tilly handed him a plate and knife. "Cut yourself one, Dawson, and you'd better make it quick. If I'm not mistaken, I just heard voices from beyond the corral."

"Well, hell's bells," he growled. "Guess I'm not meant to have any breakfast, am I?" With a quick sip of his coffee, he stood, striding to the door with agile movements Chloe thought were remarkable for a man of his years. "You gonna save me one of those?" he asked Tilly, and at her nod of agreement, he stepped onto the porch.

"I think we've got trouble," he said, his voice carrying to the kitchen. Chloe rose and followed to stand beside him. The sun had moved to hover over the treetops while they waited, and in its light, a string of horsemen rode past the corral and to the front of the barn. Three men she didn't recognize rode with Hale Winters, and they dismounted and wrapped their horses' reins around the hitching post, then, as a body, strode across the yard to join Micah as he left the porch.

Tired, sweaty and madder than a hornet just about summed up their condition if Chloe was any judge. As were her own men. From the first to the last, they slid from weary mounts and her eyes sought J.T., who'd brought up the rear, leading a horse that carried a burden across the saddle.

The animals were led into the barn, and men's voices carried to the house, but J.T.'s was noticeably silent. She watched as he dismounted and grasped the reins of his stallion and the mount he'd led. As the bay turned to pass through the door, she caught a glimpse of sandy-colored hair topping the head of the man who was draped over its saddle.

It's not Pete. The thought flashed through her mind and a surging sense of relief propelled her from the porch and across the yard.

"J.T.?" Her voice followed him into the barn, and she watched as he glanced over his shoulder and then lent his strength to lowering the unconscious man to the barn floor. Chloe was almost at the doorway when J.T.'s words halted her in her tracks.

"Don't come in here, Chloe."

Lowery stalked toward her and, had she not known she was safe in his presence, she might have flinched from the anger that set his jaw. "You don't need to be out here, Miss Chloe. We'll be haulin' Corky there to town for Dr. Whitaker to fix up. Seems like a lot of mercy to waste on a fella who'd sell us out that way." He grasped Chloe's arm as she would have moved past him, and she looked up into blue eyes that had taken on the look of tempered steel.

"Don't be pushin' J.T. right now, ma'am. He's fumin' to beat the band." His hand refused to release her and she set her jaw.

"What happened to Corky?" she asked, her eyes focusing on the long fingers holding her captive.

"J.T. beat the daylights out of him," Lowery muttered. "We caught up with him just as he cleared the boundary to the north, tryin' to catch up with the men he was workin' with." He glanced back into the barn, where J.T. was rubbing down his stallion with a dry sack. "The boss was on him like flies on honey. Took two of us to drag him off."

"Corky's a big man, bigger than J.T. even," Chloe said. "I'd have thought he could hold his own."

"Didn't stand a chance once he opened his mouth. Made a choice remark about you right off the bat, and that was all it took."

"About me?" Chloe was stunned. She'd only ever treated the men with respect, and though Corky was the last man hired and, therefore, caught the brunt of teasing, she'd thought he was satisfied to work the Double B. "I've never done anything to him," she protested, her gaze focusing on J.T.'s wide hands as they stripped the saddle from Corky's horse.

"Nah, it wasn't you. He was just mad cause he'd managed to get caught," Lowery told her, drawing her with him as he headed for Micah and the men gathered around him. Words were flying as Micah asked questions, and Hale Winters provided the answers he sought.

"One of my men got shot up when he set off chasing them. He's in town now at Doc Whitaker's place."

"Will he live?" Micah asked.

"Looks like it," Hale answered. "Caught two bullets in his leg, but we got the bleeding under control before we sent him off." Lifting his hat from his head, he slapped it against his thigh and his words were harsh. "They'd better line up a judge to sit in the courtroom, 'cause we're gonna get this gang."

Micah nodded toward the barn where J.T. stood in the doorway, pulling off his gloves and tucking them in his back pocket. "What happened out there?"

With a quick look in Chloe's direction Hale hesitated, then chose his words carefully. "J.T. lassoed Corky from his horse just as he got past the northern boundary of Miss Chloe's land. The fool shot off his mouth, cursin' and carryin' on, and then spoke unkindly about J.T.'s bride." His mouth twisted wryly. "He won't be talkin' much for a while. I think J.T. broke his jaw with the first punch. Corky got in a few jabs, but he's still out like a light."

"Well, the fool deserved whatever he got." Micah's eyes softened as he looked at Chloe. "These ladies have got a pot of coffee ready, and Tilly's got food on the stove."

"I'll go help Tilly," Chloe offered as J.T. approached the house, his gaze fastened on her. Facing him in front of almost a dozen men was not her first choice this morning, and she retreated quickly. The biscuits were out of the oven and Tilly had begun breaking eggs into a bowl while butter sizzled in the second large skillet.

"They're all hungry," Chloe told her.

"I figured as much. We'll have scrambled eggs in ten minutes and the sausage gravy is ready now." She looked over her shoulder at the table they'd lengthened with a pair of leaves from the pantry. "Think there's enough room for all of them?"

"They can take their plates out on the porch if we overflow," Chloe said, carrying plates from the buffet and shuffling them the length of the long table. "I think they'll all fit, though. They can use the dining room chairs."

"Don't let them past the kitchen with their filthy boots," Tilly warned her. "Keep the mess in one place."

They managed to eat, elbow to elbow. Tilly emptied the gravy into her largest bowl, then set about making another batch. The cinnamon rolls were eaten and exclaimed over, and Micah found himself the possessor of the largest one, handed to him separately as he leaned back in his chair. "I believe I just may move my bedroll into your bunkhouse, J.T.," he drawled, licking icing from his fingers. "If this is the kind of cookin' you're enjoyin' here every day, I wouldn't mind workin' for you."

"Well, we'll be on the lookout for another ranch hand,"

J.T. said dryly, the first words Chloe had heard pass his lips since he'd entered the house. She poured a second cup of coffee, leaning past him, and his hooded eyes flickered over her face.

"You all right?" he asked, the words so softly spoken they reached only her ear as she bent close.

Her head nodded briefly, but she felt the flush climb her cheeks as his hand left his lap to touch her, fingers brushing against her pants leg as if he would reassure her of his concern. "Are you?" she asked, finally meeting his gaze. The hand holding his fork was bruised, the knuckles skinned, and she bit her lip, her curiosity at a peak. "Can we talk, later?"

His nod was brief, and he lifted the fork to his lips, where dried blood edged the corner of his mouth. The signs of a battle were there, and she felt the residue of anger pulsing from his hunched shoulders and taut posture. The knowledge that this man was capable of protecting her and the ranch they shared was an assumption she'd made from the first. And his behavior now only reinforced her faith in him.

An outpouring of emotion gripped her, and she turned away to settle the coffeepot back on the stove. The affection she'd felt, the attraction to the man she'd taken as her husband was magnified at this moment to an extent beyond belief. If what she felt toward the man behind her could be described as *love,* she wasn't sure she was ready for it. Even now, she was swamped by heady sensations that were guaranteed to throw her life out of kilter.

"Good food, Miss Tilly," Tom said respectfully. Shoving his chair from the table, he rose and nodded his thanks, as Chloe turned to watch him walk toward the back door. "I'll hitch the wagon and haul Corky to town, boss," he told J.T. "Will we be heading back out today?"

"I want those steers brought closer to the pastures," J.T. told him. "It'll take a couple of days to handle it, but we can't afford to lose any more stock. Damn, we'd be better off to sell them at a loss than lose another bunch.''

''I figure they got over a hundred of mine,'' Hale said gloomily. ''I'd like to have got my hands on that fella out there in the barn myself.''

From the yard, Tom's voice called out a summons. ''One of you in there come give me a hand. Corky's doin' his best to get on a horse out here.''

As one, J.T. and Hale rose, and Micah spoke quietly, but forcefully, as the two men broke for the door. ''You get back here, the both of you. Shorty, go on out and see what needs to be done. We don't need any more bloodshed today.''

J.T. hesitated, but another long look from the lawman apparently convinced him of the wisdom being dealt in his direction and he returned to his chair. Within minutes, they heard the unmistakable sound of the wagon rolling from the yard. ''Tied him up and tossed him in the back,'' Shorty said from the doorway. ''Thought he'd have better sense than to try gettin' away. Stupid fool couldn't even toss a saddle on the back of his horse. Don't know what made him think he'd be able to ride out of here.''

''Well, I'm headin' back to town,'' Micah said. ''I'll send a wire to every place south of here, tell them to be on the lookout for anything with your brands on them. I'll take my deputy and ride east and south a ways and see if we can find any more tracks.''

''It's probably a lost cause,'' Hale said harshly. ''Maybe they won't be back anyway. This sort of thing usually happens in a quick series of hits and then they move on to greener pastures.''

Nightfall found J.T. soaking away his aches and pains in the long tub. Installed before Chloe's father died, it shared a room with scrub boards and copper wash boilers just off the kitchen. A pipe ran out the side of the house and drained off in a shallow ditch, eliminating the need to empty the bathwater by hand. He'd heated water on the kitchen range and carried the heavy wash boiler across the kitchen floor to fill the deep tub, then cooled it with pails of water from the pump.

Chloe paused in the doorway, watching as he slid beneath the water. The room was unlit and she hesitated on the threshold, wanting to offer something that would ease his weary soul, yet hesitant.

"Come on in," he said, as if he sensed her presence behind him. He glanced over his shoulder and sat upright in the water. "Could I persuade you to wash my back?"

"Of course. I was just wondering what I could do to make you feel better." She bent to take the washrag and soap from his hand, and he tugged at her fingers, drawing her closer.

"A kiss would help," he whispered, a dry, husky sound that made her once more aware of the newly kindled emotion she'd been dealing with the whole day long. His head tilted back and his face was pale in the dim light, his eyes shadowed.

She touched her mouth to his, and heard his murmur of pleasure as his lips opened beneath hers. The invitation was blatant and she edged her tongue between his teeth, still achingly unfamiliar with the love play he'd introduced in their bed only last night. This had probably been the longest day of her life, she decided as she knelt beside the tub, her mouth still on his.

One wet hand rose to circle her nape and he turned her head a bit, the better to deepen the kiss they shared. "You're a fast learner, Mrs. Flannery." Smacking of approval, his voice drawled the words, his teeth touching her lower lip as she drew back. "Do you think we could continue this in the bedroom? Or are you too sleepy? As I recall, you didn't get any more sleep than I did.''

She rubbed the soap briskly against the cloth, working up a foamy lather, then pushed his head forward, the better to reach his shoulders. ''Bend,'' she ordered him, her mouth damp with his kiss, her heart scampering as she considered his invitation. She put muscle into her movements, and he lifted higher in the tub as she scrubbed at the long, strong tendons that formed the firmness of his back.

''I'll wash your hair,'' she offered, cleaning the sides of his neck and dropping the cloth into his waiting hand. He bent lower and she worked up an abundance of suds in his dark waves, using the pads of her fingertips to massage his head.

''Lady, you've got yourself a job,'' he told her, his voice slurring the syllables. ''No one ever scrubbed my head before, and I think I'm gonna make this a regular thing.''

If he lasted past crawling into bed before he was sound asleep, she'd be surprised. Her lips curved in amusement as she rinsed his head with warm water from the bucket beside the tub. ''Do you have anything to wear in here?'' she asked, looking around for fresh clothing. Only a pile of dirty laundry met her eye and she rose. ''I'll go get you something to put on.''

''Don't bother,'' he told her, pulling the plug and rising from the tub. ''I'll wrap a towel around me. Just make sure Tilly's not in the kitchen.'' He stepped onto the floor and she studiously kept her eyes on his face, handing him a clean towel from the stack kept handy for the purpose.

''How about drying my back?'' he asked, his mouth twitching as if he noticed her resolution to ignore his naked flesh. Turning his back, he offered her a view of taut buttocks and wide shoulders, with a length of body that beckoned her touch. She snatched up another towel and rubbed it in long strokes down his length from nape to waist, then swiped it across the same area from side to side.

"Don't stop there," he said quietly, and as she hesitated, he turned to face her. "I'll do the rest of my back, if you'll do the front," he offered, and she looked up into eyes that burned away every notion she'd had about how they would spend the next hour or so. Either that, or his hooded gaze reflected a need he would be too weary to assuage.

"All right," she whispered, and then watched her hands as they moved the towel across his chest, the fabric absorbing drops of water from the dark hair adorning the skin before her eyes. She worked her way beneath his arms and down his sides, bending a bit as she looked down at his narrow hips. The towel draped before him, neatly covering the part of him she was trying to ignore.

"You're not going to finish?" he asked as her hands ceased their movement and she stood erect once more.

"You want me to dry your legs, too?"

He relented and lifted her chin, looking into her eyes with a heated gaze she could no longer mistake. "Not this time, Clo. I'm thinking of something else, but I reckon I've pushed you about as far as I'm gonna get for tonight."

Taking a dry towel from the stack, he wrapped it around his hips, tucking it in at the side. "Go check on Tilly," he told her. "And then we're going to bed."

Chapter Nine

She awoke in his arms, his shoulder beneath her head. A soft snore escaped J.T.'s mouth and Chloe curled closer to him, nestling her bare breasts against the soft patch of hair covering his chest. *Her bare breasts.* She stilled, then shifted her leg a bit, drawing from his arms with small infinitesimal movements, bent on retrieving her nightgown from wherever it had gone.

"Don't wiggle, sweetheart. I'm not ready to get up yet, and neither are you." His husky murmur, accompanied by a tightening of his embrace, only served to add momentum to her retreat.

"I want my nightgown," she muttered stubbornly, searching her mind for some hint of the night's events. Only to find it vacant of all but an elusive dream that consisted of J.T.'s hands removing her clothing before she crawled into the bed.

"It's in the drawer, I suspect. Besides you don't need it." One arm lowered to curl beneath her bottom and he drew her higher against himself. "I'll keep you as warm as you'll let me." His mouth found a tender spot to nuzzle, and he nudged her head back, sampling her skin.

Somehow, it seemed the better choice to remain where

she was. Not that he was giving her an option anyway. And at that thought, she gave up all notion of retreating from his embrace and, instead, slid her arm beneath his to trace the long line of his back beneath her fingertips. The sun was just rising, and surely another few minutes wouldn't hurt anything.

"I don't remember coming to bed," she whispered, tilting her head a bit more as his tongue touched the rim of her ear.

"Hm…it's no wonder," he murmured, his voice rich with humor. "Do you remember kissing me just inside the bedroom door?"

Her hand ceased its movement against taut flesh as she recalled a heated embrace, remembered leaning fully against him and resting her head against his broad chest. "I kissed you?"

He chuckled and she felt the vibration of his amusement. "Want to try it again and refresh your memory?" His teeth nipped carefully at her earlobe.

"What happened?" She sat up, catching him unaware, and then, recognizing the result of her abrupt action, grabbed for the sheet, to hold it over her breasts.

He grinned, eyeing her attempt at modesty, and then relented. "You were asleep on your feet, Clo. I stripped off your clothes and tucked you in between the sheets."

"We didn't—"

"No," he said, "we didn't. I won't ever take advantage of you, sweetheart. Besides I don't know if it was even an option." His lips twisted into a smile. "But I think I could consider it now."

"It's almost full daylight." She blurted out the words. Surely the man didn't think she would be ready to finally consummate their marriage with the sun shining through the bedroom window.

"Does it matter to you?" he asked, his eyes watchful, gauging her reaction.

"I think so," she whispered. "Maybe when everyone is asleep and I don't have to worry about hearing the men outside or Tilly in the kitchen. I think then would be better."

"You're the boss," he said agreeably, though the light in his eyes dimmed, as he accepted her reluctance.

"I am?" Relief flooded her at his easy acceptance, and she bent to kiss his lips with a hasty movement. "That's a relief. After you being so bossy yesterday, I thought I'd lost all my power around here."

"You've got more power than you ever dreamed of, Clo," he said quietly, his words bringing her curiosity to a new level.

"I guess I don't understand what you're saying," she said after a moment.

"Maybe it's for the best." He tugged at the sheet she held, and reluctantly she allowed him to drape it lower over her body. His gaze moved to her breasts and she felt the tightening of flesh as he lifted his index finger to trace the dark outline of each puckered peak. "Now," he said, his voice oozing temptation with each syllable. "Think about that all day long, and when I crawl into this bed tonight, we'll take over where we left off."

"Ma'am?" Willie stood several feet from the back porch, holding his hat before him, fingers clenching the brim as though it might be blown away if he should relax his hold.

Chloe looked up from the record book she'd discovered in her father's office, one in which he'd begun recording the dropping of foals, and then apparently decided it was not a necessary thing to continue. Absorbed in reading the unique entries, written in a scratching, sometimes illegible script, she had escaped to another time for a few moments. Willie's voice called her to return.

The book closed with a snap, as though she could not share her discovery, although Willie showed no inclination to peer past her. Indeed, he seemed about as set on vanishing at the first opportunity as any reluctant caller she'd ever encountered.

"What is it, Willie?" Her words were careful, not inviting any familiarity from the boy, but it seemed his demeanor was beyond reproach today.

"I think I need to apologize to you, Miss Chloe. I was remembering how upset J.T. got with me, that one day when he thought I was being disrespectful to you, and I decided maybe he was right on the money. And so I thought I needed to let you know that I won't be givin' you any more trouble, or lookin' at you any way I shouldn't from now on."

She was stunned. No other word quite described her reaction to the young man's words, and she scrambled for a reply. "Well, I'm sure…no, as a matter of fact, I'm not sure at all," she began. "I know you had words with J.T., but I haven't had any reason to find fault with you since, Willie." She watched as his face reddened, and his lips pressed tightly together.

"I appreciate that, ma'am. My mama counts on what I earn here to help out at home. I wouldn't want you to think I don't appreciate working for you."

"All right," she said, nodding her understanding. And then a thought winged its way past her mind and she spoke it aloud. "Did you think I might be looking at you, wondering if you're connected to the rustlers, Willie?"

"I'm not, I swear it. I got a big mouth sometimes, and my mama says I'm too smart for my own good, always talking out of turn, but I'd never do anything to bring trouble to the Double B." The words rushed from him, and Chloe felt sincerity flow through each syllable.

"I believe you, Willie. Have you spoken to J.T. about it?

Although," she continued, "I don't think he suspected you of any shenanigans, anyway."

"No, I didn't say anything to him at all. He wasn't exactly in a good mood last time I laid eyes on him. I swear, ma'am, I thought he was gonna kill Corky out there. And then—" he looked away as if he could not meet her gaze any longer "—I heard what Corky said to him about you, and I thought if J.T. was mad at me that way, I wouldn't stand a chance of comin' out of it alive."

She smiled, understanding dawning as Willie's feet shuffled in the dirt. "You thought you'd better mend your fences."

"Yeah, I guess you could say that."

"Consider them mended, Willie. And tell your mama she raised you right. You might want to practice your flirting on someone a little younger and more available next time." Her voice softened. "I wasn't young enough for you, and I was never available."

"I know that now." He clapped his hat on his head, relief wiping the apprehension from his eyes. "I've been seeing Miss Francie Higgins some when I go home for church on Sundays. She's only seventeen, but her pa lets her walk out with me on Sunday afternoons."

"I'm sure your mama will approve," Chloe said, thankful that the set-to had come to a conclusion, aware that J.T. had made an unforgettable impression on his ranch hands. And what exactly had been said about her, out there on the range, was of small concern. Only the fact that he had defended her, maybe too well, but certainly without hesitation, was uppermost in her mind. She hadn't had a champion before, and the experience was most satisfying.

"What was all that about?" Tilly spoke from the kitchen doorway as Willie swaggered his way back to the barn, apparently pleased that he was once more in favor with the boss's bride.

"Willie and I had some words back some time ago. He was pretty obnoxious, to tell the truth, and J.T. set him straight. Apparently he's gotten religion, going to church with Francie Higgins, the banker's daughter, on Sunday mornings lately."

She turned to look solemnly over her shoulder at Tilly. "I think I've been replaced in his affections by a younger woman. Francie's only seventeen."

"You'll survive," Tilly said, "and for sure be better off with a man who doesn't shuffle his feet and blush like that young'un does."

"Well, J.T.'s no foot shuffler, that's for sure," Chloe noted, holding the record book to her breasts as she rose from the chair.

Tilly held the door open for her. "You ever get your marriage off the ground, yet?"

Chloe laughed. "I turned him down this morning. I know, I know," she said with an uplifted hand and a laugh forming on her lips. "You told me to just relax and let things happen when we talked yesterday, but I just couldn't, with the sun coming up and all."

"He's got quite a temper, hasn't he?" Tilly asked, and yet it was not a query, but a statement of fact, Chloe thought. "I think the men are a little in awe of him." Tilly shot a look in her direction as Chloe sat down at the kitchen table, opening the record book before her. "You're not afraid of him, are you?"

"He'd never hurt me," Chloe said simply. "He hasn't made me any big promises. Just that one, in fact, but I trust him, Aunt Tilly. I don't know why he went off like a firecracker out there, but no one seems to hold it against him, and I'm not going to either."

"You reading up on your Pa's account keeping?" Tilly asked, apparently satisfied with Chloe's frame of mind. "He wasn't much for record books as I recall. Said he'd rather just keep things in his head."

"I'm thinking it would be good to take note of which mares J.T. is breeding and put down the results in the spring. It'll give us a better idea of our profits when it comes time to sell off the horses. He thinks we've already got enough mares in foal to more than pay for the investment he made in the stallion."

"How does he know all this stuff, anyway?" Tilly asked. "I thought he hadn't been a rancher before."

"He wasn't. I think some men just naturally have a knack for it. And I'm thankful that J.T. is one of that breed."

"You're sure steppin' back and lettin' him take over, girl. I didn't think you could do it."

"I'm willing to let him be head man here, Tilly. But I'll keep the records and have my hand in things. The place is half mine, and I'll share the decisions. Whether Pete likes it or not, that's the way it's going to be."

"Pete. Now that's another thing. Where do you suppose he is?" Tilly pulled out another chair and sat down with an abrupt movement. "I'm wondering about that boy, and I don't like the way my thoughts are moving."

"Do you suppose he's tangled up in this mess with the rustlers, Aunt Tilly? If he is, he'll end up in prison at the very least." A sob caught in her throat, and Chloe, aware of the mournful sound of her voice, winced. "I just can't bear to think that he'd betray me that way, but right now I don't know what else to make of it."

"Are the men going to be gone overnight, do you think?" Tilly asked. "J.T. didn't say when he left if we should expect them back for supper."

"I don't know," Chloe told her. "He left Willie here to do chores and keep an eye on things, and everyone else left for town. I think Winters took a bunch of his men and went along. I'll bet I wouldn't want to be in Corky's shoes today, with all those men hotter than a pistol and out for his neck.''

"We haven't had a hanging in these parts for a long time," Tilly said gloomily. "I sure as the dickens hate to see it happen now, even if the scalawag does deserve it. I'd think we'd be beyond that kind of justice pretty soon."

"Well, if rustling goes out of style, maybe the prison in Laramie will have some empty cells. But till then, I guess they'll keep on shippin' these crooks off to sit around and consider their sins." Chloe closed the book again, aware that her urge to update and improve her father's methods was off the agenda for today. "We live in a harsh world, Aunt Tilly. I guess we need to be tough."

She rose and looked at the stove where a pot simmered on the back burner. "Is that soup about done? I'll have some before I go out to work with the horses for a while."

"Done enough to eat, I expect," Tilly answered, lifting the lid to stir the contents. "When you go out, ask that young'un in the barn if he wants some dinner. I guess he deserves some food in his belly, now that he took all his courage in one hand and made his apologies so nicely."

Willie ate two bowls of soup and mopped up the remains with a slice of bread, seemingly grateful for the invitation. Between the two of them, Willie riding and putting the mounts through their paces and Chloe cooling them and brushing them down, they managed to spend the entire afternoon in good spirits.

When an approaching cloud of dust turned out to be six riders instead of the five who'd left earlier in the day, Chloe halted her trek back toward the barn and watched their approach, gripping the halter of the young gelding she'd been working with.

J.T. slowed his stud and halted beside her, his gaze

searching her face. "Everything all right here?" he asked, his voice husky, as if trail dust had roughened his words.

Chloe nodded, suddenly a bit shy as the other men glanced in her direction and then away quickly. All but the extra horseman, who scanned her with visible curiosity lighting his eyes. She turned in his direction and spoke to J.T. in an undertone. "Where'd you get the stranger?"

"Picked him up in town. Micah said he was looking for a spot to hang his hat, and I figured we'd better be filling in the gap, with summer here and not enough hands to go around." He glanced at the tall rider and motioned him closer.

"This is my wife," he said shortly. "She's half owner of the ranch, and the men call her Miss Chloe."

"Ma'am?" The rider doffed his hat for a split second, then replaced it, the usual homage given to a woman. His eyes were hooded and he took note of her in a casual way, one Chloe could find no fault with, but still sensed his interest. "My name's Cleary. I'm familiar with horses and cattle, and I work for a fair wage. Your husband said he'd give me a week or so to prove myself."

"Sounds fair to me," Chloe told him. She turned back to J.T. and assessed his stony demeanor. "Did you find anything out?" From the corner of her eye she saw Cleary move toward the barn, his horse breaking into a slow trot. And then she spoke her thoughts aloud. "Is he all right? He doesn't seem the ranch hand sort to me."

"Let's take it one day at a time," J.T. said, dismounting and walking beside Chloe as they ambled up the lane. "No, I didn't find out a whole lot. Corky's not saying much, mostly because his jaw's pretty sore. Maybe a session with the judge will help him remember who his friends were. Maybe not." He untied his bandanna with one hand and wiped his face with it.

"And then about Cleary. He's a cool one, a good rider,

packs a gun and rides light. Just a pair of saddlebags, but his saddle and boots are first-class. That tells me a lot about a man. Takes good care of his horse from what I could see.'' He looked down at her questioningly. ''Are you willing to give him a week to prove himself?''

''You already have,'' she said, and then softened the words with a smile. ''I'm not being snide,'' she added. ''This is your department. I've about had enough of picking and choosing men for the job. Corky was the last one I took on here, and I didn't do such a hot job when I hired him, did I?''

Willie appeared before them, riding his latest mount around from the corral, and he nodded in greeting as he stepped from the horse. ''You want me to walk this one, Miss Chloe?'' he asked. ''I suspect you'll have things to do now, with the men back and all.''

''That'll be fine, Willie,'' she said pleasantly. ''I'll brush this gelding down and put him out in the pasture before I go in.''

J.T. followed her into the barn and his grip on her arm turned her into the nearest corner. ''You have got the sweetest fanny, lady,'' he whispered against her ear. ''I was noticing this morning how nicely it fit into my hands.''

She peered up at him in the dim light. ''Are you out of your mind? We're in the barn with three men not ten feet away and you're talking about my body parts.''

''They can't hear me,'' he said, his voice dark with promise. ''I just wanted you to know that I haven't been able to concentrate on much else all day, just remembering...''

He took the lead line from her hand and spoke to the nearest man, his eyes never leaving her face.

''Shorty, how about taking these horses and having someone rub them down good and put 'em out back. Mrs. Flannery and I are going in the house to talk about supper.''

''Sure enough, boss,'' Shorty said cheerfully. ''The

quicker Miss Chloe gets food on the table, the better I'll like it. It's been a long time since breakfast.''

"Tilly's got things on the back burner, Shorty," Chloe assured him. "We'll be ready in fifteen minutes, guaranteed."

"We'll move right along, then," the stockman said with a grin. "I'll crack the whip out here. They'll be lined up at the trough to get the dust washed off before you know it."

His arm stretching across her shoulders, J.T. turned Chloe toward the barn door and set off for the house, slackening his pace to match hers. "It'll be dark in about four hours," he said, nodding at the sun where it stood in the western sky.

"Are you trying to tell me something?" Chloe asked, looking up into eyes that met hers boldly. Neither gray nor brown, sometimes the dark orbs hovered on the edge of black, when his body was attuned to action or, like now, when he offered a peek into the emotions that drove him.

And yet, even as she watched, his control seemingly overrode the desire he'd allowed the upper hand, and his smile was crooked as he peered down at her. "You're pretty sassy, honey," he said. "I just may make you wash my back again after supper. That'll show you your place around here."

"And where's that?" she asked, climbing the porch step, then turning quickly to clasp his shoulders. His hands rose to grip her waist and she felt the leashed power beneath his fingers.

She'd been right, she decided, looking deeply to search out the expression in his eyes. They were a gauge she'd used to measure his feelings over the past weeks. Now, the calm, yet measuring look he bent in her direction brought about a sizzling reaction in the pit of her stomach she'd only begun to recognize recently.

"Your place is beside me," he said, resolution setting his jaw firmly. "Whether that's at the supper table or in bed. I want you next to me. When I leave here in the morning, if you're not with me through the day, I want to know you'll be waiting for me when I come in that back door.''

"And where's your place in my life?" she asked quietly, sensing the serious bent his statement had taken.

"I promised to take care of you and honor you, Chloe. I'm your husband, and I'll make damn sure any man who looks in your direction does so with respect. We're partners in this place, and you hold an equal part of everything here. I'll be beside you all the way."

Well, that was certainly putting his money where his mouth was, she decided, stunned by the responsibility he had assumed. Without even blinking an eye, he'd staked his claim on her, stating his intentions in no uncertain terms. In these moments, even more eloquently than during the wedding ceremony they'd participated in, he'd offered her his full loyalty and promises for their future.

And in so doing had managed to turn her into a creature she'd never thought to resemble. A woman in love.

"Did Willie talk to you today?" he asked, closing the bedroom door behind them. Turning, he reached to latch the new lock he'd installed right after supper; then, rubbing his palms together in a gesture of male satisfaction, he leaned back against the solid barrier.

Her eyes flew to the shiny, brass addition and she fought the blush that threatened to turn her cheeks a rosy hue. "I wondered what you were doing in here. Some special reason we need a lock on the door?" she asked, and he was bright enough not to push it.

"I wanted you to know that when we're in here together, it'll be as private as you want it to be." Short and simple, an explanation that was just another sample of his willingness to do some catering to her needs, she decided.

"All right," she said agreeably, turning away to place the

lamp she carried on the bedside table. "And yes, Willie came to the house this noon and made a pretty apology for his cocky attitude. He told me about his new girlfriend in town." Looking back at him as she bent to the table, she noted the satisfied look he wore.

"Did you put him up to it?" she asked bluntly.

"I just suggested, politely, that he might want to get on your good side, and make amends for his foolishness. I think he's seen the error of his ways." He took his weight from the door and walked toward the bed, his fingers working at buttons, tugging his shirt from its moorings and hanging it over the post as he rounded the corner of the bed.

"If you'll turn around here, I'll give you a hand with getting that shirt off, Mrs. Flannery," he offered.

"Not till I have my gown out of the drawer and the lamp's blown out, you won't," she retorted. "Besides, I managed to button the thing, and I'll warrant I can get out of it by myself. But the lamp goes out first. I'm not going to be on display for anybody who wants to take a gander in that window."

"I won't argue with you about the lamp being left on tonight. You can blow it out just as soon as I get you all undone here. But you won't need that nightgown, sweetheart." He made short work of the fastenings on her shirt, yet his fingertips lingered on her skin at every opportunity, and as she watched, his eyes narrowed, his mouth thinned and a ruddy texture mottled his tanned skin.

With barely audible tones, he murmured her name, bending to touch the tip of his tongue on a bit of exposed flesh beneath her collarbone. And then he held her from him, and his hungry gaze brought a matching glow to her body, rising from her breasts to color taut and heated skin.

"You've got a randy bridegroom on your hands, sweetheart. A man who's been waiting longer than any man should have to. I'm more than ready to take you to bed and get this marriage off the ground.''

''I've been thinking about things all day, J.T., first about the rustlers, and then—'' she said quickly, then ceased abruptly as his fingertips touched her lips and his head shook a slow denial of her words.

''Not now, sweetheart. In the morning, we'll talk, or later tonight if you want to, but for now, there's just you and me and a few hours' time to fill with turning you into my wife.''

Stepping aside, he bent to the lamp, lifting the globe and blowing out the flame. The room was swept into darkness by his action, and each whispered breath was magnified by the silence that fell between them. Her shirt fell to the floor with barely a sound, and then he worked at the placket of her trousers, his agile fingers sliding the buttons loose and lowering the heavy denim the length of her legs.

She stood before him and he nudged her closer, until she was wedged between his knees as he sat on the edge of the bed. ''Take off your vest,'' he murmured and she felt his gaze on the pale rise of her breasts as the stars filtered their light through the window.

''Slide down your drawers,'' he said next, and she did as he asked, feeling awkward as she stood before him with garments gathered around her feet. He leaned closer and his breath warmed her belly, sending shivers the length of her body as his tongue touched the sensitive skin inside her navel.

Long fingers slid between her stockings and the backs of her legs, and one by one he lifted her feet to strip the remaining garments from where they lay. ''Damn, I told you this was a sweet fanny.'' Released on a sigh, the words were accompanied by his hands against her bottom and he squeezed the flesh, his fingertips rough against her skin, bringing new sensations to life.

She whimpered, bending her head to his, and he looked

up, his skin drawn tautly over the bones of his face, his mouth an unsmiling line. Was there any semblance of love to be found there, she wondered. Did he feel any of the same surging desire that ran rampant even now within her breast? Or was it simple masculine need for satisfaction that drove him?

"I don't know how long I can last, Clo," he said softly. "I've never needed anything so much in my life as I need you right now." His groan was muffled against her skin as he buried his face in the softness of her belly, and she felt the brush of his evening beard against sensitive flesh. Then the feel of long fingers cupping her and finally nudging her thighs apart.

His head dipped lower and his breath blew softly against the curling nest of dark hair he found there. *Surely not.* The words loud in her mind, she tensed, but he only held her more firmly, and then his tongue edged the tender skin from one side to the other, barely touching the line of feminine hair that felt the warmth of his breath.

"Jay?" She heard the panic thread through the single syllable and her hands tugged at his hair. For less than a moment, for the length of a single second, he lingered, and then lifted his face to her. If ever she had felt a moment's apprehension with this man, it was now.

And then his touch softened, his fingers smoothing the taut flesh of her bottom as he rose, easing her from him. Hands that promised pleasure rose to cup the firm rounding of her breasts and he dipped to kiss with almost chaste caresses the upper rise of her bosom. As if she were lifted with no effort, he swept her feet from the floor and turned with her to the bed, placing her in the center of the quilt.

She watched as he lowered his trousers and drawers, her gaze intent as he sat beside her to scoop stockings to join them, and then bent in her direction. "I'm going to make you mine, Clo," he whispered. "I want you to know when you get up in the morning that there are no boundaries between us. What we do here, in this room, is for us, for the pleasure we can find in this bed.'' His hand brushed her hair back, and then his fingers tangled in the length that spread across her pillow, and he ran it between fingertips and palm, drawing the tress to its full length before he released it.

''I want you to have it all, sweetheart. I want you so filled with me, you'll never wonder again if I care enough about you to be here for you, from now until the day I die.'' His voice thickened as he spoke the words that eased her thoughts, words she'd never dreamed of hearing from a man. And the knowledge she'd harbored within her breast poured forth in a murmured confession she could not contain.

''I love you, Jay. I didn't know what it would be like to love a man, not till now. And you don't have to say the words in return. It's enough that you know how I feel about you.'' She slid her fingers through his hair and drew his head closer. ''I don't know much about this. You already know that, but whatever pleases you will please me, too.''

His groan was taut with passion, and his body was hardened with a desire he made no effort to conceal as he lowered himself over her. Holding his weight on his forearms, he bent to take her mouth, his tongue impatient as he sought the secret places he'd only begun to explore two nights past.

Swept up in the churning whirlwind of his passion, left breathless by his desire, Chloe could only submit to the caresses he bestowed upon her body. Soft sounds of pleasure poured from her lips as he nuzzled and suckled, finding places she'd never before known could contain such shivering sensations beneath her flesh. He murmured softly, words of admiration for her firmness, for the rounding of her hips and the shape of her breasts, for the spattering of freckles he kissed with patient care.

And it was as it had been the first night, only that now

there was no call from the yard, no voices to disturb the culmination of his tenderness, his passion and the power of his possession. She felt a stinging pain, one he seemed to absorb with a sudden stillness of his movements; and then he pushed deeper within her, and his groan was harsh and aching in her ear as he withdrew, only to lay claim again to the tender flesh she offered.

As though a mountain rose before her, she struggled to find the rhythm needed to assail the peak and fly freely. For surely the rising tension he brought to life must in some way be brought to fruition. Her cry was smothered by his mouth as she sought some elusive touch that would put an end to the driving, aching need, forcing her to surge against his body.

He murmured against her lips, his words guttural, urging her movements, and she gripped his shoulders with the full force of her strength, fearing she could not endure longer without relief from the tension with which she struggled. And then, as though released by a giant hand, her body was fully, achingly, enveloped by a throbbing pleasure she could only enclose, allowing it to fill her until her breath shattered and she cried out his name.

Her moan smothered against the damp skin of his shoulder, she felt the throbbing of her inner tissues subside, and was aware only that he moved against her once more, two, then three long, pulsing strokes bringing him to a shuddering release.

He was heavy, and she welcomed his weight. Their bodies were slick with perspiration, and the breeze fluttering the white curtains swept across the bed in a soothing, cooling stream. She felt the coiling of muscle as he lifted from her and her grip tightened, her fingertips digging into the taut lines of his back.

"Don't go," she whispered. "Don't leave me yet."

"All right." Holding his weight above her, enabling her

to breathe freely, he touched his lips idly to hers, then to her cheek and forehead, tender gestures that expressed words she knew he would not speak.

And it was enough.

Chapter Ten

"There's not a whole lot we can do, Hogan." J.T.'s words were forceful, yet a note of frustration was apparent. "Until Micah gives us the go ahead, it's in his hands. The trail is dead, and we're going to have to stay put until the judge comes in at the end of the week and gets Corky up before him."

"We're just gonna let this bunch of outlaws hit and run and get away with it?" Hogan's voice was rough, raw with anger, and J.T. shook his head in quick denial.

"Hell, no. We're going to double the number of men keeping watch at night, and the rest of us will take turns doing double duty on the chores. We've got a ranch to run, and I'll be damned if I'll let a gang of rustlers put a halt to the operation." He strode toward the barn, and Hogan was hard put to keep up.

"I want every man armed to the teeth, and be sure they've all got enough ammunition to do some good if they need it. Put the new man with Willie. I don't know which of them will be watching the other more closely, but I've a notion Cleary is a force to behold if his back's against the wall. Micah wouldn't have given him the nod if he didn't trust him."

"All right, whatever you say goes, boss. I know Winters has hired on a couple of men that look more like gunfighters than ranch hands to me. I feel like we're heading for a battle here before we know it."

"That may be," J.T. agreed. "But we're going to be ready for it, one way or the other. I've put a couple of shotguns handy for Chloe and Tilly. They're better off with them than a rifle, I figure. And I'm staying pretty close to the house. You're in charge of the rest of the operation out there." His hand waved toward the north, where the herd had been gathered into as small an area as they could manage.

"Keeping track of the horses will be up to me, and whoever isn't needed on the range. Have the men take turns, and be sure they're not asleep in that damn cabin the next time someone decides to cut the fence."

Hogan shook his head. "You know as well as I do that Corky did that job for them. It's just too bad that Tom…" He paused as if he rethought his words. "Hell, I don't know what would have made a difference. We all thought the man was on the up-and-up. And I know damn well Chloe is beatin' herself over the head, thinkin' she was the one that hired him on."

"I think she's more worried about Pete," J.T. said. "Not knowing where he is or what he's up to is preying on her mind right now."

"You think he's put in with the rustlers?" Hogan's lips were set firmly and his hands clenched at his sides, forming fists that twitched with the obvious urge to vent his fury. He shot a glance toward the long lane, where even now Chloe was leading a horse, bending her head to speak to the animal she held on a short line. "She's lookin' kinda frayed around the edges, ain't she?"

"Yeah," J.T. agreed, knowing that part of Chloe's drawn look was due to the lack of sleep she'd encountered during the night before. And it was his fault, though he could not bring himself to regret one moment of the pleasure he'd found in her arms. They'd spoken softly, murmuring words that blended into the background as he'd sought her throughout the night, unable to leave her untouched, his hands ever smoothing across her skin, his mouth seeking hers in gentle assurances of his concern.

And she'd gloried in it. As surely as he'd watched her sleep in the dawn's light, he knew that in spite of the shadowed lids, her eyes would be shimmering pools of delight when she awoke, that her memories would be replete with the pleasure he'd brought to her virgin flesh. Chloe was a bride to be cherished, and even as he watched her near, he renewed his vow to handle her with care.

"Got everything sorted out?" she asked, halting before them, her eyes touching on Hogan's taut features before she looked fully into J.T.'s eyes. "It looks like you've managed to get everyone headed north this morning, Hogan."

"Yeah, we're covering the herd as best we can," he told her. "I'm leavin' myself to check on the horses. Too bad we don't have a couple more bodies to ride the north edge of the ranch, but the men are covering as much ground as they can."

"What about the new man?" Her gaze was sharp as she spoke the words.

"He'll do well, I think," Hogan said swiftly. "J.T. feels the same way, Chloe. He's with Willie, and we all know he's on his best behavior these days." His grin was quick, and J.T. cast him a cautioning look. Best that Chloe was not aware of the extent of his talk to the boy, and the rest of the men had taken it upon themselves to let their own opinions be voiced. Willie would mind his p's and q's. That was almost guaranteed.

"Don't be too hard on him," Chloe said with a grin. "He's just a boy, feeling his oats. I'll bet little Miss Francie

Higgins can keep him in line. And if she can't, his mama will.''

She turned aside, circling them with the gelding close at her heels. ''Anybody working with another horse yet? Or am I done for the morning?''

''I'm on my way,'' J.T. told her, turning to follow in her footsteps. Hogan kept pace, veering off to where his saddled mount waited near the barn door. Settling his hat more firmly against his brow, he lifted a hand and then touched his heels to the sides of the black mare he rode.

''I don't know what I'd have done without him after Pa died,'' Chloe said quietly, her hand rubbing in a distracted movement against the nose of the animal she led.

''Well, he's as loyal as the day is long, honey,'' J.T. told her, meaning every word, knowing that he could give no higher praise to the man Chloe had entrusted her ranch to during those difficult days while she got her feet beneath her.

''How many horses have you worked with this morning?'' he asked, tilting his head to look deeply into her eyes. ''Are you all right? I'm afraid…''

She laughed aloud. ''Don't you dare apologize for one thing, Flannery. Keeping me up half the night was about the nicest thing you could have done. *Nice* isn't the right word for it, I guess,'' she temporized, ''but the other things I'm thinking are best left unsaid until you slide the lock in place on our bedroom door tonight.''

A sense of relief he hadn't known he needed flooded him, and he allowed his smile full force. ''You're not sore?'' The words were a whisper, and her quick grin assured him that she did not share his concern. The urge to hold her against his body was sudden, and he fought it for a moment, then gave in to the desire he could not contain.

She melted against him, lifting her face to his as though she sought the morning sun, and would find it in his countenance. "You make me happy, Jay. I can't say it any other way. I won't be repeating what I told you last night. I won't put you on the spot thataway, but know that the words are in my heart."

Almost struck dumb by her honesty, he could only bend and touch his lips to hers, murmuring soft assurances as he held her curving form to his own hard body.

Cleary appeared at the kitchen door while dinner was being dished up and, with a single rap of knuckles, announced his presence.

"Come on in," Tilly boomed. "You don't need to wait for an invite, boy. It's time for dinner and there's more than enough to go around."

"Yeah, that's why I'm here," he said quietly. "Hogan said I should bring out food for all the men's noon meal. He'll send half of them back to the house for supper later on. If you want to send extra, the rest of us will make do overnight."

"Is there much food left in the cabin?" Tilly asked, a frown appearing as if she already was forming a list of supplies to send back with him.

"I saw canned goods and a lard tin full of coffee when I was there last time," Chloe volunteered, standing in the kitchen doorway. "If you wrap up the rest of the roast for sandwiches and send along the soup you made yesterday, they can have that later on, along with a loaf of bread. There's plenty of biscuits and ham sliced up for their dinner and we'll give them the potato salad you just made."

"Ma'am, that sounds like good food to me," Cleary said vehemently. "Best news I've had all day."

"Are things going well?" Chloe asked. "Nothing happening?"

"Calm as you please," he answered. "The men are making regular patrols around the perimeter and keeping a close eye on the herd. It's kinda hard to keep them on a tight leash, with all that open country leading off into shallow valleys and such, but they're doing their best.''

"You much of a cowman, Cleary?" Chloe asked, and was gratified when his shrug and quick grin made modest work of his reply.

"I can handle most anything that comes my way, Miss Chloe." His gaze was straightforward and his eyes clear of subterfuge. She'd lay odds that he was more than he appeared, but if Micah and J.T. were satisfied with him, she'd toss her vote his way, too.

"I'll bet you can," she said, turning to relieve Tilly of her burden as she stepped from the pantry. Hands filled with food, a jar of potato salad beneath her arm, she welcomed Chloe's aid, and in moments, they had sliced ham and the chunk of roast beef into sandwich-size slabs and were wrapping them in waxed paper. The packages were thick and the waxed covering held the juices and grease within its folds, ensuring the meat would stay moist and edible throughout the day.

"That sure looks like enough food to last them till morning," Cleary said, reaching to pack it into the saddlebags he'd carried into the house with him, taking care with the towel-wrapped loaf of bread. He hoisted the bags from the table and tossed Tilly a grin. "I'll bet they never give you a day off, do they, ma'am?"

"Not lately," Tilly answered smartly. "You just keep a good eye on those steers, mister, so Chloe here can rest easy."

His eyes narrowed and Chloe sensed the return of his normal caution as he nodded. "I'll do that," he said, opening the door to leave. He looked back at Chloe and nodded once, a silent message she pondered as she watched him stride from the porch to where his horse lingered beneath the nearest tree, reins touching the ground.

J.T. was right. The man rode well, had a horse between his legs that followed his command with barely a movement to be seen of either reins moved or knees pressed against the animal's barrel. And the boots and saddle were of top quality, as J.T. had pointed out. As was the man, she was willing to bet.

"I wonder where Micah found him," she mused, turning back to Tilly as she reached for three plates to set the table. J.T. would be in shortly, ready for dinner, and as that thought entered her mind, she hastened to finish readying the kitchen for the noon meal. In moments she had pulled the bell cord on the porch, allowing the clanger to touch each side of the bell just once, the sound that would announce a meal, not an emergency.

And in her mind rang the echo of Tilly's murmured reply. "That Micah's got something up his sleeve. I'd lay odds on it, and I'm not even a gambling woman."

The next days passed by in a flurry of activity, the workload heavier with the men doubled up on guard duty, leaving the chores to the hands of Chloe and whoever was left to work with the horses. Usually J.T., but sometimes Lowery, was there, and Chloe knew that the best talent available was at hand. They were both men who rode as if attached to the animal they handled, their every movement precise, as if they danced in unison with the horse's fluid movements, bodies lithe and elegant in the saddle.

Today, Lowery had taken on the duty of training and putting the green-broke animals through their paces. A buyer was coming from a rancher's group in Montana, and J.T. was doing his best to have the chosen horses ready to sell. Already, he was looking beyond this year's stock to the foals that would welcome spring next year, the results of the breeding he'd accomplished thus far with the paint stallion he kept close to the barn. And Chloe had begun to share his excitement, even buried as it had been beneath the worry of rustlers and the added work entailed by their presence.

Her arms were weary from the brushing, her legs ached from the miles she'd walked today, cooling the horses down. Time after time, hour after hour, she paced, with only the intermittent currying and cleaning of her animals to break the monotony of the task she'd taken on.

And her mind churned with thoughts she could not dump onto J.T.'s broad shoulders, as willing as she knew he was to hear her fears voiced aloud. As ready as his listening ear would be, she could not speak aloud the dreadful thoughts that woke her in the hours of the night. The image of Pete dangling at the end of a rope filled her mind, as she had seen it so vividly against her eyelids just before dawn. She groaned aloud at the tortured lines of his face, a face she'd beheld with such reality, that, even knowing it had been a dream, she could not escape the memory.

"Penny for your thoughts, sweetheart," J.T. said from beside her, and she jerked to attention, aware that her mind had wandered far from the animal she was supposed to be grooming.

"You don't want to know," she muttered, bending again to her task.

"Well, they weren't of me, I'll warrant," he said, touching her arm to cease the regular movement of the brush she held. "You looked like you'd just lost your last friend. And I know better than that, honey."

"You're the best friend I've ever had," she said fervently, adding additional muscle to the long strokes she took across the gelding's side. "And after last night, I don't think I'm in any danger of you running off anywhere."

His laughed aloud. "Now that's better. I declare, ma'am, your cheeks are about as rosy as those flowers Tilly keeps watering by the porch."

"I needed you to cheer me up," she admitted. "I've had too much time to think lately."

"About Pete?" he surmised and she nodded glumly.

"You can't do anything about him, Clo, except think good thoughts, and I'm not sure even that will help. Unless he turns up pretty soon, I'm afraid he'll be considered a part of the shenanigans that're goin' on around here."

"Have you heard from Micah?" she asked, her thoughts turning to Corky's presence in the town jail.

"Yeah, I'm afraid Corky's not going to get a trial of any sort. The judge came in and Micah sent word that he sentenced him to prison. He's giving him three days to come up with some names. Promised him a shorter sentence if he'd come clean, but I don't hold much with Corky spilling what he knows. We'll just have to wait and see."

"Did Micah talk to you?" she asked, turning to hear this latest bit of news.

"No, he sent word with Hale Winters last night, and Lowery told me about it. I think Micah's looking for something to happen in town, maybe a jailbreak. Those rustlers would like to get their hands on Corky. They're probably worried about him blowing the lid on them, I'm thinking."

"Is the judge still around?"

J.T. nodded. "Yeah, he told Micah he'd advise him to find another deputy and to put a man in the jail around the clock. He hasn't any real authority, but Micah thinks he's right on the button."

Chloe's heart beat more rapidly as she listened. "What do you think?" she asked finally, watching closely as J.T.'s mouth grew taut, as if he hesitated to reply.

"I think we need to be ready for anything, Clo."

Supper was a silent affair, with only four eating around the table, Hogan hastening back to the bunkhouse afterward for as much sleep as he could manage before another long day faced him. "I'll go on out early on and replace Lowery," he told J.T. And then he turned to Tilly. "Can you make up a batch of biscuits for the men? Anything fresh tastes good out there."

He lifted a hand when Chloe would have spoken. "Nobody's complainin', Chloe. It's just a fact of life. We've got them all spoiled with good grub. But, they're earnin' their way, keepin' those cattle underfoot and takin' turns on guard."

"How about the new man?" she asked, and Hogan chuckled.

"He's keeping Willie moving right along. Looks to be handy with a rope and his horse is well trained. Hope he'll stick around when this is all over. We can use a man like that, maybe a couple more like him when things get off the ground and we're doing more with training the new colts we'll be seeing the next couple of years down the road."

J.T. walked out with Hogan, and Tilly waved Chloe off. "I'll clean up in here. Go on out and sit on the porch for a bit. Enjoy the cool air and wait for J.T. to come back."

It was a welcome suggestion and Chloe stood at the end of the porch, her eyes cast upward as the first stars began to appear. Depression fell with the darkening sky, and she thought again of Pete, her heart aching with futile pain. He'd never been strong, maybe feeling he had taken a back seat to her years ago, she decided, when she and their father had bonded so closely.

And yet, she'd always hoped that the intimate beginnings, when they'd shared their mother's womb, might have instilled in Pete a deeper love for his sister. Searching her mind, she thought of his lapses, his chronic need for rebellion, and achingly pondered the ways and means she might have found to help him during his last stay on the ranch.

Probably her marrying J.T. had been the final straw for Pete, knowing he was finally on the outside looking in. Yet, she could not regret one moment leading up to that point. *"If only…"* Her lips whispered the sad phrase, and as if prompted by the melancholy of her mood, she saw a figure, riding slowly, but with purpose, toward her.

Stepping down from the side of the porch, she hastened to meet the solitary horseman, never giving a thought to danger, intent on discovering who the visitor might be. "Pete?" she called out hopefully. "Is that you, Pete?"

"Yeah, it's me," he answered, his voice muffled, as if he feared being discovered in this place. He halted beneath the lone tree at the side of the house, and dismounted, holding his horse's reins and watching as Chloe approached. "I didn't know if you'd talk to me," he said quietly.

"Where've you been?" Even to her own ears, the words were accusing, and she watched as he turned back toward the saddle. "Wait," she cried, rushing to catch hold of his shirt. "I've been worried about you. Don't get angry right off, Pete. Just stay here and talk to me."

His back was stiff, unbending beneath her hand, and she untangled her fingers from the cotton fabric, brushing against the nap, as if she would apologize for her hasty words. "You always accuse me first, don't you?" he said, anger rimming the words. "It's always my fault, no matter what goes wrong."

"That's not true," she said, denying his claim, stung by the unfair accusation. "You're the one who left in the first place, the one who ran out and brought me to my knees. If it weren't for J.T.—"

"Damn J.T." he said roughly, spinning to face her. "This whole thing was his fault, cheating me out of my money and then taking the ranch."

She caught her breath, stunned by the fury radiating from him. "You hate him that much?" she asked sadly. "He just happened to be there that day, Pete. If it hadn't been him, it would have been someone else, and that someone else might not have been as good to me as J.T. has.''

"Yeah, I saw how good to you he was," Pete sneered. "Snatched you right off the shelf and said a few words in front of a preacher, and now he's got the whole kit and caboodle for himself.''

"We've been over this before," she told him. "And you'll never see past that image, will you?" She stepped back from him, sadness surrounding her as she saw the futility of this moment. "Why did you come back this time?" she asked. "There's no money for you here, and with the rustling—"

"What rustling?" he asked sharply. "What's going on now? You think I'm in on a thing like that?"

It sounded like bluster to her ear, and yet, she could not accuse him without proof, and she shook her head. "I don't know what to think. I just know that the night we got married, rustlers hit during the party and we lost a lot of steers out of the north range.''

"Well, I didn't have anything to do with it," he said staunchly.

"Where did you go when you disappeared that night?" A dark voice cut through the night, and J.T. appeared from the opposite side of the tree, stepping closer as he spoke.

"That's none of your damn business, *brother,*" Pete said, sarcasm oozing as he faced the bigger man.

"Well, I happen to think it is," J.T. persisted. "You ran off, and within a couple of hours we lost a good-size chunk of the herd.''

"Yeah, well I heard in town that Corky's the man you need to be accusing," Pete blustered. "I heard they're out shoppin' for a new rope right now.''

"He's going to prison in a few days, Pete. They won't be hanging him." His voice softened. "Aren't you afraid he'll mention your name?"

"I got nothing to do with it." Pete sounded sullen, defensive, and Chloe could bear it no longer.

"Stop." She spread her hand wide on J.T.'s chest, her heart aching as J.T. inhaled, aware his anger was at the boiling point. "Let's not do this tonight. Pete—" turning to her brother, she motioned toward the bunkhouse "—go on out and get a good night's sleep. We'll talk in the morning."

With a haughty glance in J.T.'s direction, Pete nodded, then led his horse toward the barn, and Chloe was left to face the fury of the frustrated man behind her. His first movements were harsh as he spun her to face him, and then she tipped her head upward to meet his gaze in the shadows. *Damn.* He caught his breath as he watched the tears flow, and his anger was deflected by concern for the woman who stood between her brother and disaster. "Chloe." Her name was all he could speak, and then she was gathered to his chest and he felt the shuddering sobs she could not contain. "Don't let him pull the wool over your eyes, honey," he said quietly. "You're too softhearted where that boy's concerned, and he'll take advantage."

"You really think he's part of the whole thing, don't you?" she asked, lifting her face to peer into his eyes.

"Yeah, I do." And he was uneasy at the thought of harboring him even for one night within the boundaries of the ranch, lest he'd just let the enemy through the gates, he thought glumly. Yet, maybe close at hand was the safer of two choices.

"What did he say he wanted?" J.T. asked.

"He didn't." Her voice held a note of surprise and she stiffened. "He just said he…" She paused and looked toward the barn, where a light glowed within and Pete could be seen unsaddling his horse in the aisle. "I don't know why he came back." Puzzlement wrapped the words, and her shoulders slumped. "I was just so happy to see him, and I thought surely he wouldn't show up here if he was guilty of anything.'' Her laugh rasped against his hearing and she lifted a hand to her mouth. ''You're right. I'm gullible.''

''No, just tenderhearted,'' J.T. said, denying her words even as he expelled a sigh of relief. Maybe she was beginning to see Pete in a new light, finally. ''I'll take a walk out and tell Hogan to keep an ear open for him. We'll talk in the morning, and Pete will come up with some answers, or he's on his way out of here, Chloe.''

It was an hour later before J.T. crawled into their bed. Curled into a ball, the sheet almost over her head, Chloe huddled in the middle, and he scooped her against himself. ''You awake?'' he asked quietly, aware that she relaxed against him with only a moment's hesitation. He pushed her hair from her face, tilting her head back, and found her mouth with his own.

Warm and soft beneath his lips, she responded, not with passion or desire, but as if she needed the comfort of his presence. He kissed her, without demand, but with purpose. Coaxing her into his arms was not the problem. Chloe was willing to be held. Easing her to a state of loving might take some doing, but the need to enforce their intimacy was uppermost in his mind. A bulwark against Pete's influence must be formed, and to his way of thinking, such a thing could be best erected by the claiming of Chloe's body and the firming of their growing relationship.

''I don't think I want to do this,'' she murmured as his tongue edged her lower lip.

''Sure you do, honey,'' he said, his voice low and coaxing. ''I need you, sweetheart.'' His hand rubbed idly against her back, easing her nightgown up until he found the soft skin of her hip beneath his fingertips. She shifted idly, and shook her head, a quick movement signifying reluctance.

But he would not cease, only murmuring words of admiration for her as he feathered his kisses across her face, coming up on his elbow, the better to accomplish his purpose. She rolled to her back and he slid his hand the length of her thigh, lifting her knee and shaping the muscles of her calf in his palm. "You're so sleek, honey," he murmured. And then he sought the soft flesh of her inner thigh, where his fingers lingered, brushing the tender skin as he found her mouth again and breathed warmth against her soft lips.

"Kiss me back, Clo," he whispered. "Please." And she did, hesitantly at first, and then as his fingertips touched her hidden folds, she trembled against his hand and a tiny sob escaped her lips.

"You don't play fair," she cried softly. Almost reluctantly, she rose to his touch, and he stifled a surge of satisfaction at the helpless note of desire in her voice. "I didn't want this tonight," she told him, pushing against his chest, and yet her fingers brushed against the curls.

"I'll stop if you say so," he said slowly. "But I don't want to, Clo. I think you need me as much—"

"I do," she whispered, her words tangling with his. "I just feel like things are not right somehow, and I don't know how to fix it."

"Don't think for now. Not at all," he coaxed. "Just let me love you."

"You didn't bargain for this when you married me, did you?" she asked sadly.

"I'll take anything I can get when it comes to you, Clo," he told her firmly. "I've never needed a woman so much."

"Needed?" The single word was wistful, and he lifted his head from her throat and heard the plea behind its utterance.

"Wanted, maybe?" he asked quietly. "I care about you, sweetheart. Enough to be a part of your life until the day I die. But I won't make you do anything you don't want. Just say the word and I'll kiss you good-night."

Her sigh was deep and she lifted a hand to his cheek. "I'm being pouty, aren't I? Acting like a silly child, when what I want is to be…I want to be your wife, Jay. Maybe I just needed some persuasion." She buried her fingers in his hair and with gentle pressure guided him to the front of her gown.

His mouth touched the soft fabric and he bit carefully at a button. "Won't come undone," he muttered. And laughed as she inched her fingers through the buttonhole beneath his mouth. She eased the next opening apart, then another and he waited, impatience building as she exposed pale skin to his view. The bodice fell wide apart as her fingertips reached the bottom of the row of small buttons, and he dropped his cheek to touch the pearling of soft flesh as it peaked against his whiskered jaw.

"Damn, you're beautiful," he whispered, turning his face to catch the rigid bit of skin between his teeth. She gasped, a taut whisper in the night, and her hands clutched for purchase at his head. It was all he needed, that single sound that told him she was with him, and his mouth opened fully over the firm, plump treasure she offered.

"Jay." The desire was there now, and he rejoiced at her generosity, yet he lingered, not willing to press her too rapidly into the final movements of this act of loving. He would make it last, draw out her pleasure, fulfill the yearning that throbbed even now beneath his hand, where slick, wet folds urged his possession.

"Jay." Desire became demand and her fingertips pressed more firmly against his head as her hips rose, thrusting against him.

He answered, a low, hungry sound, a guttural blend of desire and triumph. And found that in the giving, he received. In the pleasuring, he found satisfaction beyond his expectation, and as her cries of passion rose to fill his hearing, he found she had woven her way into his heart. And he was struck by the sudden knowledge that he was no longer alone. That this woman made him vulnerable. Vulnerable and afraid.

Chapter Eleven

"You're outta your mind, lettin' him stay on here." Hogan vented his opinion with a glare, his hat pushed back, his hands fisted against his hipbones. "You've done nothin' but set loose a coyote in the henhouse, J.T.," he snarled. "I know Chloe's a soft touch where he's concerned, but I gave you credit for more sense."

Aware that the man's anger was honest, J.T. ignored the lack of respect in Hogan's words. Another time, or from another man, his reaction would have differed greatly, but Hogan was as much a part of the Double B as Chloe herself. "I won't fight her over her brother," J.T. said calmly, even though his every instinct was to agree with Hogan's stand. "We'll have to keep an eye on him."

"Damned if I'll follow him around like a nursemaid," Hogan said, defiance lighting his eyes. "You gave him a bunk last night, J.T., you can just handle him yourself." He breathed deeply, looking off across the yard to where Pete stood on the porch with Chloe. His shoulders twitched, and then he grunted, a curse dropping from his lips as he swung back to the silent man watching him.

"You gonna fire me?"

"Hell, no," J.T. said with a harsh burst of laughter.

"That'd be like cuttin' off my nose to spite my face. You run this place, Hogan. What would I want to do a fool thing like that for?"

"I'm not gonna apologize," Hogan warned him.

"Didn't expect you to. A man has a right to his own opinion."

Pete looked up, his narrowed gaze touching the two men who watched him. And then he spoke to Chloe again, and her eyes flashed to where J.T. stood, a fleeting message within their depths that he sensed rather than saw.

"Get on out here, Pete. You've got a day's work to do if you're planning on earning your keep." J.T.'s tone was harsh, and he made no effort to soften his stance as Pete jumped from the porch and headed toward him. "I want the barn cleaned and the tack looked after. The rest of the men have their hands full keeping track of the herd. You'll pull chore duty for the next day or so."

"Keeping me close by?" Pete asked snidely. "What's the matter? Afraid I can't hold my own out on the range?"

J.T.'s fingers formed a fist, and he subdued the urge to slam it into Pete's mocking expression. "I'm afraid if those men get a gander at you, they'll chop you to bits, boy. You're not very popular around here right now."

"Never had any trouble till you started causing it," Pete said snidely. And then he stalked past the two men and snatched a pitchfork from the barn wall. Grasping the wheelbarrow, he headed for the back of the barn, and J.T. glanced toward the house where Chloe watched from the porch. She lifted a hand, then dropped it into her pocket, her movement slow.

"I'll be out in a while," she called, and he nodded.

"I'm headin' out now," Hogan told him, untying his horse and easing into the saddle. Sacks of provisions hung heavily from behind the saddle, and he moved cautiously. "J.T.," he began, his reins taut as the horse pranced his impatience. "Should I send Cleary back up here? Maybe he needs to know who Pete is. You know, just in case he runs across him."

"You're thinking the same thing I am, Hogan. Spit it out. Cleary's here because Micah wants him around. I've accepted that, and I'm putting my faith in Micah's good sense. Tell him about Pete, and don't spare the details. He needs to know what we think. And whether Chloe likes it or not, Pete's under the gun as far as I'm concerned."

"You said it all, boss." Relaxing his hold on the horse he rode, Hogan allowed the animal to set out, and in moments they were gone, a cloud of dust concealing their movements.

The days were slow, and J.T. watched and waited. His suspicions ran high, as did the tension among the men who were working shorthanded. Torn between staying close at hand, in order to watch Pete and be with Chloe, or working with the men, he chose the former, spending the hours with training and keeping Pete busy at mundane tasks. The young man was silent, dark looks betraying his anger, and J.T. felt he was walking a tightrope, uneasy, yet certain his gut instincts were on target.

Micah showed up the third day, sweeping his hat from his head, looking toward the house as if seeking a glimpse of Tilly. "How's it going?" he asked, leaning on his saddle horn, his narrowed eyes taking in J.T.'s impatient demeanor.

"You tell me," J.T. answered curtly. "They still holding Corky in a cell?"

"Yeah. The judge gave him another couple of days to ponder his sins. The man's gettin' edgy as hell, to tell the truth. Heard him hollerin' this morning, wantin' to know what's goin' on. Maybe the judge has the right idea, keeping him off guard this way. I'm thinking the rest of the gang will be anxious to have it done with, and hoping Corky keeps his mouth shut." He shrugged idly. "Then too, they might be down in Silver City counting their money by now.''

"It's a waiting game either way," J.T. said. "But I think Pete's got something up his sleeve. He's been keeping an eye on me for two days, like he's waiting for me to get out of his range."

"He working or just shuffling his feet?" Micah asked, tossing a look toward the barn.

"A little of both, trying to stay in Chloe's good graces, mostly.''

"How is she?" Micah asked, his gaze flickering toward the back door. And then his eyes lit. "Say there, Tilly. You got a cup of coffee for an old man?''

Tilly stood behind the screen, a solid presence, and J.T. grinned. "Go on in and talk to her, Micah. Give her something to think about, other than fretting about Chloe.''

Not waiting for a second invitation, Micah stood down from his horse and tied the animal to the hitching rail before he sauntered to the porch. Tilly held open the door and he walked past her. She released it with a snap of her hand and it caught him smartly on his rump, and J.T. heard her muffled laughter.

"We'll lose our cook if you keep encouraging him," Chloe said from behind him. He turned to watch as she tilted her hat back and grinned at him. A smile he hadn't seen form in three days, a welcome glimpse of white teeth and curved lips. He couldn't resist, and swept her into his embrace.

"I've missed your smile," he murmured, bending to drop a series of kisses against her cheek. And then he released her. "You smiled last night, though, now that I think about it.''

"How do you know?" she asked with a flash of sassy eyes. "It was dark.''

"I knew," he told her. And was silent, watching as her

mouth pressed together and she flushed, as if her memories were warm in her mind. "I knew, Chloe. It did my heart good."

"Mine, too," she admitted quietly. "You're good to me, J.T., and I appreciate it. I know it hasn't been easy for you to have the worry of Pete being here. I keep wondering where you're getting all the patience it's taking to deal with him. And I keep waiting for something to happen."

"You, too?"

"Me, too." She touched his shirt with her index finger. "I've curried and brushed those horses till my arms ache. I've watched you riding and working and wondered how long we can keep marking time this way. What's going to happen?"

"I don't know. But I feel a storm brewing, and it's not good. The weather's changing and the herd is tired of being held so tight. A good lightning bolt will be enough to cause real problems out there, and we're sitting on a powder keg, Chloe."

"Why don't you take a ride out and see how the men are holding up? Things are fine here, and Micah will probably stay for a while."

"Maybe." He hesitated, then made up his mind. "All right. I'll just have a word with Micah first."

From behind the barn, a shrill trumpet announced the presence of the paint stallion, and Chloe looked to where Pete stood at the barn door. "Your stud is edgy, too, Jay. Is he just tired of being kept away from the mares?"

"Probably. Lowery's wanting to ride him, working the herd, and he could use the exercise, but I'd rather keep him near the barn."

He was gone in fifteen minutes, a quick kiss his farewell, and Chloe watched him leave. She headed for the chicken coop, where the hens gathered around the flat wide pan in the middle of the fenced-in enclosure, clucking and pecking

their way through the morning's offering of feed. A bucket
of water scooped from the trough in hand, she opened the
gate and squeezed through, holding the dusty, gray hens
aside with one foot, lest they escape into the yard. She bent,
filling the water basin for them and watched with a grin as
they gathered there to drink, tipping their heads back, allowing the water to run down their throats.

"Silly things," she murmured. "Nothing to do but eat
and lay eggs and let that fancy pants rooster chase you
around." The cock stirred from beneath the shade of the
coop as if he'd heard his name mentioned and stretched long
legs, strutting between the members of his harem and sending them scattering with a sharp peck.

"Mean old thing," Chloe said, tossing the residue of the
water in his direction. He crowed, a distinct challenge, and
she laughed aloud. "Men are all alike," she said, scolding
him roundly. "Between you and that stallion…" And J.T.
Flannery, she thought, remembering his words. *You smiled
last night.* And she had, she remembered, opening the gate
and closing it behind herself.

Cocky. He'd been downright cocky. She deposited the
bucket by the trough, her mind filled with the memory of
his touch, his kisses, his body possessing hers.

The man in the shadows of the barn watched, cursing
beneath his breath as he wondered what thoughts ran rampant in his sister's mind.

"He's making a fool of you," he whispered. "And I'm
gonna hit him where it hurts."

The storm rumbled its way across the range, lightning
flashing, bringing J.T. up from the bed with a sharp excla-
mation. "Damn, it couldn't have come at a worse time,"
he said with impatience, running his fingers through his hair.
"Middle of the night's a bad time to hold that herd in place
with this kind of commotion."

"You can't do much about it now," Chloe said from the bed. "There's no sense in getting wet for nothing. The men will handle it."

"I feel uneasy," he told her, searching for the trousers he'd dropped beside the bed right after dark.

She sat upright and sighed. "I'll get up and make you coffee."

"Don't bother. I'll just find my slicker and—" He jerked, his attention caught by lightning from outside the window, and hopping on one foot, he clutched at his trousers, hauling them on as he bent low to peer toward the barn. "Something's going on out there," he said harshly. "The door's hanging open and I can see a light inside."

"Probably Tom checking the horses," she said. "He's in charge for tonight."

"Maybe," he said tightly. "But it doesn't look like Tom." He stomped his feet into his boots and snatched a shirt from the drawer, buttoning it as he headed for the door.

Chloe grabbed for her robe and pulled it around herself, aware of the lack of sleepwear beneath it, but anxious to follow J.T. through the house. The kitchen was dark and she reached for the lamp, striking a match to light the wick. The glass globe slid in place and she looked up to find J.T. shrugging into his slicker, his hat pulled low. A frown pleated his forehead, and she felt a moment of apprehension at the taut look of his features.

Without a word, he pulled the door open and was gone, the screen slamming behind him. Wind blew in a gust across the yard and she saw the bucket spin crazily from the trough toward the tree. From over J.T.'s head a flame licked high into the night, and she swallowed the horror that gripped her.

Fire. The menace that threatened the livelihood of every rancher, every farmer with barns and livestock to protect.

And J.T. was heading for it, running full tilt, his slicker flying behind him.

She reached for her own rain gear, her fingers awkward as she tugged it over her robe, then pushed her feet into the boots she'd left by the back door.

"What's going on?" Tilly came through the doorway from the hall with a rush, her bulky form covered by a quilt she'd apparently snatched from the bed.

"Fire," Chloe said, the single word an explosion of horror as she burst through the door and across the porch. Standing stock-still in amazement, she watched as flames licked from the hayloft window to curl over the edge of the barn roof. So rapidly it spread; so quickly destruction followed in its wake, and she was sickened as she heard the sound of horses inside the barn, frantic as they kicked against the stalls.

Most of them were in the pasture, but the barn held the milk cow in the nearest stall, and she knew the stallion was there, somewhere, unless J.T. had already taken him to safety. Two mares, tempted by the rich timothy hay, had nosed through the fence and eaten their way into a bellyache and J.T. had put them in solitary stalls for the night after dosing them down. She heard their shrill whinnies as she reached the barn door and ducked as a piece of burning wood fell beside her.

"I'm coming," she muttered, lifting her long gown with one hand, wondering where J.T. had gone. And then, as she released the first mare, turning with her to lead her from the barn, she heard a groan from behind her.

"J.T.?" She called his name, but the man who rose from the floor next to the wall was not her husband. Tom's face blurred before her, and he staggered in the glow of the fire, one hand pressed against the side of his head.

"Tom?" She led the horse to where he stood and grasped his arm. "Come on, Tom. You've got to get out of here," she told him, and he allowed her to lead, pushing on the wide door as they passed through it, and then took the mare from her grasp.

"I've got her, Miss Chloe," the man said, his voice slurred.

Chloe turned back without a word, hurrying past the patient cow, who lowed and jerked her head within the stanchion, begging her freedom. "I'll be there, Bossie," she said, entering the stall with the second mare, uncaring of the animal's shifting and frantic movements, set only on removing her from the peril of a ceiling full of hay coming down from above.

"Chloe, get the hell out of that barn." J.T.'s voice was strident, his words sharp and nearby, and she ran with the horse she led, stumbling and tripping her way to the doorway.

"Take her. I'll get the cow," she panted, and thanked J.T.'s good sense for doing as she asked. The cow was a simple matter, only too willing to back from the confining wooden contraption that held her prisoner, and was led outside in moments.

The rain, the blessed, heavenly rain poured in torrents, taking her breath as Chloe left the burning barn, and she looked up into the heavens with thankfulness. It sizzled on the barn roof, sending clouds of steam skyward as it cooled the wood and soaked the hay beneath.

"Will it be enough to put out the fire in time?" she asked as J.T. reached for her.

"Yeah," he said harshly. "It's only gotten a good hold here at the front, and the wind's blowing the rain right on top of the fire."

The window in the loft was wide-open, and even as Chloe watched, the fire subsided. J.T. set her aside, issuing a warning glance. "Don't go back in. Send Tom in as soon as he gets his head clear. We'll check it out."

The front part of the barn was damaged, the wall burned out in one spot, thankfully allowing the rain to soak down the hay behind it. In moments, she watched as J.T. pitched the last of the smouldering stuff from the window to the ground below. The stench was acrid in her nose, and she wondered how he stood it, tall amid the smoking mess around about his feet, there, where surely the smell was filling his lungs.

Even as she watched he lifted the kerchief he'd tied around his neck and allowed it to drape his nose and mouth. Beside him, Tom took a stand, following J.T.'s lead, getting rid of the rest of the hay that still held danger in its depths. And then they halted, looking upward as the rain poured down, blowing against their stalwart forms and, even now, seeping through the ceiling and falling to the barn floor.

It was over, the threat held under control, and Chloe closed her eyes, whispering a prayer of thanksgiving for the gift of rain.

"Somebody set that fire." From behind her, Tilly's gloomy voice spoke Chloe's own fears, yet she felt obliged to deny it.

"Might have been lightning," she said firmly, turning to face her aunt.

"You and I both know better than that," Tilly said sharply.

"Pete?" Chloe's whisper sounded loud inside her head, and she repeated it, stunned by his absence, aware that unless he had an awfully good reason for not being here, the finger of suspicion pointed directly at him.

"Yeah, Pete." From the barn door, J.T. repeated his name. "He took the new stallion, Chloe. He set the damn fire and took the paint stud." Tom stood beside him and nodded.

"Caught me broadside, Miss Chloe. I went in the barn, followed him in fact, when I heard him leave the bunkhouse.

He had a saddle and was heading for the stud when I came in.''

"He knocked you out?" she asked, already knowing the answer.

"Yeah. Caught me with the saddle. I wasn't lookin' for it, and he laid me out like a log."

"He could have killed you," she said dully, thinking of Tom on the barn floor with the fire blazing overhead.

"Well, he worked fast, I'll give him that," J.T. said. "And now he's long gone, and I'll bet we'll find trouble riding with him."

"What are you going to do?" Chloe asked, watching as the two mares wandered the middle of the yard, the cow ambling peacefully toward the tree by the house.

"Saddle a couple of horses and head north to the herd." He looked up at the barn. "I think we've got it all out, Chloe. The rain will take care of the rest if we've missed any. See if you can tie those mares somewhere or put them in the pasture with the cow."

"All right," she said, unwilling to cause him any delay. "Go on. Do what you have to."

He strode past the barn to the pasture fence and a shrill whistle brought half a dozen horses toward him, his own among them. Within minutes, he'd led two of them toward the barn, tying them at the hitching rail while Tom brought out saddles and bridles. The blankets smelled smoky, but the tack room was undamaged, and Chloe whispered thanks for that.

She watched as the two men rode into the darkness, her heart aching at the turn of events, even as her anger rose toward her brother. She'd given him her trust, again and again, and now could find no reason to excuse his actions.

Pain overwhelmed her as she watched the silent, slow-moving men approach just before noon. There was a certain air of satisfaction in Lowery's face as he doffed his hat to stand before her, yet Chloe felt the hesitation in his voice as he spoke.

"Boss said to tell you he'll be back as soon as he can, Miss Chloe. He went on into town to see the constable. Hale Winters and his bunch is with him and they're turnin' in six rustlers at the jail." His jaw was set and his eyes flashed an angry message. "They tried their best to clean us out last night, but between the Winters's crew and the rest of us out there, we chased them down and got the best part of the herd back where they belong."

She hesitated, fearful of voicing her fear. But Hogan saved her the choice, riding up behind Lowery to sweep his hat from his head and face her with a somber expression that told the tale. "We got the stallion back, ma'am. Pete just about ran him into the ground out there. The boy musta been crazy to do that to a horse. I'm surprised he didn't get dumped and trampled."

He slid from the saddle and nodded at Lowery, who seemed relieved to be excused from the conversation. Grasping Hogan's reins and leading his own horse, he turned toward the barn. "Damn, sure is a mess, ain't it?" Lowery muttered, scanning the damaged front of the building.

"Nothing we can't fix in no time flat," Hogan said. "Wish everything else was gonna be that easy to mend." And then he walked up onto the porch where Chloe sat, unwilling to move from the chair that supported her, unable to catch a deep breath as she faced what must surely be bad news.

Hogan sat beside her, and in a movement unlike his usual reticence, reached for her hand. "I was gonna let J.T. be the one to tell you this, honey, but I think we've been together long enough for me to be the one carrying the bad news."

Her heart ached and her breathing hitched as he spoke. It was bad, worse probably than she'd anticipated. For Pete would end up in prison for sure if he'd been caught with the rest of the rustlers. And she wasn't sure she could face the reality of the dream that had haunted her for the past days.

"Pete was one of them, wasn't he?" she said, and it was a statement of fact that rang with certainty. "I didn't want to face it, but there isn't any other answer." She looked into Hogan's face. "Will he just be put in jail? They won't hang him, will they?"

"Not a chance," Hogan said sadly. "Miss Chloe, Pete didn't make it through the shooting. He took a bullet through the head."

"He was wounded?" Even to her own ears, the words were foolish. Yet she persisted. "Did J.T. take him to the doctor?"

Hogan shook his head. "You know better. Don't make me say it, honey. Just know that it wasn't anyone else's fault. Pete brought this on himself. Stealin' that paint stud was the last straw. And then trying to use the animal to rustle your cattle was the finishing touch."

The vision of Pete at the end of a rope vanished, and another appeared, one even more tragic as she thought of him being readied for a grave. "He's dead, isn't he?" The words were dull, whispered in a monotone that needed no reply. Yet, Hogan supplied it.

"He's dead, Miss Chloe. Along with two others. J.T. had to make a statement at the constable's office and appear before the judge with the prisoners. He'll be home right soon, though."

Deep within her chest a raw wound opened, and Chloe was seized by a wrenching pain that threatened to take her breath from her body. She'd done this. As far-fetched as the idea might be to another, she knew that accepting J.T. into her life had pushed Pete from her. That her brother's final acts somehow were connected to her own happiness, that he'd been unable to accept the turning of her back on him, as she'd embraced a marriage with the man who had taken Pete's inheritance.

"Miss Tilly?" Hogan called out for help and Chloe glanced at him, not able to comprehend his panic. "Miss Tilly, can you get out here?" Hogan called again, and Tilly slapped the screen door wide, her startled gaze shooting from the foreman to the woman who bent double in her chair, forehead against her knees, as if her bones were not sturdy enough to hold her erect.

She reached for Chloe, lifting her with an amazing strength, and held her upright. "Honey. You gotta breathe, girl. Come on now, take a good hold of yourself." Hogan grasped one arm, and Tilly hoisted Chloe toward the door.

Her feet dragged across the boards beneath them and Chloe saw the dust rise, small particles that reminded her she hadn't swept the porch this morning. The sight of Tilly's wide shoes, made for a man, but guaranteeing comfort for a big woman's feet, took her attention next and she tried to match her own movements to those of the black, laced foot-wear that shuffled in step with her own.

The kitchen floor appeared then beneath her feet, and she slumped into a chair beside the table, hearing the murmur of voices beside her. A damp cloth met the back of her neck and, bending forward, she fought to focus on the small flowers that covered the oilcloth before her eyes. Yellow with dark centers, they flowed in a seemingly endless array, and her eyes searched out the limits of their advance across the wide table.

"Breathe, girl," Tilly said, her voice harsh, her hand rubbing in circles against Chloe's back.

"I can't." It hurt too much to inhale, the pain of betrayal and death overwhelming her natural instincts for survival, and Chloe could only lay her cheek against the cool oilcloth and close her eyes. A sob slid from her lips and she tried to gather it to herself, unwilling to release the pain so readily, as if she must store it within her body, clutch it to her breast and dwell in its midst.

The back door opened, a muted sound of boots on the floor announcing the arrival of another, and without opening her eyes, she felt J.T.'s presence beside her, knew the tender weight of his hands on her head and shoulders, and then was lifted in his arms.

Without words, he carried her to the bedroom. Without murmurs of comfort or whispered instructions he placed her on the bed. And without haste, he drew her clothing from her, until she was garbed in the briefest of undergarments, stockings stripped from her feet and only a sheet covering her.

And then he sat beside her, holding her hands in his, rubbing her fingers and breathing unevenly. He watched. Eyes closed against the sight of him, she knew of the dark expression he wore. Her heart twisting in her chest, forming lesions on its surface she knew would never heal, took her attention. But she sensed his despair. And within herself, she ached for the chasm that spread between their souls.

"Shut the door." His words were flat, low and final, and she heard the closing of her bedroom door. And then he rose and she listened to the sound of his gun belt being hung over the chair, heard the rustle of clothing as he stripped from his outer garments. He was there, pulling back the sheet, coming down behind her, sliding his arms around her and drawing her against the heat of his vibrant body.

But it was no use. She would never be warm again.

Chapter Twelve

The coffin was covered by a layer of dirt, its weight flattening the handful of flowers Chloe dropped into the gaping hole. And still she stood to one side, watching as the men took turns with their shovels, working in tandem to cover the final resting place of her brother. A wound that would never heal, she thought, a spot on the top of this hill where the sun would shine and the rain would fall, but where flowers would not grow, nor grass creep to cover the barren ground.

The cemetery outside of Ripsaw Creek was a sad, lonely place, yet one she had visited several times over the past years. Her mother was there, her father's grave adjoining and now Pete occupied his own spot, several feet away. A simple stone, with only the last name of her family stood guard, and she leaned to brush the dust from its surface. Her hand held the residue, and she wiped it uncaringly against her dress. A black dress Tilly'd found at the back of her closet and brought forth as appropriate garb for this most forlorn of days.

J.T. stood beneath the solitary tree marking the top of the hill, watching. He'd waited silently as she spoke briefly to townsfolk, most of whom were distinctly uncomfortable in her presence. Not knowing where to look, fumbling for words to comfort her, patting awkwardly at her back as they passed by, the line of mourners and curious onlookers was short. Thankfully short, for she could not abide much longer the knowledge that she was an object of pity among the people who knew her.

Pete was a rascal, a scalawag Tilly called him. Yet, he was her brother, and her heart ached that his life was cut off and wasted, his reputation in shambles and that there had been no last words of reconciliation between them before he died.

The eyes watching her were dark, flat and lacking any sort of emotion, and she met J.T.'s gaze with a curiously barren look of her own. The face that had become so dear to her over the past months bore the flesh and bone structure of a stranger. No remorse touched those harsh lines. Only a waiting, watchful stance that enveloped him in darkness.

His hat pulled low over his eyes, his gun belt in plain view, the holster against his thigh, he was a symbol of all she despised right now. The triumph of law over lawlessness, the hand of death dealt her family. She'd told him as much, and her heart clenched within her breast as she recalled her words upon awakening yesterday morning.

No matter who pulled the trigger, you were there, J.T., and you should have stopped it. Spoken without forethought, they'd spewed from bitterness and grief, and he had listened and turned away.

"That was the wrong thing to say to him," Tilly had said, disgust alive in every word. "That man cares about you, Chloe, and you've just driven him away."

And perhaps she had, Chloe decided, for J.T.'s hand had only touched her waist, guiding her up the hill to the grave an hour past. His body behind her, he'd offered silent support and she had ignored his presence, so caught up in the grief and pain she could not bear to be comforted, lest she forget for a single moment the anger she felt.

Now he left his chosen spot and walked to where she stood, alone and bereft, watching as the final shovelful of dirt was tamped atop the grave. Where the raw ground spoke of a man buried beneath the weight of earth, and the sorrow of the woman who wept.

For the tears had begun. Now that it was over, now that the visitors were on their way back to their everyday existence in Ripsaw Creek, she found hot rivulets coursing her cheeks and sobs forcing their way from her mouth. Her hand lifted to halt the torrent, but to no avail. A handkerchief pressed into her fingers and she grasped it from J.T.'s hand, mopping at the visible signs of grief, even as she hugged the pain to her bosom.

"Come on, Chloe. There's nothing more for you here." His words were harsh, but his hands touched her with gentle care as he turned her from the grave, and she allowed it, walking at his side to where the buggy waited at the foot of the hill. His curved palms touched her waist, lifting her, and she fell onto the seat in a twisted mound of fabric as the skirt of her dress tangled around her legs.

"Let me help you," he said quietly, tugging and straightening the mess of her skirts, tucking the voluminous folds around her legs. It wasn't worth arguing over, and she allowed him to fuss, then sat upright, looking straight ahead as he climbed to the buggy seat and took up the reins.

The ride back to the ranch was silent, Chloe having eschewed the idea of a gathering afterward in which food would be eaten and trite phrases of comfort strewn in her direction. The buggy halted before the back door, and J.T. lifted his arms to her, grasping her waist to bring her to the ground before himself. He held her there and she was silent, looking dully at the front of his black coat.

He'd found a white shirt to wear with a black string tie,

and on the homecoming trip had undone the tie, allowing it to hang beneath the stiff collar. His chest rose and fell as he inhaled sharply, and she shook her head, an abrupt movement as his words erupted.

"Chloe—"

"No, please don't say anything. I don't think I want to talk to you right now."

His hands fell from her and he stepped back. "Do you want me to move to the bunkhouse?" he asked, his voice totally without emotion.

She looked up at him, shaking her head. "I can't put you out of the house. You own half of it, remember?"

"All right." He nodded and bowed his head, a gesture she thought smacked of sarcasm. His mouth was firm, a harsh line that offered no words of argument, and as she moved past him, he followed her to the porch, politely held the door for her to enter the kitchen, then stood silently as she swept across the floor toward the hallway.

From behind her, Tilly's voice was choked. "How'd it go, there at the end? I couldn't stand to watch any longer, J.T., once they were fillin' in the grave. I had Micah bring me on back to fix dinner."

"We stayed till they were done," he said. "Where's Micah?"

And then Chloe was inside her bedroom and the door closed behind her, muffling the words spoken in the kitchen. She leaned against the portal, her eyes closing, their lids scratching against her eyeballs and yet, the tears were gone. She'd shed them all, she realized. Now she would put aside the mourning and find work to do.

The black dress was a pile of dingy rags on the floor within moments, and she scooped it up, rolling it into a ball to be burned. The sight of those yards of funeral attire was an abomination, and the sooner they met the trash fire, the better she'd like it. Her movements more vigorous now, she stripped from her undergarments, petticoats cast aside as she found trousers and a shirt in her drawer.

Long black stockings rolled down her legs and sailed across the room toward the bundle she'd tossed next to the door. She sat on the chair to draw plain cotton footwear into place, then tugged her boots on over them. As if in a dream, she looked around the room, searching for any trace of funeral attire she might have missed, then placed J.T.'s handkerchief amid the tangle of stockings and black petticoat and dress.

Passing through the kitchen, she carried the bundle of clothing against her chest, refusing to meet Tilly's gaze, only looking at the floor as she strode to the back door and shoved her rump against the frame to push the screen door open. A murmur followed her into the yard and she ignored it. J.T. stepped from the porch close behind her and she paid him no mind, intent on locating a spot that would suit her purpose.

"Chloe." He called her name, his hand touching her shoulder as he paced next to her. "What are you doing, Chloe?"

She shrugged the weight of his palm aside and hesitated inside the barn door. "Willie, are you in here?"

"Ma'am?" The youth stepped from outside the back door and approached. "What do you need, Miss Chloe?"

"I want to set a fire. Bring me some kerosene and a match, please."

Willie's wide eyes veered from her to seek silent advice from J.T. and to his credit, the bigger man only nodded and stood aside. The kerosene lantern was lifted from a peg and Willie followed as Chloe walked the length of the barn, out into the sunshine and across from the corral, where the manure pile and a trash heap used for burning household refuse lay.

Without ceremony, she dumped her burden atop the pile

and motioned to Willie. Obligingly he dribbled kerosene on the clothing, then stepped back as she took the box of matches from him. "Go away," she muttered darkly, and the youth retreated swiftly, casting a last look at J.T., who waited in the doorway.

"Don't set yourself on fire," he said mildly as Chloe struck a match and dropped it to meet with the sodden fabric. The kerosene drew the flame like a wick, and the dress caught fire with tiny licks of gold, following the trail of the liquid Willie had poured upon her clothing. She watched as though mesmerized and, as the heat began to rise, felt J.T.'s hand on her elbow, drawing her away from the pyre.

Her eyes burned, seared by the smoke, and she blinked a bit, then peered through her lashes, coughing once as the wind blew a waft of acrid haze toward her. The ashes lifted on a stray bit of breeze, then settled against the trash beneath, and the fire caught hold with gusto, burning the various bits of paper and leavings Tilly had sent out after breakfast.

"Come on," J.T. said harshly. "Whatever you hoped to accomplish is done with, Chloe. You've buried Pete, and probably yourself with him. But there's no point in standing here getting all smoked up and choking yourself on the remains."

"I'll do what I want to," she said stubbornly. "I got along before you got here, and I'll still get along after you leave one of these days."

"I'm not going anywhere." He turned her to face him and she was forced to look up into his eyes, his hand beneath her chin in a gesture that offered no tenderness. "I told you a long time ago, I'm in this for the long haul. You're my wife, like it or not, and I'm here to stay."

"So stay, then," she said, and felt her jaw harden as his fingers softened their touch. "You do your work and I'll do mine. As to being your wife…" she closed her eyes against the power of his dark, penetrating glare ''—it's all legal and binding, I suppose, but I don't have to...'' She could not say the words, couldn't even imagine the deed. And yet, should J.T. push for his legal rights, she could not deny him.

''No,'' he said agreeably, ''you don't have to do anything you don't want to, Chloe. I can only hope you come to your senses one of these days and open your eyes to the truth. Before it's too late.''

She spent long hours with the horses, the knowledge that the sale of those animals would put her operation in the black, once J.T. made the arrangements for buyers to arrive. The cattle herd was once more at the northern edge of the Double B, and the men rotated position, staying on the range for days at a time, then coming back to the ranch proper to take chore duty.

Chloe's skin took on the hue of copper, where her sleeves were rolled high above her elbows and the sun touched the skin of her throat and the nape of her neck. She wore the same braid sometimes two or three days in a row, only scraping the flyaway tresses from her face and pinning them in place. Muscles ached at night, but she was uncaring, just thankful for the blessed sleep that possessed her when she placed her head on the pillow.

And behind her in the wide bed, long hours after she sought the comfort of pillow and quilt, she felt the presence of J.T., never touching, never speaking, only there. He was gone when she awoke, and only the impression of his head on the pillow and the rumpled covers he left behind gave notice of his presence.

It was too much trouble to order him into another bedroom, she decided, after the first night. He obviously was not interested in conducting a marriage in the bed they shared, and for that she was grateful. The distasteful idea of denying him his rights made her shudder, but the thought of his hands on her body was beyond imagination.

She'd loved him. Of that there was no doubt, and deep within her soul, she loved him still. But the barrier of what he had allowed to happen was an obstruction she could not deny.

"You ready for breakfast?" Tilly asked as Chloe stood in the kitchen doorway. It was another bright day, the sun above the treetops in the east, and Chloe tugged at her belt, noting the need of another hole to be punched in the leather.

"I'm not very hungry," she said, distracted as she looked down at the loose fit of her trousers. "These pants don't fit the way they should," she said, tugging them higher.

"You've lost weight," Tilly said flatly. "You don't eat enough to stay alive these days."

"I eat plenty," Chloe said disagreeably. "It's too hot to stuff myself."

"Well, you're looking like the wrath of God, is all I got to say," her aunt stated harshly. "You've got J.T. on a tight leash, and the men steer clear of you, and I'm not sure you even like me anymore."

"Don't be silly," Chloe said, hurt rising within as she considered Tilly's words. "You know I love you, Aunt Tilly. I couldn't run this place without you."

"Hell, I know you *need* me," Tilly said. "I just don't think you give two hoots and a holler about anything or anybody but yourself anymore."

The pain increased as Chloe absorbed the taunt, and she halted beside a chair, her fingers gripping the back. "I'm sorry," she said after a moment. "I didn't realize you felt that way." She slid the chair from the table and slumped onto the seat. "I'll have something to eat if there's anything left over."

"I saved you a plate, just like always," Tilly told her, sliding the warm offering from the top of the stove. Scrambled eggs, surrounded by bacon and topped with a slice of toast were piled high on the plate, and she dumped it with a decided lack of ceremony in front of her niece.

"Grab a fork and dig in," Tilly said, turning back to the sink. "J.T. said to tell you he'll be out on the range today, in case you're interested."

She was. For the first time in two weeks, she felt a twinge of guilt as she chewed and swallowed, aware of Tilly's displeasure with the state of affairs in this household. "What's going on out there?" she asked, sipping at the cup of coffee that appeared by her plate.

"Nothing special. Just deciding which part of the herd he's going to take to the stockyard and put up at auction."

"Don't I have any say in that?" she asked, thinking of years past when she'd trailed behind her father and Hogan as they culled the steers from the herd.

"Apparently he didn't think it mattered to you. You haven't said two words to him since the funeral," Tilly said accusingly. "I guess he figured you were content to work with the horses and drive yourself into the ground walking and grooming them and suffering in silence."

"Suffering in silence." Chloe repeated the words beneath her breath. "Is that what you think this is all about?"

"I dunno as I care," Tilly said, casting her a look of disgust. "I just know you're not the girl I thought you were. You've taken out your anger at Pete on the best man that ever rode this ranch, and you don't give a good gol durn about how much you've hurt him or anybody else."

"My anger at Pete?" Her voice rose on each syllable, and Chloe pushed back from the table. "My brother's dead, Tilly. And for all I know, J.T.'s gun held the bullet that killed him."

"For all you know, it could have been half a dozen other men," Tilly said sharply. "You've chosen to blame J.T. instead of leveling your anger where it belongs. And I, for one, am sick and tired of your shenanigans.'' She banged a kettle on the stove and turned to pump vigorously at the red pitcher pump beside the sink. Water spewed forth and splattered into the dishpan, and Tilly swiped her hand across her face.

"Well, I guess I know where I stand," Chloe said. Aware of her aunt's anger, unable to admit her own wrong, she sailed from the kitchen and off the porch, kicking at a clod of dirt as she headed for the barn.

And then she halted, looking up into the blue sky above, where puffy clouds formed overhead. The sun licked down and she blinked at the brilliance of its glow, feeling the sharp tears that formed as she inhaled the morning air. Life was for the living, her father had said once. And then he'd died, leaving her to carry on.

Now she was left to move ahead once more. And life was passing her by, the rest of the ranch continuing to prepare for the days ahead, the men guided by J.T., the herds of horses and cattle following the regime set for them by his program. It would not do, she decided, to be left trailing in the dust.

"You gonna be helping me today?" Lowery asked, leading his latest project toward her. "This one needs a good, long, cool-down." And indeed the horse showed evidence of a hard training session, she thought, his nostrils flaring, his shiny coat slick from the hour he'd spent beneath Lowery's weight.

"Not now," she said distractedly. "I'm going up to the north range and check on the herd. Tilly said that's where J.T. went this morning."

"Yeah, he did." Lowery watched her from beneath beetled brows. "What's got into you, Miss Chloe? You haven't ridden out in weeks."

"Well, then it's about time I did, don't you think?" she asked sharply. In moments she had whistled down her mare and saddled the feisty animal. Unused to being ridden over the past days, the horse shifted and skittered beneath her touch, and Chloe welcomed the battle to be fought with the saucy mare.

Head bowed, tail a flag in the breeze, the mare set off, and Chloe felt the first surge of life through her veins explode with a vigor that erupted in laughter. The mare stretched out, straining at the bit, and Chloe gave her the freedom she demanded. It was a hard ride, and she bent over the animal's neck, eyes narrowed against the wind, her hat flying behind, caught only by the rawhide strand that held it.

At the top of a rise, she drew up the reins and the mare pranced between her legs, eager to set off again, but Chloe tugged her hat into place and looked north from beneath its brim, seeking moving specks across the horizon that would pinpoint the whereabouts of her herd. Nothing moved beneath the glittering sunlight, and she loosened the reins, allowing the mare to pick her way down the slope and across the lush pastureland.

Rain had blessed them with grass, abundantly thick on all sides, and Chloe noted flowers blooming, watched as a line of trees appeared to delineate the stream flowing from north to south at the eastern edge of the property. She veered in that direction, thinking of the horse between her knees, and then followed the shallow stream to where it deepened into a pool of water the men were wont to use as a bathing area.

Sliding from her horse, she led the mare to the edge of the stream, her hearing attuned to the sound of birds and the splashing movement of running water ahead. The mare bent to drink, tossing her head so that the water spewed and silvered in the air. And all was alive and luxurious suddenly, the lush surroundings impelling Chloe to step closer to the cool stream. She bent to dip her hand into the sparkling flow, above where the horse drank, and she wet her face, then rubbed her hands together, watching as the dust of the ride disappeared into the water.

To her left, a shadow moved and she looked up quickly, aware that someone watched from beneath low-hanging branches. Long feet, calves that melded into thighs and then formed the loins of a man met her vision, and she lifted startled eyes to meet the gaze of the man who stood silently before her.

"J.T." She breathed the sounds beneath her breath, and his mouth formed a sardonic smile of welcome.

"Well, well," he said quietly. "I didn't know I'd find you here." His hand motioned toward the pool behind her and she glanced back at him quickly, noting the drops of water that dwelt in his body hair, the slick sheen of moisture he wore. "I couldn't resist the idea of a swim," he told her. "It was a hot and sweaty morning. I needed cooling off." And beneath his words she heard a tinge of danger.

"Cooling off?" Her thoughts were confused as she sought another target for her attention. His body was ropy with muscle, strong and tall, and she felt a rush of apprehension as she considered her position. Alone, with a man whose eyes were carefully stripping her clothing aside as he watched her. A man with the power to toss her to the ground, should he want to, and press his perfect body against hers in a dance of male possession.

"I haven't had much relief from the tension you've managed to generate lately, Mrs. Flannery." He took a step toward her and she retreated, stumbling on a small hillock. One hand flashed out and grasped her arm, and he jerked her upright, hauling her against himself. "And now you've shown up and offered me a chance to—"

"I'm not offering anything," she said harshly. "I rode here to water my mare, and I had only begun to enjoy the peace and quiet, when you made your presence known."

"I was here first," he reminded her softly, although his

eyes were hard, dark orbs, rimmed by shadows. His face was gaunt, she thought, dark with the sun, but the bones were taut beneath the flesh, his nose a sharp blade above an unsmiling mouth. "On second thought, maybe I won't wait for an offer," he said, his hands lifting from her waist to snatch her hat from her head. Long fingers pierced the plaited strands that circled her head, and he tugged and pulled at her pins, dropping them onto the ground as his hands made short work of the braids.

"Don't do that," she said, swatting at his efforts, tossing her head, only to feel the stinging pain of hair being pulled as he refused to relax his grip.

"You're hurting yourself," he told her. "Stand still." His hands dropped to her shoulders and he shook her, a strong, harsh movement that stunned her into silence. And then he continued with the untangling of her hair until it submitted to him. It hung around her shoulders and down her back finally, a dark cascade that made her scalp ache. She felt disheveled and breathless, fully aware that he'd set in motion some sort of ritual that would not be brought to a halt until he decreed it to be so.

"Get undressed," he told her. "You need a bath."

Words flooded her mouth, but she swallowed them, knowing he would not be swayed from his purpose. Her hands rose to touch the buttons on her shirt, and he watched, impatience dancing in dark eyes as she slid them from the holes. His hands were rough, jerking the shirt from her, and then he looked down at the belt she wore, and he grunted, his eyes flashing a message to hers as he shoved her trousers down her legs without loosening the restricting leather.

"You're nothing but skin and bones," he muttered, baring her to his sight.

"Well then, I won't hold much appeal, will I?" she said smartly, her heart racing as she taunted him.

"I didn't say I wanted you to spread your legs," he told

her with total lack of feeling. "I only said you needed a bath. You haven't combed your hair in two days. And you smell like a horse."

"So do you." She felt snippy as she spoke the lie, for he was clean, and his scent rose to surround her, musky male flesh, with a fecund aroma that filled her nostrils. Her face burned as she considered his accusation, his scornful words. It was true. She'd neglected herself, bathing haphazardly, washing in bits and pieces, as if it mattered little. For indeed it hadn't.

Now it looked as if she would be given the full treatment, and she waited, defiance and a dark sense of anticipation alive in her as he reached for her bare flesh, his fingers firm, but not painful as he lifted her and carried her in his arms. He stepped in at the edge of the pool and lowered her into the water, dropping her the last several inches, her rump sinking to the sandy bottom, her hair floating over her head.

She sputtered and rose, an awkward movement that angered her. "Are you trying to drown me?" And looked into eyes that pierced her soul.

"What do you think?" He turned from her and reached for a rag and a bar of soap he'd left on the bank, then turned back, his hands busy with forming suds on the dingy piece of cloth. It touched her shoulder and she flinched. It scrubbed over her back and she stiffened.

He brought it across the soft curve of her breast and she ceased breathing.

The fabric was rough, but his touch gentled, and she stood in water lapping at her hips and allowed him his way. The soap was rinsed, then replaced by more suds and he moved on. Across her other breast, across her belly and along the sides of her hips, his eyes intent on what he did, his hand moving slowly, the pressure of fingers bringing life to flesh she'd thought dead to his touch.

The breeze whispered across her, and flesh peaked as she

shivered, bringing her breasts alive with a taut, uplifting movement she could not halt. His eyes strayed there, and, as she watched, his body stirred. Below the surface, his arousal throbbed, nudging at her hip, reminding her of his masculine beauty and the swelling of his manhood.

He slid the cloth beneath the water, washing her bottom, the suds floating away as they disintegrated. And still he laved the cloth over her skin, as if the movement of his hand against her flesh mesmerized him, and the pressure of his fingers gave him pleasure. His growl was against her ear as he bent closer, a wordless sound she recognized, and she jerked away, looking up into the intensely primitive message she could not mistake.

"I won't," she told him sharply, even as she recognized defeat in the yearning of her own body.

"You will," he countered, and lifted her, one hand on each side of her waist, tucking her neatly against himself, until her legs bound her to him, wrapping around his thighs as she fought to keep her balance.

"Open for me," he said, and it was an order, a demand she'd thought never to hear from him. Tenderness vanished, only passion remained, and the desire that lit his gaze fueled a fire deep inside her body, one she'd thought was extinguished forever.

She widened her legs and enclosed him, feeling the depth of his single stroke as if a sword pierced her very soul. There was no pain, for she was softened and ready, her anger and apprehension blending with an excitement she could not contain. He withdrew, a slight movement, and pressed farther within, and she grasped him with strong interior muscles that seemed to have a mind of their own.

Her cry rose and he captured it in his mouth, his tongue sweeping past her teeth to plunge the depths of her throat. It should have repelled her, but she savored the thrust. It should have disgusted her to be so used, but she groaned and fought for a better grip on his shoulders.

It should have left her cold, this blazing force of his desire, shed with ruthless impact upon her newly slender form, but it brought her instead, in mere moments, to a climax that forced sobs from her lips, and took the breath from her body.

He pumped harshly against her, as if his own release was too powerful to be vented in silence, and his voice rose in a roar of defiance, piercing the air like an animal in a fight for supremacy, sounding his triumph aloud for all the world to hear.

And then he held her, his arms around her trembling form as he climbed from the water and stood, legs widespread on the grass beneath the canopy of green that sheltered them.

She could not move, could barely breathe. Limp, she slid from his grasp and shivered, her mind swimming, only aware of the bonds that held her to this man. Not the strength of muscled arms, although they clasped her upright. Not the sturdy frame that she leaned against, though it provided a resting place for her.

But the compelling knowledge that they were man and woman, husband and wife, that she was his mate, and he had bound them today with a primitive blending of their bodies, branding her as his own.

Chapter Thirteen

She dressed, silent and filled with a peace she could not comprehend. She had allowed J.T. to spend his pent-up frustration on her body, and that was knowledge she shrank from. Yet, in her heart of hearts, she recognized her own participation in the act that had taken place. She could not, would not, blame him unduly, for she had not cried for mercy, not begged for him to cease his aggressive behavior.

Indeed, she had been pushed beyond her own capability to respond, and had more than allowed him his way. She flushed deeply as she pulled her trousers up and tied an awkward knot in the leather belt. And heard his smothered chuckle as he watched.

"I said you were skin and bones," he reminded her. And then he bent to her, his fingers undoing the tangle of leather. "I'll put in another hole for you," he offered, drawing his knife from his pocket and pressing her to sit on the ground before him.

Kneeling beside her, he placed the length of her belt on a piece of rock and held his knife tip against the leather. With a sharp movement, he impaled the strip and turned the knife to widen the tiny slit. In seconds he'd completed the small task, and he stood, pushing the knife back in his pocket, and offering his hand.

She glanced up, unsure of what would meet her gaze, but his face was impassive as he offered the choice. Either accept his help or rise on her own. She placed trembling fingers against his and felt his warmth enclose her hand, drawing her upward until she stood inches from him.

"Don't look at me like that, Clo," he said harshly, emotion coating each syllable.

"How do you want me to look at you?" she asked, reaching for her shirt, loath to pull the sweaty material over her damp skin, yet even more unwilling to stand before him naked.

"I have a clean shirt if you want to use it," he offered, as if he could read her mind, sense her distaste for the soiled fabric.

She held the plaid cotton before her breasts and cut a cautious glance upward, then nodded quickly. "Tilly will wonder at me, leaving with one shirt, returning with another. She was pretty put out with me this morning," she offered.

"Do you blame her?" he asked, turning aside to reach for his saddlebag, there beside the tree where his own shed clothing lay in a crumpled pile. He bent, oblivious to his nudity and searched briefly within the leather bag, bringing forth a well-worn, but clean shirt, and handed it to her.

"No." She slid her arms into the sleeves and sorted out the buttons, aware that the length hung almost to her knees. She thought of Tilly's frown and the gesture of reconciliation she'd offered. "But she saved me breakfast."

"She's saved you a plate every day for weeks," he told her. "You've hurt her, Clo, and I don't know if you did anything to make it up this morning, but you owe her a debt you'll probably spend the rest of your life working at."

"You think I don't know that?" She felt a pout curl her lip as she tucked the shirt beneath her trousers, pushing the abundance of material as far as she could. "I suppose I owe you one, too," she said stiffly, latching the belt, sliding the metal into the newly formed hole.

"Not in my book, you don't," he said quietly. "You don't owe me anything." He stalked to where his clothing lay and snatched up his trousers, balancing lightly as he stepped into them. And then he turned back to her, catching her unaware as she fed her eyes on the pale flesh he covered with casual movements.

His words held a harsh tone she had not expected. "I'll lay odds you're waiting for an apology from me, aren't you?"

She shook her head, dragging her gaze from him as she rolled drooping sleeves higher. "You didn't force me," she said after a moment, glancing back at him, concentrating on his hands, fisted against his hips.

"I was harsh with you."

She nodded. "Yes."

"I probably left bruises."

Her gaze shot up to meet tired eyes and she only nodded. "You didn't ask permission, that's for sure, but then…"

"Then, what?" he asked. "Did you hate it so much, Clo? Have I lost you entirely? Did I push you too far?"

She shook her head. "I'm your wife, Jay. You had every right. I've turned my back on you for weeks, and I knew when I found you here today that you were up against the wall, and you wouldn't put up with much more." She sighed and sat on the ground to find her stockings and pull them on, then looked up with a half smile.

"Maybe I needed to know I'm still alive." She shifted and grimaced. "At least there's that to think about. My pa used to say…" She thought of the words that had flooded her mind earlier and repeated them now.

"Life is for the living." She rose and stood before him.

"Pete's dead, but I'm alive, and there's a ranch to run and horses to tend and my aunt waiting back at the house."

"And I'm here, Clo."

She looked up at him, searching his features, seeking some sign of the anger he'd spent on her. But there was none to behold, only a strange lassitude that puzzled her. "I know you are. I'm aware that you probably didn't fire the shot that killed Pete, but there's a big circle of blame surrounding you, and I can't seem to get over it. Tilly said I'm taking my anger at Pete out on you. Maybe she's right."

"You'll have to figure that out for yourself," he told her. "I won't fight with you over it. If I caused you pain today, and you're wearing bruises because of me, I guess I'll apologize for that, but I'm not sorry for what happened between us, and if that makes me less than a man in your eyes..." He lifted his hands in a gesture of helplessness, then dropped them to his sides.

"I wanted you angry, Clo. I wanted your fury to burn away the barriers you put between us. I guess I succeeded, a little, maybe." He turned her, his hand on her shoulder, to where her mare waited, reins touching the ground. "Go on home. I'll go back up and lend a hand for another hour or so and then I'll see you at supper."

"When will you take the steers to auction?" Hesitating, reins in hand, she turned back to him.

"In a week or so. We'll be gone a week or ten days maybe."

She nodded. "I figured as much. It's a long haul to Cheyenne, and then back again."

"Have you ever gone with them?" he asked, and she searched for a hidden message in his query. Her nod was short, and she jammed her hat in place as she mounted the mare.

"I have. But I won't this time." And with that quick

reply, she'd shut the door once more, she realized, and wept bitter tears as her mare found the way home.

For all the words spoken, the lines of communication opened, it might as well have never been, J.T. decided after supper was behind them. He sat on the porch, watching as Chloe shut the chickens in the coop for the night, his gaze following her slender form as she held her shirtfront from her body, and recognized that she had picked up eggs, passing through the nesting hens.

Now, she approached in the twilight and climbed the steps to the porch, taking three paces to the back door. "I've got a few fresh eggs," she told Tilly, who sat by the table with a catalogue in front of her.

"Put them in the crock," Tilly said, nodding toward the pantry, and Chloe moved obediently to do as she was asked. Tilly looked through the window and J.T. moved a bit, letting her see his presence there. She nodded and gathered up her periodical. "I'm going to the parlor."

"All right," Chloe said from the depths of the pantry. "Do you need anything from the smokehouse for breakfast?"

Tilly glanced again at the porch and mumbled a reply. "A piece of ham would come in handy. Have J.T. take down one of those shoulder pieces hanging out there."

Chloe walked across the floor and out the door. "I can do that," she said. "I'll bring it in."

J.T. walked behind her to the smokehouse, held the door open as she stepped inside and then followed her in. It was dark, an eerie place with meat hanging from the rafters. Strange shadows formed as his eyes adjusted to the pale glimmer of moonlight through the roof venting. Chloe grumbled words beneath her breath and sighed.

"I can't reach quite high enough. Lift this piece from the hook, will you?"

He obliged, recognizing the aggravation she felt when her height prevented her from accomplishing her aim. "You don't like being small, do you?" he asked, pushing the door open, inhaling deeply of the night air.

"Most of the time I hate it," she said, her voice a liquid pout, and then she looked upward, and he heard her indrawn breath. "A shooting star," she whispered, and he saw her in a new light, as for a moment vulnerability touched her features.

"Did you wish on it?" he asked, aching to grant whatever it was she yearned for.

She glanced up at him and shook her head. "Foolishness," she muttered. "The things I wished for all my life seem silly now."

"Like what?" he asked, leaning against the door to hold it shut as she shot the bolt. Her look in his direction held a touch of scorn.

"Happy ever after, mostly," she said sharply. "I know better than that now. I thought my father would live forever, that my brother would buckle down and we'd be a team."

"Didn't you wish for something just for you?" he asked.

"All that was for me."

"How about pretty dresses, and men to court you, and a family of your own?"

"I'm not like other women. I don't need fancy things to please me, or pretty words to flatter me."

"Well, I'll grant you there's a difference between you and the women I've come up against over the years. You're tougher and stronger and more capable than any four of them put together. But you're still female enough to need a little…" He hesitated, searching for the single word she could accept as a genuine balm to her lonely heart.

"I think you need to be cherished, Clo."

"Like today?" she asked bluntly.

"No, not like today. That was all about anger and pain

and need, honey. I didn't do any cherishing, I'm afraid.''
He spoke hesitantly as she turned aside and looked toward
the house where the light from the kitchen window beckoned. "Childhood dreams come true sometimes, Clo. Mine
did.''

"Yours?"

"Yeah," he said, walking beside her toward the house,
his hand on her shoulder. "I was just an ordinary kid, with
the usual ideas. I wanted horses of my own and a place
where I could be in charge, instead of answering to someone
else. My father ran a tight ship, and crops were the most
important thing.''

Her footsteps lagged as they neared the house and she
listened, tilting her head a bit. Encouraged, he went on, remembering the days of his youth. "Pa used mules for the
most part, had a mare to pull the buggy, but making money
hand over fist was his aim in life. He said playing with
horses was foolishness. Told me I needed to tend to the
business of growing cotton and making money.''

"Did you live in the South? Well, of course you did,"
she said, answering her own query. "I should have known.''

"Does it show?" he asked, shooting her a lazy grin.

Her arms crossed over her breasts as she looked up at
him, scanning his features, a smile twitching. "Once in a
while, I hear a trace of…something.''

"Must be when I forget myself," he said quietly. "Anyway, in the course of events, the home place burned to the
ground, with my folks inside when it happened. My
mother—" He thought of the woman who had given him
life.

"They both died there that day. By the time I heard about
it, it was too late to do more than sift through the ashes.
And to tell you the truth, I didn't care enough to stick
around and claim my inheritance, what there was left of it.

I just lit out and worked my way north and west, looking for a spot to hang my hat.''

"Well, you found one. You wanted a place of your own, and you managed to win it in a poker game," she said flatly.

"That's about it," he admitted. "I was willing and able to buy land by that time, but this fell into my lap, and I'm not stupid enough to walk away from a sure thing when I see it coming."

"And me?" she asked. "Was I a sure thing, too?"

"Never," he told her. "I spent the first little while waiting for you to put a bullet in me. Never saw a woman so mad as you were."

"I had a right," she snapped, taking the first step to the porch, and then pausing, as if she considered the claim. "Maybe not," she whispered, meeting his gaze. "I was mad at the wrong person, Jay." She reached for the meat he held but he shook his head.

"I'll bring it in." It seemed safer not to agree with her assessment, he decided. Enough that Chloe was able to admit some small degree of wrongdoing. She didn't need him to rub it in. He followed her into the kitchen and crossed to the pantry. A hook from the ceiling provided a place for the smoked meat he carried, and he hung it there.

She turned from him and blew out the lamp, then crossed into the hallway, calling a good-night to Tilly before she went toward her bedroom door. And there she stopped, her hand on the doorknob, her nape vulnerable as she bent her head.

From behind her, he watched her fingers grip and turn, saw the inhalation of breath that lifted her shoulders, and felt her reluctance as she slipped through the open door into the dark bedroom beyond. Suddenly, he felt the worst sort of bully, recalling his rough treatment of her at the pool, remembering the tender flesh he'd handled so heedlessly.

Beneath her clothing she wore bruises. He'd almost guarantee that fact, and now he was champing at the bit to renew his assault, his aching loins full and pulsing with a desire she brought forth simply by being here.

"Jay?" She'd turned to face him, there in the darkness, and the sound of his name on her lips was a hesitant summons.

"Yeah." He'd learned early in life to press for the advantage, and he'd been doing just that for the past months. This was no time to back off, now when she was off balance, when he'd taken her by storm. He crossed the threshold and closed the door behind himself, then watched as she found her way across the floor, around the end of the bed, her shirt a pale shadow in the darkness.

He sat on the chair to pull his boots off and dropped them heedlessly to the floor. Rising, he stripped from his clothing. Naked, he approached her, and she lifted her face to him. His hands cradled her head, long fingers sliding beneath her hair to hold her. And then he bent to her, his mouth hungry, avid and searching.

She whimpered, and her lips fell prey to his assault, her hands lifting to clutch at his wrists, their bodies separate, only their mouths forming a bond. And then she sagged against him, as if her legs would not hold her upright.

"Things are going to be different, Clo." His voice was low, his promise given harshly, warning her of his intent. "When I crawl in that bed tonight I won't be staying on my side. I'm done with leaving you alone. If you're grieving for your brother, I'll understand. I'll hold you when you cry, if need be. But I won't be accepting the blame for his death."

"I'm done crying," she told him, and indeed, her voice was clear of tears. Sorrow remained, but he'd expected that. She lifted her face to him again and spoke words of promise. "I won't turn you away." And then she spoke a sad warning. "But I can't help how I feel."

"Fair enough," he said, triumph racing through his veins with each heartbeat. A fair shot at winning her was all he asked, and reinforcing the bond he'd established would be no hardship. And this time…this time, he vowed silently, he'd take his time, evoke every moan, every whisper of yearning he could draw from the depths of her being.

This time… His hands gentle against her flesh, he divested her of the clothing she wore, lifting her against his chest, placing her on the bed, and then watching as her arms rose, inviting him to her.

This time… He covered her, sheltering her from the night air, enveloping her in the embrace of his body, capturing the soft sounds of her passion as she rose to meet the hardening of his loins, the thrust of his desire.

This time, he vowed, there would be no haste in his taking of her woman's flesh, no frenzy in his touch, no careless handling of what she entrusted to his care. Only the quiet, slow, tender wooing of a woman worth whatever it took to win her to himself.

"You sure you don't want to go along?" J.T. stood by his stallion, offering her a last chance to change her mind, and Chloe shook her head in refusal. A trace of disappointment darkened his eyes, and she smiled.

"I've got plenty to do here," she said. "By the time you get back the fella from Bar X will be standing here, money in his hand, to buy the extra horses."

"If he shows up before I get back—"

She lifted a hand, halting his words. "I know. I'll make him wait." Her lips twisted ruefully. "I've learned a few things in the past months, Jay. You're tougher than I am. I can respect that."

"You'll be all right here?" he asked, and then shook his head. "I'm missing you already. Lowery will look after things, but he knows to listen to you, Chloe. Willie and Tom will keep an eye on the rest of the herd, and Cleary..." He looked past her to where the tall cowhand stood near the barn. "Cleary will be in charge."

"Who is he?" she asked quietly, and was not surprised when he only shrugged.

"He's here, just in case," J.T. told her. "Micah feels better about things with Cleary around, and I'm not gonna argue with him, not till we know every damn rustler has been caught and we've gotten the rest of the cattle back. Micah seems to think those steers are in a canyon north of here somewhere."

"What do you think?" she asked.

"Hell, I don't know. I'm just anxious to get this herd sold and things back in order here. When I get back, we'll probably take another look, but in the meantime, Micah's got an eye open. Winters's bunch is joining the rest of us on the trail, and we'll sort out our herd when we get to Cheyenne."

He bent to brush his mouth against hers and she returned the kiss, aware of the men watching, yet not willing to send him away without the warmth of the farewell due him as her husband. He swung into the saddle in a single lithe movement and straightened his hat, slanting her a long look of satisfaction.

He was cocky, she decided, too damn cocky for his own good. And yet, she could not deny his right to the arrogance that fit him like a tailor-made suit of clothing. He was a male animal, aggressive and confident. And for a moment she regretted her decision to remain behind, repented her pride that would not allow her to follow in his dust during this venture, rued the days she would spend without him.

The days were long, the nights longer. Micah stopped by twice during the first week, spending time in the kitchen with Tilly, while Chloe excused herself from their company to work with the horses. Again this morning, he'd arrived, looked around and greeted her nicely. Then hightailed it into the house, leaving Chloe feeling like leftovers.

Watching from the pasture fence, she laughed as a half-broke gelding pawed at the ground. Leather creaked behind her and she turned her head as Lowery approached. Sitting low in the saddle, his rope spinning in a lazy orbit, he rode through the gate she opened for him, and the watching animal tossed his head. The rope sailed in an effortless, drifting circle, settling on the gelding's neck, then drew taut as Lowery's horse dug in his heels and halted. One last fluid shiver ran down the flank of the roped gelding before he yielded to the tug on his neck, following Lowery to the gate.

"You make that look so easy," Chloe told him, reaching to unlatch the opening for him again. She swung the gate aside and then back in place as he led the gelding toward the back of the barn. "I never caught on well to swinging a rope. My pa said it was all in the wrist."

"You do all right," Lowery said with a grin. "I've seen you rope a steer or two." He slid from his mount and approached the brown animal he'd captured. A bit slid into the gelding's mouth with care and the bridle eased into place. "Now this one," he said, motioning at the brown gelding, "this one's got some manners already. He'll make a good cow pony. Just enough spunk to keep a man on his toes." And with that the gelding tossed his head and sounded a shrill whinny.

Lowery tightened his grip on the reins. "See what I mean?"

"You like what you do," Chloe said, watching as Lowery tied the reins to a handy metal ring on the side of the barn.

"Been doing it all my life, seems like," the man answered, smoothing a saddle blanket in place before he lifted the heavy saddle from the ground.

"Do you think we're ready for the buyers?" she asked.

"Ready as we'll ever be," he told her, tightening the cinch and moving aside as the gelding shifted uneasily. "Don't worry, Miss Chloe. Those ranchers know what they're gettin' when they come here. Your pa always had good solid horseflesh for them, and they've passed the word along. Not everyone breeds horses. Most everybody hereabouts concentrates on the cattle business."

"What about when the foals drop next spring?" she asked. "J.T. seems to think the paint stud will give us a good bunch of horses to work with."

"He's right," Lowery said simply. "The man knows what he's doing, Miss Chloe." He led the gelding toward the corral and turned back for a moment as he slid open the gate. "You were smart to marry him." A grin touched his lips. "Or maybe he was smart to marry you. I don't know which."

"Chloe?" Through the barn, she heard Micah call her name and she answered the summons, cutting through the large structure to where he waited beyond the big front doors. He was peering upward where new boards gleamed with paint. "Got this thing all fixed up, I see."

"Didn't take long," she told him, joining him in his perusal. "Had to put in some new flooring and a lot of roofing. Worst part was we lost more hay than we could afford." One more sin to add to Pete's list, she thought with a twinge of bitterness.

"Got a wire from Cheyenne yesterday. J.T. said to tell you they're headin' home. Won't take but a couple of days, now that they're not pushin' a herd of steers in front of them."

"Is that why you came out here this morning?" she asked.

"Partly," he said. "Partly because I wanted to see Tilly." He looked down at Chloe and she thought, not for the first time, that he was looking weary. "I guess you're the one I need to talk to, Chloe. Seeing as how Tilly's young 'uns aren't here, you're the only family she has in these parts.''

''What's wrong, Micah?'' she asked quickly, and then his hand lifted to rest on her shoulder, and she felt reassurance in the touch. His bronzed skin took on a ruddy hue as she watched, and his nostrils flared. Faded blue eyes met hers and she recognized that for the first time since she'd known him, Micah Dawson was searching for words to say.

''Nothing's wrong, Chloe. In fact, everything is getting better by the minute. Your Aunt Tilly and me…we've been talkin' about things. And I told her I wanted to kinda sound you out a little.''

Light glimmered in Chloe's mind, a vision of Tilly's beaming smile aimed in Micah's direction making itself known, and Chloe laughed aloud. ''Go ahead, sound me out,'' she invited. ''Tell me you want to marry my aunt, Micah, and next you can tell me you're willing to come here to live with her, because I sure as the dickens won't be willing to send her to town with you.''

He looked disgruntled for a moment, tugging at his waistband, then snapping his suspenders with a fretful motion. ''Hell, you took the starch out of me with that one, Chloe. Didn't even give me a chance to give you the spiel I've been working on.''

''Am I right?'' she asked eagerly. ''You want to marry my aunt?''

''Yeah, I guess you could say that.'' He shot a look toward the house, and a grin appeared as the screen door slammed and Tilly appeared on the porch. ''All clear,'' he called, waving a hand in her direction. ''Come on out here.''

Chloe met her halfway, her step eager, dust puffs rising behind her as she ran to embrace the woman who approached. Hands shoved into apron pockets, Tilly looked past Chloe to where Micah waited, and Chloe was stunned by the look of affection the older woman wore. And then she reached for her niece, and Chloe was smothered against ample breasts and surrounded by loving arms.

"I told the old geezer you'd be happy for us," she boomed. "He wanted to do things right and proper though." She held Chloe away from her momentarily, searching her face. "We're not goin' anywhere, you know. Micah can move in here with me. We got more room than we know what to do with, I figure. At least till you start having babies and filling up those bedrooms upstairs."

No wonder J.T.'s wire had taken second place in Micah's thoughts today. He'd been about more important business. "I'm happy for you Aunt Tilly," Chloe managed to say before she was caught up again in a majestic embrace. "But won't Micah need to be close to town?"

"He's about done with bein' a lawman," Tilly announced. "Once we get this mess with the rustlers all cleaned up, and things on an even keel, he's gonna hand in his badge. I figure you and J.T. can use another hand around the place."

"Now, you told me you were gonna stay out of that part of it, Tilly," Micah said reprovingly. "I'll handle lookin' into a job here once J.T. gets home."

"You can move in anytime you want," Chloe burst out. "I'm a full partner in the place, and I can hire a new man if I've a mind to." And then she hesitated. "Well, after you get married, maybe, would be better.

"When will it be?" she asked, turning back to Tilly.

"Soon," came the reply from Micah. A single word that spoke his intentions, Chloe thought.

Lowery had to hear the news when he appeared, the foam-flecked gelding on a lead line. And Chloe left him to talk with Micah while she led the horse down the lane and back. *J.T.'s on his way home.* The words sang in her mind as she walked, and she repeated them over and over, in time with her footsteps. The soonest would be… She calculated in her mind the distance he was traveling, and recognized with a grin that tomorrow might see his arrival.

The horse behind her shook his sides with a great resounding shudder, and she laughed aloud at him as specks of foam flew through the air. "You sure had a workout," she said, and the gelding tossed his head. "How about a good rubdown?" she asked, turning in a wide circle to approach the barn once more. And was rewarded by a firm nudge against her shoulder as the horse pressed her forward. Pausing by the water trough, she waited until the gelding drank deeply, then returned to the barn.

"Miss Chloe?" From the east, a rider trotted into her line of vision, and Chloe heard her name called in strident tones. Tom's hat hid his features as he neared, and he was off his horse in a single movement, the animal sliding to an abrupt halt. "Is Micah here?"

"Up at the house," she told him. "What's wrong, Tom?"

"Plenty," he said, a ripe curse sounding beneath his breath. "There's trouble again, and Cleary sent me after Micah and Lowery. He said for you to keep a close eye on things and keep your gun handy."

"I'll get you a fresh horse," she told him, taking his reins and looping them across the hitching rail.

In moments, she came back with a black gelding, and Tom hastened to her side, a towel-wrapped package in his hand. "Thanks, ma'am. Tilly gave me something to eat, but I'll have to take it with me." He lifted his gaze and searched the corral. "We'll need Lowery up on the range. You better send him along."

She nodded agreement. "I got a fresh saddle blanket for you," she told him. "Yours needs drying out." A flip of her wrist sent the piece of tightly woven cloth over the horse's back, and Tom reached for his saddle. "Let me hold your food," Chloe offered, standing aside as the cowhand worked. "What's going on out there?"

"We found tracks where a small herd moved across the northeast corner of the range, and Cleary set off to follow. Hogan and Willie are keeping an eye on the herd." His movements were quick as he tightened the cinch and tugged the stirrup down, and then he hoisted himself into the saddle and reached for the wrapped package Chloe held.

"Thanks, Miss Chloe. Sorry I left you to take care of my horse. You tell Lowery to get himself up yonder just as quick as he can."

"He'll be right behind you," she said, stepping back as he turned in a tight circle and joined Micah. With a lifted hand, Micah looked toward the house, and the horses moved out at a fast trot.

"I put the bay in the pasture, Miss Chloe. He was in pretty good shape. What's goin' on up here?" From the barn, Lowery's voice was sharp and curious and Chloe repeated what she'd been told. His look was dubious as she spoke, and he shook his head as if he would defy his instructions. "I don't like leaving you here alone," he said. "J.T. won't like it, that's for sure."

"I think maybe I'll head on out there, Lowery," she told him, itching to take her place with the men, frustration riding her as she thought of waiting inside the house while the men took charge.

"Don't think that's a good idea, ma'am." Firmly, he scotched the idea and she was taken aback.

"It's my herd and my ranch, Lowery. I'll do whatever needs to be done."

"You'd better do what Cleary says, ma'am. Boss kinda left him in charge, him on the range and me tending to business back here."

"Well, neither of them is here now, and Tilly can tend the cow and the chickens without me holding her hand." She set her jaw as she spoke, and was rewarded by a nod from the man in front of her.

"I'll wait for you, then," he said.

"No, go on ahead. I'll get some things together and take some food along. I'll be an hour behind you." She lifted her chin, a defiant gesture, and Lowery gave her a last glare before he turned away.

Chapter Fourteen

Leaving Tilly alone was difficult, especially when the woman frowned and predicted dire happenings. Chloe doggedly packed an abundant supply of food into a sack and trudged to the barn with it. Her own horse stood on three legs near the pasture fence, and she approached the mare with a frown. Tail swishing and head tossing, the pretty black whinnied, a shrill command, and Chloe stepped inside the gate.

"What's the matter, girl?" she asked, holding out her hand as she approached. The mare took a step forward and her limp was apparent. "Let me take a look," Chloe said, lifting and bending the slender leg, the better to inspect the mare's hoof. A cut across the tender frog was dark with dried blood and Chloe muttered beneath her breath.

"I can't ride you today, can I?" she said, leading the animal out the gate and toward the barn. "We'd better get you fixed up." The mare limped in her wake, and Chloe slowed her steps, her first thought for the well-being of her horse. Aware that she was not going to make an appearance anytime soon where the scattered ranch hands were trying to keep things under control, she struggled to set aside her impatience.

With the medicine kit from the tack room in hand, she returned to her mare and in moments had cleaned the cut. After applying a thick gob of salve and a heavy bandage, she wrapped the hoof and tied the mare into a stall. Hay filled the manger before her and a portion of grain served as an apology for leaving the animal indoors.

"Now to find another horse," Chloe muttered, returning to the pasture. The green-broke geldings were not her first choice, requiring a rider's full attention, their training not complete. In the far north end of the pasture, the paint stallion bent his head to the grass and she watched him for a moment. J.T. would have a fit, she supposed, should she decide to ride the stud. And yet, he was the likeliest prospect available.

Time was passing and she was dithering, and being aggravated wasn't adding to her good disposition. A cow pony near the fence, left to his own devices, once Hogan had deemed him too old to ride in the roundup, lifted his head and watched her approach. With bridle in hand, she stood before him and he bent his head agreeably as she slid the bit between his teeth. It was a simple matter to climb on bareback, her lasso in hand.

The stallion watched suspiciously as she rode near, his tail at half-mast, his head high. Eyeing her awkward swirl of the rope and the presence of a high-flung circle over his head, he reared and obligingly made himself a target. The pony Chloe rode dug in his heels and the stud hit the ground with his forefeet and shivered, the rope taut around his neck. Backing and then turning, she headed for the gate, and led the stud into the barn.

"J.T.'s gonna have a fit when he finds out you rode that animal," Tilly predicted moments later as Chloe called her from the kitchen. On the porch, arms folded at her waist, Tilly glared stubbornly. "And when you get thrown, who's gonna be there to help you?" she asked. But she brought the bag with supplies toward the stallion, reaching to hand it up to Chloe, wary of the stallion's tossing head.

"I won't get thrown," Chloe assured her. "My mare can't be ridden, and I can't trust any of the others."

"You can't tell me there's not another horse in that pasture fit to ride," Tilly said, her jaw set, disbelief darkening her gaze.

Chloe had the grace to look chagrined. "Probably more than one, but none of them can travel like this paint. I've been wanting to ride him since the first day he got here. Just haven't had a chance."

"You mean J.T. wouldn't hear of it, most likely."

Chloe shrugged. "Doesn't make any difference now, does it. They need me up there to help keep the rest of the herd in one place. They're short-handed and it won't hurt me to do something to earn my keep." She laid the reins against the side of the stallion's neck and he turned immediately, his training visible as he bent his head and lifted his feet in quick movements. Chloe's heart beat more rapidly, her cheeks flushed with the anticipation of riding the animal, who was rigid with power, awaiting her command.

She rode like the wind was propelling her, at one with the animal who seemed to sense her excitement. With seemingly little effort, he flew across the meadows, skirting stands of tall pine trees and setting a pace that filled her with admiration for the strength of the horse and brought her to a realization of his worth.

The sound of cattle lowing reached her before she saw the first scattered animals beyond the third ridge she crossed. Micah was nowhere to be seen. Lowery rode at the west side, Tom on the east, and between them the herd shifted and swerved, as if prodded by an invisible force. Normally silent and slow-moving, they were agitated, as if a storm hung low overhead or some unseen force urged them to move from their pastureland.

She halted the stallion, looking down at the men who rode the perimeter of the herd, breaking away to chase down a stray, then returning it, their ponies working in precise movements. Beyond them another ridge loomed, and to the north of it lay a series of canyons. Allowing the herd to stray in that direction would mean disaster. Keeping the group intact was the only way to have any sort of control, and it was taking every bit of perseverance and skill the two men had to hold the cattle where they stood.

"Ma'am?" From behind her a quiet voice caught her attention and she pulled the stallion up short, turning him to face the man behind her. A cowhand she did not recognize eyed her closely from the back of his mount, and as she watched, his hand slid the revolver from his holster. Tied to his thigh, it was a lethal weapon, and she felt a moment of shame as it was lifted and aimed in her direction.

Intent on the scene before her, she'd been caught unaware, and her aggravation turned to anger. "Who are you?" she blurted, feeling the stallion's unease as he pranced beneath her.

"Makes no never mind," the man said, his eyes on the horse she rode, his hand steady as he pointed the revolver. "You just ride on down there aways, nice and quiet, and let those men of yours see you with this gun on your back, you hear?"

"If you belong to that gang of rustlers that already managed to get away with part of my herd, I'm sure as hell not going to help you snatch any more of them," she said, her words filled with a fury she made no attempt to contain. "Go ahead and shoot me, if that'll do you any good," she told him. "I don't know what you think you're going to do, one man against those two."

Whether her voice carried to where Tom and Lowery rode, or whether the movement of the two riders caught their eye, the men working the herd looked up, almost at the same moment, and Tom's shout rang in the air.

"Miss Chloe, what's goin' on up there?" He spun his horse in a half circle and rode toward her, reaching behind his saddle to pull the rifle from the leather sheath holding it.

The man before her leveled his gun in Tom's direction and Chloe dug her heels into the stallion's sides. The horses collided, the paint stud turning aside, destroying the rustler's aim as his shot missed its mark. And then the man aimed again and Chloe recognized that she was the target this time. "Call him off," the rustler said, his voice a harsh command.

There was no need. Tom's horse skidded to a halt less than fifty feet away, as he recognized Chloe's danger. "You shoot her, you're a dead man," Tom said quietly. "J.T. Flannery will hunt you down and make mincemeat outta you."

"I don't intend to shoot her," the man said roughly. "Not unless you force me." He held his reins taut, his horse prancing beneath him, and his head jerked to one side. "You ride on ahead of me, ma'am." And then he looked at Tom and Chloe saw a bleak expression cross his features.

"Turn around, cowboy. Head back where you came from. Now."

"Do as he says, Tom," Chloe told him. "And if you shoot him," she said to the rustler, "I'll see you hang for murder."

"I don't need a rope around my neck, ma'am. I just want you to do as I say."

Tom looked from one to the other, and over his shoulder, Lowery could be seen watching from the back of the herd. They milled in a tight circle, the stray bullet startling them into motion. His horse was fighting the bit, head tossing as the herd moved erratically.

The rustler pointed his gun upward and another shot rang

out. The herd bolted, running full tilt to the north, and Chloe
shouted a command at Tom. "Stop them. Help Lowery."

The man beside her reached to grab her reins, and jerked
the stud's head in his direction. "Come on, I told you," he
commanded. With a harsh, wrenching movement, he urged
her horse to follow, leading her down the slope and to the
west. The stallion went, unable to resist the bit's pressure
against his mouth, and Chloe was thrust forward in the saddle as he stumbled on a hillock.

She grabbed for the saddle horn, lurched to one side, and
as the stallion fought the bit, tossing his head, kicking his
hind legs in a futile effort at freedom, she was thrown from
the animal's back.

The ground rose to meet her and a sharp pain vibrated
inside her head. The sound of rushing waters filled her mind,
confusing her, and she struggled to gain her feet, only to
lurch forward again. This time she floundered, and without
the ability to break her fall, she landed with solid force. Her
cry was muffled, and she lay spread-eagled on the slope,
her forehead pierced by the sharp edge of a rock.

"Damn, she sure is bleedin' like a stuck pig." The pronouncement seemed aimed at her, Chloe decided. Unable to
open her eyes, lest the light make the pain any more intense,
she only groaned, uncaring if she was heard or not.

"You get hit in the head, it's gonna bleed thataway,"
another voice chimed in. "One of you tie a bandanna around
her forehead and pad it good."

She felt hands touch her, rolling her over on her back
carelessly, and she cried out at the pain of bent arms forced
beneath her. Peering between her lashes, she saw a starkly
brutal face, framed in a red glow, and she muttered words
of anger.

"Just shut your mouth, lady. If you don't behave, I'll just
let you bleed to death." His hands were rough, placing a

wad of some fabric against her forehead, then tying a length of cloth to hold it in place.

It was blood that colored his image, she decided. Her own, most likely, and that thought was no comfort at all. The pain radiated through her head, running down her neck and shoulders and converging in the aching muscles that fought the rope binding her hands. There was no use in it; she was well and truly hog-tied, her feet crossed at the ankles, her knees bent and looped with the same rope.

"Just rest easy there, ma'am." Now that voice was familiar, the same polite, casual tones that had greeted her ears to begin with. And if she could get her hands on the miserable… Her mind failed to come up with punishment harsh enough to fit his crime.

She'd been careless, oblivious to her surroundings, aware only of the men who fought to keep her cattle under control, and had allowed this wretched piece of humanity to blindside her. Anger at herself was matched only by the fury that she directed at the man who spoke to her.

"You know you're going to at least end up in prison, don't you?" she asked, her voice hoarse as she fought the twin sources of pain that confused her mind and brought fresh rage to sweep through her. Her hands tingled from the ropes binding them, and her head banged a furious rhythm. She blinked at the rosy hue edging her vision and resisted the urge to move her head again.

"You're just makin' it harder on yourself, ma'am," the outlaw said, casting a look toward the men who watched from several feet away.

The truth of his words sank in and Chloe inhaled deeply, willing her voice to be reasonable. "Will you roll me over? My hands are—" She broke off as he stooped to do her bidding, and she was rolled unceremoniously to her side. He eased his fingers between the ropes binding her and she felt a loosening of her bonds. Her fingers curled and twitched in an attempt to regain feeling, and the horrible urge to shed tears of anger was almost overwhelming.

Only the thought of their scorn should she use so obvious a female ploy for sympathy dried the evidence of her pain. She gritted her teeth and chewed on the inside of her lip, unwilling to appear weak in front of such monstrous creatures.

"Leave her be," the roughest of the bunch said, motioning with a crooked finger at the man next to her. "She's not gonna be feeling much of anything pretty soon."

"You said we wasn't gonna kill her," the soft-spoken rustler said accusingly. "I don't hold with shootin' women."

"You want her telling everybody what you look like, that's one thing. I'm not about to give her a chance to draw my face on a Wanted poster. I'd just as soon not see a picture of myself hangin' on the wall of the county sheriff's office any time soon."

J.T., wherever you are, I sure hope you know I need you. The fervent cry of her heart seemed loud in her ears, and she recognized the movement of her lips as she whispered his name. "Jay."

The canyon walls were steep, and she saw them from an angle as the ugly one slung her over the back of a horse, leaving her to dangle on either side of the saddle. He'd untied her legs first and she felt the tingling of pins and needles as they came to life, straining to balance herself as the horse moved at a plodding pace. Heading for the ground would be a disaster, with no way of protecting her head, and she tensed her muscles as she tried to curl against the flat leather saddle beneath her body.

The sun was absent, and the depth of the canyon they traveled made it impossible to tell the time of day. Shadows surrounded her and ahead she heard the sound of cattle.

Probably hers, she thought, as anger boiled to the surface again. The men rode single file, and the horse carrying her brought up the end of the line. It wasn't the paint stallion, and for that she was grateful. He would never have been so placid as the packhorse beneath her.

And wouldn't J.T. have a fit when he discovered his stud was gone. Probably make more fuss over the loss of his breeding stock than his uncontrollable wife. Now, that wasn't fair, she thought, scolding herself on his behalf. He had feelings for her. She knew it, as surely as she knew she was his wife. No man could be as caring as J.T. and not give more than two hoots about the woman he shared a bed with.

She tried to visualize him, wherever he might be. Even now riding hell-bent-for-election toward home, the money from the sale of their cattle tucked into his pocket. He'd no doubt make a stop at the bank in town, to leave it in Mr. Webster's care. And she thought of the message he'd probably receive once he hit the edge of town. Everyone within miles around would know by now that there was trouble on the north range.

Once J.T. found that she'd managed to get herself neck deep in the mess, he'd be on his way. And if he got himself killed on her account… She gritted her teeth as the black thoughts flashed through her mind, and her head bounced against the saddle, reminding her of the wound that was still seeping blood. The pain washed over her and she groaned beneath her breath, unwilling to draw attention to herself.

It was no use. The last rider, the one holding the lead rope that kept her horse in line, halted and hauled the lead line to himself, bringing Chloe's inert form closer. ''You sure are a mess, drippin' blood all over the place, ma'am.''

And wasn't that what she wanted to hear? Chloe closed her eyes, her head aching, her arms feeling like someone had cut them off above the elbows. The voice beside her was lower now, and she strained to hear the harsh whisper. "I'm gonna get you outta here, lady. I won't be a part of killin' a woman. Just keep your eyes open and be ready."

And with that, he moved on ahead and her horse obligingly followed.

Keep your eyes open. Dizzy from watching the view at such an angle, she ignored his command. The path beneath the horse's hooves was rocky and narrow. Scanning her mind, she tried to remember the area they rode, recalling the early days when her father had shown her this desolate part of the country. Canyons formed like widespread fingers splayed across the landscape, and getting lost was always a real possibility, her father had said.

It was doubtful that J.T. had explored beyond the north range, and he'd be at a loss trying to find her here. Micah, now, was a different story. The man knew everything there was to know about this part of the country. He'd put his life on the line more than once in years past, hunting down and bringing back men who'd tried to hide from the law. And in that small comfort she put her hope.

That, and the fact that one of the rustlers was having a spell of remorse.

Mr. Webster wore a frown as J.T. entered the ornate bank lobby. "Thought you'd be in a hurry to get home," he said, his hand outstretched to clasp J.T.'s in greeting. "I understand Micah and the rest of your crew are scouring the canyons, looking for the rest of the rustlers and your wife."

J.T. halted where he stood, his mind attempting to make sense of the statement. "What the hell are you talking about?" he asked harshly. "Why would my wife be lost in a canyon?"

"Not lost," Mr. Webster said. "Taken hostage, from what I understand."

J.T. spun in place, then looked back impatiently. "Who has her?"

"Don't know for sure, but she disappeared yesterday, late afternoon. They were looking for her to show up, and when she got there, some fella pulled a gun and stampeded the herd. Miss Chloe told the men to tend to the cattle and by the time things were under control, she was gone."

And wasn't that a garbled mess, J.T. thought, his mind attempting to make sense of the story. Chloe. He should have known she'd get into some sort of trouble, leaving her on her own. And where was Cleary, the man he'd depended on to keep an eye on things? His footsteps rang out on the fancy marble floor of the bank lobby as he stalked to the door, and Hogan watched his approach with apprehension.

"All done with your business already?" he asked, handing J.T. the reins to his horse.

"Hell, I forgot." J.T. reached into his pocket and pulled forth the reason for this stop at the bank. "Give it to Webster. Tell him I want a receipt, and then you head on home. I'm taking Shorty with me. Something's gone wrong at the ranch."

His horse was trail weary, and yet he pushed the stallion to the limit, leaving Shorty behind as he rode the familiar road toward the Double B. Silence met him as he tied the horse to the hitching post near the house, and the back door was locked when he attempted to enter the kitchen.

His fist thumped loudly on the frame, and from inside he heard Tilly call out a reply. Her footsteps vibrated the porch as she hustled across the kitchen floor, and he called her name. "Let me in, Tilly. What's goin' on?"

Eyes reddened and face pulled into lines of worry, she faced him through the screen door, then pushed it open, grabbing his arm to drag him inside. "Never been so glad to see anybody in my life, J.T., and that's the truth. The whole bunch of them set out yesterday afternoon, Micah with them, and Chloe an hour or so behind.''

"Where'd she go?" He cared little about the rest of them right now, his mind set on finding his wife.

"A fella from Hale Winters's place stopped by early-on this morning and said Chloe got herself taken away by somebody holding a gun on her. Tom and Lowery were fightin' to keep the herd from stampedin' north, and they were afraid to shoot, lest they hit Chloe."

"Where's Cleary?"

Tilly lifted her shoulders and shook her head. "I don't know anything else to tell you, just that Chloe's up there somewhere and Micah's trackin' her."

"Get me something to eat and I'll take it along," he told her, turning back to the door. "Make it enough for three. I'll take Hogan and Shorty with me. But first I've got to get another horse. Mine's done in."

"Don't be looking for the paint stallion," Tilly said sharply. "Chloe rode him out of here."

"Chloe rode the stud?" His words were quiet, but his fury was apparent. He felt the heat of anger rise within him as he thought of Chloe handling the paint. Not that she wasn't a good rider, but the horse had been kept pretty close to the barn, and was sure to be a handful. "I'll find her, Tilly," he said, and the look he sent her was a promise.

"Come on, lady. Eat up, or go without," a voice snarled from beside Chloe, and she allowed her gaze to move upward to where the flat-faced rustler watched. His eyes were shiny, avid on her countenance, his mouth slack and wet, and a shudder of revulsion began at the base of her spine and shot upward.

He squatted, the toe of his boot nudging her leg, and reached one hand to touch her hair. She jerked, a reflex she could not control, moving her head from his filthy fingers.

His laughter was quick and harsh. "Don't be so high and mighty, lady. You just may be wishin' for somebody to be nice to you before this thing's over with." Ripe with innuendo, his words were accompanied by a leering grin, as he allowed his gaze to rest on her breasts. Beneath the cotton shirt she wore, she felt her flesh shrink and shrivel at the thought of his hand touching her there.

"Did you sleep good last night?" he asked, and she shook her head in mute reply.

"I should've come over and kept you company," he suggested. "Maybe tonight."

J.T., where are you? The words resounded in her mind, as she thought of what the creature beside her insinuated with his threatening words. And then the husky man hoisted himself to his feet and walked away, leaving her with a mouthful of beans that threatened to choke her as she swallowed.

Beyond the circle of men, five of them in all, a rope corral held a small herd of horses, the paint stallion among them. He looked ordinary, except for his distinctive coloring, she decided, standing with an assortment of nondescript mounts. Yet he stood out in her eyes as she noted the sleek sides and black spots that denoted his ancestry. If she could find some way to get on his back, he would outrun the rest of the remuda effortlessly. Even without a saddle, with only a bridle to control him with, she'd be willing to take a chance on making an escape.

In fact, she decided glumly, she'd settle for a halter and a piece of rope right now.

"Come on, ma'am." Her captor approached, holding out his hand for the plate and she scooped up the last bit of beans. A single swallow of coffee remained, and she drained the cup quickly.

"I need some privacy," she told him, feeling a flush of embarrassment creep to cover her cheeks. She'd wiggled and squirmed and contained the discomfort as long as she could, but drinking the coffee had made it apparent that she could no longer hold her tongue. "You'll have to untie my feet, so I can find a place to—"

He nodded quickly. "I figured as much," he said. "I'll be back." And he was. Within minutes, he'd untied her feet, loosened the rope around her waist and led her by its length, her feet stumbling as she walked to an area where an out-cropping of rocks provided shelter.

"I'm hangin' on to the end of this rope, lady," he told her brusquely, and she sensed that his discomfort matched her own.

It was no time to argue with the man, and she waited until he turned his back and then sought a spot for her use. A tug on the rope hastened her on her way, and her fingers awkwardly redid the buttons on her trousers, then pulled the belt tightly around her middle. She looked down at the rough hole J.T. had punched, that day at the pool. It seemed ages since, and she closed her eyes for a moment, recalling the pleasure she'd found there, the memories assailing her mind, bittersweet.

The horses were being saddled as she trudged back toward the men, and she dreaded the thought of being slung over the saddle once more. But it was not to be. Rough hands lifted her and she was placed in her saddle. Not atop the stallion, much to her dismay, but on a nondescript black with dust imbedded in his coat and a tangled mane showing lack of care on the part of his owner.

A loop was passed around her hands and then fastened to the saddle horn and she was led to where the group waited. From ahead, she heard the bawling of cattle and one of the men rode up beside her, nudging her horse into movement, then tugging at the lead line as he rode ahead.

"Want to see what we're takin' to market, ma'am?" he asked, taunting her with a grin. A sharp jog in the trail curved right within the steep, rock-walled bottleneck they traveled, and she looked ahead to see a wide, boxed canyon. With cliffs on all three sides, the cattle were effectively caged by sheer, straight walls, as though the canyon had been formed by eons of water flowing its length.

Steers milled within a roped-off corral, a fire was glowing at one side, and she saw branding irons pushed into the midst of the burning coals. Another part of the herd grazed several hundred yards beyond the temporary corral, and she felt bitterness rise within her at the sight.

No doubt some of her own herd were here, awaiting a new brand that would cover that of the Double B, and make it possible to sell these animals without leaving a trail that would lead back to her ranch. The operation was obviously larger than any of them had thought, and the men who sat in the jail in Ripsaw Creek were only a part of the gang.

She was limp in the saddle, her head pounding in time to the rough gait of the horse she rode, and when the gelding came to a halt, she allowed herself to be pulled from his back with no protest. Again, she was forced to sit at the base of a tree, and her feet bound, while the second rope tied her upright. In front of her, the cattle were being branded, a slow process since they were full-grown steers and not nearly so easy to contain as they had been as young bullocks.

The noise from bawling cattle, men calling back and forth, and the echoes reverberating from the canyon walls surely must be audible, she thought. And yet, they seemed unconcerned as they worked, sweating and filthy from the dust rising in the air. She tilted her head back, eyeing the tops of the walls, scanning them in the hope of some trace, some small shred of evidence, that there were others watching.

For the whole of the afternoon, she watched, narrowing her eyes, the better to note any change in the horizon above the canyon, focusing on each bit of rock formation, casting abrupt glances to the sides in the hope of catching a glimpse of a new bit of color, a spot of shadow or gleam of metal visible to her eye.

She was given another few moments of privacy toward the end of the afternoon, and she was grateful to Gus for his attempts at kindness. *Keep your eyes open and be ready.* Had it been a dream, those words uttered so softly just yesterday? She watched as Gus took his turn at the branding, noted his silence as the other men made jokes at her expense, and ignored the leering glances tossed in her direction by two of the men. And yet, she could only wait.

J.T., where are you?

"She's under that tree, the one with the low-hanging limbs." Micah's words stirred hope as J.T. followed the lawman's murmured directions and pointing finger. "Don't look too much the worse for wear."

And if that was supposed to be encouraging, J.T. could only brush aside the words as a panacea to his anger. "I don't see any way to get to her," he said beneath his breath.

"Cleary's on his way," Micah told him. "Down there at the mouth of the canyon. Keep an eye out. And have your rifle ready."

Chapter Fifteen

"Ma'am? We're gonna be movin' out right soon." Gus stood before her, his expression somber. Bending, he released the bonds on her ankles and she stretched her legs, wiggling her feet, encouraging the circulation to flow unimpeded. "You're gonna be ridin' right close to the front of the line, right in the line of fire, just in case any of your ranch hands are nearby."

Chloe was silent, alert to a change in the atmosphere as the rustlers broke up camp, putting in motion an exodus from the box canyon. Her captor hoisted her from the ground and she staggered, her knees weak, her feet still feeling the effects of being bound. He pushed her forward, and as she stumbled, quickly held her upright and drew her back against himself.

"Keep your eyes open," he muttered against her ear and then shoved her in the direction of a group of horses. The paint stallion's muzzle brushed across a patch of grass and, as she watched, one of the men jerked on his halter, sliding it from his head and replacing it with a bridle. The man clutching Chloe's arm dragged her toward the paint, and she caught her breath as excitement rushed through her veins.

Quickly, he loosed the bonds from her hands and retied

them in front of her. "No saddle for you, lady," he growled, lifting her with ease to place her on top of the stud. "You just hang on as best you can." Gripping the trailing reins, he mounted another horse and led her from the group.

"What's happening?" J.T. eased down beside Micah as the small train of horses left the middle of the box canyon and slowly made its way to the opening at the far end. Chloe was atop the paint stallion, with no saddle beneath her, and only the horse's mane to grip. In front of her rode two men, one towing a pack animal, the other holding the reins of Chloe's mount.

"They're movin' out," Micah said quietly. "That's quite a herd of cattle they got. And I'm thinking they figure that Chloe's their ticket to a clear trail." He backed from the edge of the cliff and waved a hand at the men who watched from a hundred yards away. "We need to move out, quick and quiet. It'll take half an hour to get to the other side of the neck of that canyon, and that'll be the place to make our move."

"It'll take them an hour to get those cattle through the gap," J.T. said. "Why do you suppose they're pushing Chloe on ahead?"

Micah shot a look at him and J.T. faced the reality of Chloe's position. "She's their shield."

"You got that right," Micah told him. "They know we're not gonna start something with her out in front."

"Then…" J.T. paused, holding his horse's reins in one hand as his mind returned to Cleary. "Won't they notice Cleary on their way out?"

Micah grinned. "Sure will. He's their rear scout, Flannery."

Careful to keep her heels from the stallion's sides, Chloe rode behind Gus, casting long looks to right and left, then up to the cliffs that rimmed the canyon. Ahead, a lone rider emerged from a thicket and sat atop a pale horse, whose dark mane and tail stood out sharply against the golden animal.

"Cleary." She whispered the single word as she recognized the tall cowhand, and her heart sank, knowing that J.T. had been deceived by a man he trusted. She lifted her chin, facing him, unafraid, even though her better judgment told her she should be pliable and biddable before these men.

Their eyes met and his gaze was dark, his eyes holding no trace of recognition as he swept a casual look over her. "I see you got us a hostage," he said to Gus.

"Yeah, this is the missus, just fell into our hands like a ripe peach," Gus told him. "We figured the man in charge wouldn't want to take the chance of anything happening to his bride." He tugged at the stallion's reins and pulled Chloe forward. "Her brother told us the man's right fond of her."

"My brother?" Chloe whispered the phrase, and her eyes closed, reminded once more of Pete's betrayal.

Gus pulled her mount along the trail, and then as they reached the canyon's mouth, moved with her off to one side, looking back at the cattle that had begun to head in their direction. "I want to tell you something, ma'am." His mouth barely moved as he spoke, his attention seemingly on the approaching herd. "Your brother was tryin' to pull out of this deal that night you had a fire in your barn. When your fella caught up with us and there was a gun battle, a good share of us got away. Your brother got shot. It wasn't none of your people who killed him, ma'am.

"You see anything going on up top?" he asked, raising his voice in Cleary's direction. A swift, negative shake of the man's head seemed to reassure him and he turned his horse toward the mouth of the canyon.

"I think they're on the range, still tryin' to follow tracks," Cleary said, riding in their wake. "There's a mess of tracks out there, but I dusted over the trail when I came in behind you."

Gus looked back over his shoulder, then he lifted a hand at Cleary and the second rider. "Let's head on through the narrows. We want to be well in front of that herd when they come out the other end."

Chloe's mind swam with the words Gus had uttered. *It wasn't none of your people who killed him....* Pete had tried to make things right. Clinging to that thought, she gripped the dark mane of her mount and followed, aware of Cleary at her rear, and a bawling herd of cattle not far behind.

"First and foremost, we need to make sure Chloe is out of the line of fire," Micah said. They'd ridden hard, the length of the canyon, back from the cliff's edge by a quarter mile, to where the ground sloped in a gradual manner on the south side of the rocky formation. It had been longer than the thirty minutes Micah had allotted to the ride, and now they rounded the stand of trees at the base of the ridge.

"Spread out, but stick on the south side of the mouth of that canyon," Micah said, his voice low, yet carrying to the men who followed his lead: "Watch for Cleary. He'll be responsible for getting Chloe out of the way."

"I sure as hell wish you'd let me in on things beforehand," J.T. told him, snarling the words in anger. "I feel like an idiot, hiring Cleary without knowing what was going on."

Micah sent him a long look that smacked of regret. "Didn't have a choice, son. Cleary came in here from the U.S. Marshal's office and I just did what I was told."

The men around them scattered, their horses hidden behind rock formations and within the trees. With almost twenty guns aimed in the direction from which Chloe would be coming, J.T. could only hope there weren't any itchy fingers touching a trigger.

He watched as Micah placed his ear to the ground, lifted his head to peer toward the canyon mouth, and then bent to listen again. "Horses coming," he muttered beneath his breath. "And a rumble, real low, but it sounds like the herd's on the move."

J.T. crawled to the side of the pinnacle of rock he'd taken as shelter and squinted past the low cover that stretched before him. From the opening ahead, a flash of movement caught his eye, then the sight of a horse, moving at a quick trot, its rider leading a pack animal behind.

Close at his heels was a second rider, the reins of another horse in his hands. The familiar colorings of the paint stallion met his gaze and J.T. swept fearful eyes to the rider. She was bent forward, her hands clutching the mane, as he'd last seen her, and to her rear rode the man he'd hired as a ranch hand.

Cleary. His hat pulled low over his eyes, he held his rifle in one hand as he rode, and as J.T. watched, Cleary's gaze swept his position. He looked past, then his eyes returned to where J.T. hovered at the edge of the rocky site. His rifle lifted in a subtle salute as he rode closer to Chloe's side, and J.T.'s muscles clenched as Cleary called out to the second man in the small train.

"Gus. I'll take her now." It was an order given in a tone of voice that expected to be obeyed, yet the man who turned to face Cleary made no move to heed the summons. Instead, he pulled Chloe's mount closer and, leaning toward her, grasped her hands in his.

"What's goin' on?" J.T.'s words were an amazed whisper as it seemed the two men would tussle over the woman between them, and then Cleary nodded, and a knife blade flashed in Gus's hand.

Without missing a step, the paint veered to the right as

Chloe leaned over and grasped the reins, her hands free of the ropes that had bound her. Close behind, Cleary spun to a halt and turned his gun on the first rider. The man had looked back, obviously wary of the commotion behind him, and as he drew his own gun from the holster, Cleary's rifle lifted into position. His aim was true and the man fell from his mount, rolling on the ground, even as he dropped the lead line for the packhorse.

From the mouth of the canyon behind them a spurt of cattle appeared, widening to a stream that quickly gained speed as the steers reached the open range. Interspersed in their midst were riders who moved to the outside of the herd to maneuver. Taken up with keeping the herd under control, the men seemed oblivious to Cleary and his charge, and as J.T. watched, the man leaned toward Chloe and she nodded agreement, following his lead.

Gus glanced once in their direction and rode ahead to where the rustler lay on the ground, his horse beside him. Dropping from his saddle, he lifted the wounded man and draped him over the saddle, then snatched up the reins and mounted his own horse.

"Don't shoot him, Cleary," Chloe said quickly. "He told me from the beginning he'd help me escape."

"Move out," Cleary told her harshly. "Take cover behind those trees. I'll be right behind you."

She turned the paint, and encountered resistance, the horse's training urging him toward the herd behind them. And from the men riding point in front of the thundering steers came a shout. "The woman's getting away!" One of the rustlers turned his mount in a tight half circle, heading in her direction.

She clung to the paint, digging in her heels as he heeded her hold on the reins, and bending low over his neck, she headed due south, where Cleary's instructions had bid her go. Behind her, shots were fired and men shouted, and racing beside her was a dun-colored pony with one of the rustlers astride.

He cursed loudly, aiming his gun in her direction, forcing her toward a rocky area. Behind her, another gun spoke and the rustler fell from his horse. She glanced to her right, spying Cleary as he rode apace, and then watched in horror as he jerked in the saddle and fell against his horse's neck. Blood covered his shoulder, quickly soaking his sleeve, and his gun fell to the ground.

The paint stallion obeyed her hand on the reins and turned back to where Cleary's horse stood, eyes rolling in his head, pawing at the ground as the reins fell to either side of his head. Chloe edged as close as she could, grasping Cleary by the belt and calling his name.

"Can you get on behind me?" she asked as his eyes squinted at her, and his mouth opened as if he would speak.

"Yeah." The single word seemed to take every bit of his energy, but the stallion stood as if made of stone as Cleary lifted himself from the saddle and fell across Chloe's horse. "Go," he said, sagging on either side of the stud's barrel behind her.

She moved ahead cautiously, aware of gunfire, and the pounding hooves of the cattle behind her, praying that they would not veer from their path. The stand of trees concealed them as she rode past the edge of the wooded area, and as the ground sloped upward, she slowed the pace of the stallion.

Beneath a tree, she halted, looking quickly over her shoulder lest they be followed, and then with a sigh of relief, slid from the stud. Leaning her forehead against his shoulder, she murmured words of praise, then lifted the reins to twist them around a branch. Beside her, Cleary slid to the ground, crumpling at her feet, and she bent to him.

Blood flowed from the front of his shoulder, and she tore the tattered remains of his garment from the spot where the bullet had erupted, taking flesh with it. Sliding from her shirt quickly, she tore off a double strip from the hem and knotted it together. Then, folding the rest into a thick pad, she pressed it against the gaping wound. The strip reached from his shoulder, across to his waist on the opposite side, and the rest of it she managed to slide beneath him.

Cleary watched her, lifting his head and breathing fitfully, groaning as she moved him to tie the bandage in place. He was sweating profusely, his countenance almost gray, and as she worked, he lost consciousness, his head falling to the ground.

Loading him back on the horse was impossible, and Chloe could only kneel beside the wounded man and wait for help to arrive.

"Chloe?" She heard the familiar voice and rose quickly, lifting her bloodstained hands from the man at her feet. J.T. rode beneath the overhanging branches of a tree, then straightened in the saddle and their eyes met, his making a swift survey of her, her own gaze unable to swerve from his face.

"I put some pressure on the wound, but he's still bleeding," she told J.T. and his attention turned to the man on the ground. He slid from his horse and reached for his saddlebag, opening it quickly and removing a towel.

"This ought to do the trick till we can get him back to the house," he said, folding the heavy fabric and sliding it into place beneath the wadded material of Chloe's shirt.

"What happened?" she asked. "Did you get all the rustlers?"

"A couple of them took a bullet. The rest gave up when they saw there wasn't much chance of getting past us."

"They were going to use me as a hostage," she said. "If it hadn't been for Gus and Cleary..." She inhaled deeply, thinking of the men who had paid so little attention to her well-being, and were so willing to put her life in peril.

"Micah knew Cleary would watch out for you," J.T. said, feeling for a pulse in Cleary's neck.

"He'd have had a hard time if Gus hadn't cut my wrists free," she said. "And Gus told me—"

"Later," J.T. said, cutting her off mid-sentence. "We need to get Cleary loaded up and on his way to a doctor."

"Let me look for his horse," she said, hurrying through the trees to where the sounds of men shouting and cattle lowing could be heard.

And then she halted, watching as Lowery rode toward her, Cleary's horse in tow. Beyond him men worked the herd, while others stood in a circle, hands over their heads, as two cowhands took their weapons and then tied their hands.

"Those fellas are in for a long walk," Lowery said with a grin. "Hale Winters's boys are takin' them to town." He looked beyond Chloe to where J.T. knelt next to Cleary. "They didn't kill him, did they?" Lowery asked, his grin turning to concern.

Chloe shook her head. "No, he's still alive, but he's got a nasty hole in his shoulder."

"He'll probably be back on his horse in a week," Lowery told her. "My guess is it won't be the first time he's had a bullet in him." He turned his horse and headed back to the milling cattle. "It'll take a while to get these animals sorted out, Miss Chloe. You and the boss better take Cleary back to the house."

You and the boss. She mulled over his words as J.T. lifted the wounded man to his horse.

The man she'd married had taken control, and she'd allowed it. Yet it rankled and she determined to dig in her heels.

* * *

Tilly decreed there was no need for the doctor to be called out so late in the day. For by the time Cleary was installed in a bed on the second floor, the sun had been below the horizon for almost an hour. Washing the wound in carbolic soap, then stitching the raw edges of the wound with heavy thread was a job Chloe was only too glad to give into Tilly's able hands.

J.T. knew she'd done her share of stitching in times past, but as she watched, her face turned pale, and he reached to catch her as her legs gave way beneath her. In moments she was seated on a chair, her head held between her knees. J.T. squatted by her side, one big hand on her nape, the other holding a cold cloth against her forehead.

"Just stay right there," he said sharply. "I don't want to scrape you up off the floor."

"I don't know what's wrong with me," she muttered. "I never get puny at the sight of blood."

"Could be the past two days kinda got to you," he said, sarcasm alive in his tone. "Maybe it has something to do with ridin' off on the paint stallion and gettin' yourself in a peck of trouble. And then being the cause of a man getting shot when he tried to rescue you."

"Are you going to be mad at me forever, or can I look forward to a little sympathy after while?" she asked in a whisper.

"I just can't believe you went off half-cocked, Clo. I told you—"

She lifted her head abruptly, and the cloth he'd held against her face dropped to the floor. "Listen to me, Flannery." She snarled the words, her eyes flashing temper at him. "You're not going to spend the rest of our lives together telling me what to do, and you'd better get that through your head right now."

He looked fully into her eyes, then surveyed the bruised lines of her face. One hand reached to brush her hair back, and his heart thumped an extra beat as he saw the lump on her forehead, dried blood caking the jagged cut that ended at her hairline.

"What happened to your head?" he asked, cutting off her protest midsentence.

"I got dumped and landed on a rock." She spit the words in his direction and brushed his hand aside. Angry tears fought to be shed, and she lifted one hand to brush them away.

"Don't touch that cut," he said gruffly, fearful of dirt entering the open wound. "Why didn't you tell me you needed stitches on your forehead?"

"You didn't ask." Chloe set her jaw and rose from the chair, making her way to the dresser where a pitcher of water waited next to the china bowl. She lifted the pitcher and found it taken from her grasp.

"I'll do that," he said, pouring the bowl half full. "I washed up downstairs. My hands are clean."

Chloe looked up at him and he felt his heart lurch within his chest. The anger had been a cover-up, his worry about her well-being making him cross and fit to be tied. And now he looked into weary eyes that begged silently for understanding. He reached for a clean cloth and wrung it out in the water, then pulled the chair closer.

"Sit down, Clo," he said quietly. "Let me bathe that cut and see how bad it is."

"It's already healing," she said, obeying, as if her legs would no longer hold her upright. And then she lifted her face, closing her eyes as he held her hair back and washed the edges of her wound.

"You need me up here?" Micah stepped through the doorway, surveying the two patients. "I'd better be getting to town. Don't know where we're going to put that bunch of rustlers. If I had my way, there'd be a hanging party tomorrow after the judge holds court early in the morning.

But I don't think that's gonna happen. They'll probably all get sent to Laramie to prison.''

"Micah!" Chloe jerked in her chair and made an effort to stand. Only J.T.'s hands on her shoulders kept her bottom pressed against the seat.

Micah turned to her, frowning as if he caught the edge of panic in her voice. "What's the problem, Miss Chloe? I know you're averse to hangin' anybody, but the law's the law, and doggone, a few years back that's what would have happened to them. And I'm not sure it wouldn't be a good idea now." His firm tone left no room for appeal, and J.T.'s private opinion was much the same.

One look at Chloe told a different tale, however. And her voice trembled as she spoke. "The man, Gus...the one who cut the ropes and turned me loose. He told me early on that he'd help me, Micah. Said he didn't hold with hurting women."

She closed her eyes for a moment as J.T. nodded his agreement. "I saw him cut her free," he told Micah.

"That's not all Gus had to say," Chloe whispered, and J.T. bent low to hear her words. "He said that Pete was killed by one of the rustlers. Gus told me Pete was trying to get out of the whole thing that night."

J.T. felt a load lift from his shoulders. He'd never known, had not been absolutely certain that his gun wasn't the one that felled Pete from his saddle. For sure, he had never deliberately aimed at the man, but in the heated exchange of bullets, the possibility had remained. And it was that possibility that had almost severed the ties that bound him to Chloe.

She leaned her head against his shoulder now, and he nodded at Micah over her head. The lawman's eyes were narrowed, his lips pursed, and then he spoke to Chloe. "I'll see what I can do, Chloe. I'll put Gus in a separate place, and if the judge will listen, we'll see if we can get him a shorter stay in Laramie than the rest of them. I'd say the man is owed a debt, even if he is a low-down rustler. Must be some good in him.''

Chloe shivered, and J.T.'s arms circled her, holding her slight form against himself. ''Come on, sweetheart,'' he whispered. ''Let me clean you up and we'll tuck you into bed.''

To her credit, she made no protest, uttered no claim of well-being. Only allowed him to thoroughly wash the wound on her head with carbolic soap, wincing as it burned the tender skin. And then he followed Tilly's instructions and applied a bandage with salve smeared thickly across its surface. He thought Chloe looked like a waif, a wide-eyed child, as he led her from the room.

And if he noticed Cleary's gaze following, he set the knowledge aside, aware that J.T. Flannery was the man doing the job of undressing, washing up and tucking in the female creature he'd taken as wife.

''She's some woman.'' Cleary's voice spoke the words in an undertone, and Tilly mumbled a reply, the sound lost as J.T. picked Chloe up and carried her to their bedroom.

Her clothing was filthy, and he piled it in a heap for disposal in the morning. She shivered as she stood naked before him, and his hands were gentle as he washed her from top to bottom, leaving only her hair untouched by soap and water. It was snarled and dusty and only a thorough sudsing would accomplish much, he decided. And Chloe was not in fit condition for that tonight.

Her nightgown, folded neatly in a drawer, had not been used of late, and he shook it from its folds reluctantly, knowing she would welcome its warmth tonight. Sliding it over her head, he regretfully covered the firm breasts and rounded hips that drew his gaze. And then watched as it drifted to the floor, until only her pink toes were exposed to view. A quick flip of his wrist tossed the quilt and sheet aside and Chloe was deposited on the fresh bed linen. Before her head touched the pillow, her eyes closed and a sigh escaped her lips.

His own ablutions were taken care of quickly, his body yearning for the closeness of his marriage bed, and in moments he'd blown out the lamp and found his place beside her. She nestled closer in her sleep, and he blessed the day he'd found a place in her life. His arms surrounded her, lifting her gently, holding her against his chest, her feet tangling with his calves and her nightgown pulling up to expose the lush curves of her bottom.

His hand rested there, holding her firmly, his own need put on the back burner as he breathed soft words into her deaf ears. No matter that she could not hear him speak the tender scoldings that poured from him. It counted for naught that she slept through his litany of worry and pain as he'd watched her struggle to ride the paint, hands bound and body aching.

And even when he murmured soft words of praise for her bravery and courage as she'd brought Cleary from the midst of the conflict, she only muttered beneath her breath and wiggled closer to him. He smothered a chuckle then, aware of the stalwart spirit of the woman he'd married. The strength that drove her to do as she saw fit, damning the consequences. The future would indeed prove interesting, J.T. decided.

You're not going to spend the rest of our lives together telling me what to do. She'd spit the words at him, and there was not a shred of doubt in his mind but that she would battle him on that point for years to come. But for tonight, he could allow her the space she needed. Tonight, he would hang a second moon in the sky if she asked.

Chapter Sixteen

Nursing the patient was a task shared by Tilly and Chloe. Carrying trays at mealtimes up the stairway fell to Chloe's lot after her first glimpse of Tilly's cautious treading of the steps. "I'll do the running up and down," she said firmly, and Tilly gave her little argument.

Listening for Cleary at night fell to Tilly, since their bedrooms were directly across the hall from each other. And changing the bandage on his wound was the last thing she did before she sought her bed at night. It was healing well, she told J.T., only a bit of festering causing fever, but that would soon fall prey to the healing poultices she and Chloe applied daily.

On the fourth day of their vigil, Cleary pronounced himself able to come to the table for breakfast, and the sight greeting J.T.'s eyes as Chloe assisted the patient down the stairs, was enough to make his blood boil. Cleary's arm was draped across Chloe's shoulder and she watched attentively as he took his good old time finding his way from one step to another.

Chloe murmured soft words, and Cleary laughed aloud at her, his grin fading as J.T. caught his eye. "Your wife's quite handy to have around," he said.

And as if the words were a challenge, J.T. bristled. "I think so. Bottom line though, is that she's *my* wife." He stood a few feet from the foot of the stairway and Chloe's frown made him seethe. "I don't suppose you've decided you're gonna leave us anytime soon," he said quietly, but with enough emphasis to make Chloe dart him a quick glance.

"Tilly says I need another day or so to rest my shoulder before I ride a horse," Cleary said, obviously smothering amusement as he read J.T.'s expressive face aright.

"I think we need to talk," J.T. said shortly. "Right after breakfast, in fact. In the study." And then his gaze touched Chloe, a stern look she ignored as J.T. added a single word to his demand. "Alone."

Breakfast was hearty and J.T. noted that Cleary's appetite was pretty well restored, the man plunging into a plate full of ham and eggs, with pancakes on the side. Tilly, appreciative of his words of praise for her food, fawned over him unduly, J.T. thought. And Chloe rose quickly as she noted his coffee cup was empty. The fact that she paused by his own chair to refill his was but a minor detail. Cleary was obviously the man of the hour.

And in the study, half an hour later, the man from the U.S. Marshal's office sat comfortably in a chair near the desk, his half smile an aggravation J.T. could not tolerate.

"You know, I resent the fact that you came here under false pretenses," he said, seating himself behind the big desk. "I told Micah I didn't appreciate you taking a job here without telling me what was going on."

"I just do what I'm told," Cleary said briefly, and then crossed one long leg over the other, examining his boot as he spoke. "I was sent by the Wyoming Cattle Owner's Association. I used to be what they call a stock detective, and when this mess came up, they asked for me. My boss said to get in with the rustlers if I could. And then to hire on a a ranch and play cowboy for a while. Micah knew what the story was.''

"Well, it could have caused some real problems,'' J.T. told him. "You don't know how close you came to getting shot by me when I saw you down in that canyon and realized you'd been playing a double-edged game by being part of the gang.''

Cleary shrugged. "It was good cover, and they believed my story. It was the only way I could see to find out where the herd was being held. And now, let me tell *you* something.'' His pause was short as he considered his words. "If I hadn't been there, I'm not sure what would have happened to your wife, Flannery. Gus was swinging both ways and if push came to shove, I don't know if he'd have been able to take her out of range of the bullets.''

J.T. lifted a hand as if to brush aside the man's statement. "I don't like being made a fool of. And lying to me puts you in a position that isn't favorable to any sort of friendship between us.'' He'd might as well spit it all out, he decided. "And another thing. I don't like the way you look at my wife.''

"Looks don't do much harm, as far as I can see,'' Cleary said easily. "And in the case of your wife, she hasn't got eyes for anyone but you, anyway. I'd think you'd know that.'' His gaze shifted from the perusal of his boot, and focused on J.T.'s face. "You've got yourself a good woman, Flannery. If my being nice to her and appreciating the care she's taken of me has made you sit up and take notice, then maybe you'll recognize that the woman's dotty about you.''

J.T. was silent, dwelling on the man's casual assumption of Chloe's feelings. "You know, if I doubted your word on that score for one minute, you'd be flat on your back, Cleary.''

Cleary smiled, yet his eyes were wary. "I'm not sure my shoulder would stand for that,'' he said. "Guess I'd better get my gear together. If I can manage it, I'll head for town in the morning. Micah said when he stopped in yesterday that the judge is back. There'll be a quick trial, and they need me there as witness.''

''Will Chloe's pal, Gus, be sent to Laramie to prison with the rest of them?'' J.T. had evaded the subject for the past days, but now that things were coming to a head, it seemed a good time to make a stab at keeping Chloe on an even keel. She'd not done much talking since that first night, and right now his aim in life was to get his wife back to being the woman he'd married.

''I plan to vouch for him,'' Cleary said. ''He could have kept her in the forefront of the action, and she'd probably have been killed in the process. There sure wasn't anyone else looking out for her.''

''Except you,'' J.T. said dryly. ''And those of us who were watching when things began to happen.''

Cleary shrugged and smiled. ''I was just doing my job, Flannery. And your wife returned the favor when she loaded me on that stallion with her and hauled me into the trees. Not to mention stopping the blood flow.'' He sobered and shifted in the chair. ''I suspect the bottom line is that I owe her my life.''

''She's tough,'' J.T. said quietly. ''Tough and strong. She's a rancher, through and through, the way her father raised her to be.''

Cleary glanced up and J.T. caught sight of a look that might be construed as envy on the man's face. ''And you,'' Cleary said with emphasis, ''you're the lucky son of a gun that managed to talk her into marriage. Women like Chloe don't come down the pike every day.''

J.T. nodded his agreement. ''I just happened to be at the right place at the right time. And smart enough to take advantage of a situation that Lady Luck threw in front of me.''

* * *

Micah showed up the next afternoon before supper and spent a few uncomfortable moments with J.T. on the back porch. His assumption that J.T. was aware of his suit brought about a moment of dead silence as he casually mentioned that he'd spoken to the minister of the small church in town. J.T.'s ear caught the unspoken innuendo.

"You going to make a stab at church-going?" he asked.

"I've been going to church for years," Micah answered, his defenses well in place.

"Then what are you talking to the preacher about these days? Something going on that I'm not aware of?"

J.T. watched as Micah shot a look of inquiry at Chloe, who stood in the kitchen doorway, primed, it seemed, to call the men in for supper. She lifted her hands in a helpless motion and backed away, leaving Micah to J.T.'s mercy.

He had none to offer. Cleary's leaving had done little to calm his temper, what with Chloe and Tilly being so gracious and giving instructions to the man to see the doctor in town. And now Micah seemed about to set things topsy-turvy here, with an agenda of his own in motion.

"I asked Tilly to marry me," Micah said bluntly, his jaw set, ready, it seemed, to take on any challengers. "We're gonna set a date tonight."

"I'd think you'd have said something to Chloe about that, seeing as she's all the family Tilly has hereabouts. I know the woman's old enough to do as she pleases, but there's a matter of simple courtesy involved."

"I already did," Micah said with a look of satisfaction. "And she's all for the idea. And she told me and Tilly both that we're welcome to stay on here after the wedding. Said there's lots of room upstairs for us, and she doesn't want to take a chance on Tilly moving away. I think Chloe needs her here."

"And you're going to ride back and forth to town every

day?'' J.T. looked skeptical as he voiced the query. ''I can't see that going on for long.''

''Nope,'' Micah said firmly. ''I'm getting beyond the time when I want to be out lookin' for rustlers and such. Not that we've had much trouble with them before this last batch moved in. But Ripsaw Creek's growing. It'll be time to get us a sheriff, instead of just a town constable.'' He removed his hat and J.T. noted that the man's hair was more silver than brown, a fact he hadn't considered before.

''Getting too old for the job?'' He couldn't resist the dig, even as he recognized Micah's words to be valid. The man had to be nearing sixty, maybe even older, and by rights should be able to take life easy.

''Nope, I'll work till the day I die, I suspect,'' Micah said. ''Just not at tossing drunks in jail on Saturday night or lookin' for the stray bad man. It's a job for a younger man, I figure.''

''What kind of work you going to be looking for?'' J.T. asked, thumbing his hat from his forehead. He stretched out in his chair, boots crossed at the ankle.

Micah cleared his throat. ''Seems like there oughta be an opening somewhere hereabouts for a man who's good with horses.''

''You think so?'' J.T. slid upright and then stood. ''The women have supper ready. Might's well go see what Tilly's cooked up.''

From the bunkhouse, Hogan and Tom headed toward them and J.T. motioned them to be on their way. ''Time to eat. I was just going to ring the bell.''

Micah was left to ponder throughout the meal, and J.T. enjoyed his silence. Having the last word seemed to improve his mood lately.

''You still talking to me?'' Chloe asked, looking in the mirror at J.T.'s reflection as he stood in the bedroom door.

way. "I think I can count on one hand the times you've said two words to me in the last five days."

"You've been busy, and I didn't see much of you. Guess there wasn't much to talk about," he said, unbuttoning his shirt and letting it hang over his trousers as he sat to pull off his boots. With a muffled grunt, he tugged at one, then the other, avoiding her gaze, as if undressing was the most important thing on his mind. And so it seemed to be, Chloe thought, her brush strokes reaching through to her scalp as she wielded the instrument.

Naked in less than a minute, J.T. walked across the room, and Chloe's eyes widened as he stood behind her. "You gonna take all night messin' with your hair?" he asked, deliberately slurring his words as his voice deepened and his eyelids lowered to effectively obscure the dark orbs from her sight. His hand reached to take the brush from her fingers as she sought for an answer, and she tightened her grip.

"I know how to brush my hair without your help." If he wanted to be ornery, she could match his mood with very little effort.

She found her fingers pried from the wooden handle as his big hand lifted the brush from her grasp. "I have no doubt of that," he said, his voice a rusty sound that drew her attention. One hand gathered up the dark length of her hair and the other pulled the brush through it. "I was just wondering," he said, his voice a slow caress, "whether you were missing your patient tonight."

Chloe rose, an abrupt movement that brought quick tears to her eyes as J.T.'s grip on her hair pulled her head back. She reached behind her, her hands coming in contact with the hard muscular length of his thighs, and then her fingertips brushed against the full length of a male arousal, and she caught her breath.

"Find something you like?" His grip on her hair lessened, his fingers sliding through the strands, and then he turned her toward himself, tossing the brush to the top of her dressing table. She felt her face flush, wishing desperately that the telltale warmth would not so blatantly give away her confusion and embarrassment.

"Haven't seen enough of it lately to know whether I like it or not," she said, and then pressed her lips together, regretting her sharp tongue and the words she'd harbored in her heart for the past days. She'd had no intention of speaking them aloud, but J.T.'s crude question had triggered her quick temper and now she rued her big mouth.

His grin was immediate and his hands moved to the front of her dressing gown, sliding the buttons from their moorings with deft movements. "I think we can fix up that lack in no time flat, sweetheart." No matter that she gripped the front of her robe and the nightgown beneath it, she was no match for his strength and the power of his desire. He tossed the garments aside and Chloe straightened her shoulders and stiffened her spine as he tilted his head to one side and conducted a long survey of her body.

"I'd say you're about the best-lookin' woman I've ever seen, Mrs. Flannery," he announced in a low voice. "And I don't see any bruises that'd keep me from making love to you tonight. You got a problem with that?"

She felt anger rise, knew a moment of pure fury as he lifted her and tossed her in the middle of the bed. And then he covered her with his body, and her breath left her lungs with a *whoosh*.

"I want to tell you, lady," he began, his words a hushed whisper as he leaned over her. "I've been looking at you for the past few days, wishing I dared put my hands on you and all I saw was your sweet little fanny moving away from me, trottin' around after that idiot who got himself shot and then took over a bedroom in this house."

She felt a stirring in her depths as his narrowed eyes focused on her face. They were dark, flaring with an emo-ion she suspected rode the line between desire and aggra-vation. The foolish man was jealous. And that thought pleased her immensely. She wiggled beneath him, moving her legs to either side of his.

"You're my wife, and don't you ever forget it," he whis-pered, one hand moving to tilt her face upward as he bent to place his mouth against hers.

"Did you think I had?" she murmured, even as his lips parted and his tongue touched her upper lip.

"That man had eyes for you." She thought she heard a note of petulance in his voice, and she smiled against his kiss. "I won't have it," he whispered, his breath warm against her cheek as he dropped a series of small kisses there.

"I don't blame you, but you sure don't have anything to worry about," she said quietly. Her fingers touched his cheek, a gentle caress she could not resist bestowing. "If another woman looked at you, I'd have a genuine hissy fit, and she'd be running for her life."

He lifted his head. "Is that so?" A hopeful light took the place of aggravation and then he grinned, his smile match-ing hers. "You'd have a hissy fit, would you?"

"Is that what you're doing?" she asked, her fingers slid-ing down to anchor themselves in the curls that covered his chest.

He thought a moment and then nodded. "I guess I am. I've been half mad at the world ever since Cleary got here. Especially when you and Tilly were giving him the royal treatment, after he'd lied his way in here and played both ends against the middle."

"He was doing as he was told," she said. "I thought he would have explained that to you."

"He did. Didn't make me feel any better."

"And then Micah came courting and you felt left out, didn't you?" Her arms snaked around his neck and her fingers slid into the depths of dark hair. ''In all the fuss that was going on we didn't get a chance to talk about him and Tilly.'' She paused and waited a moment, until his eyes met hers. ''That's my fault, Jay. I should have taken time to tell you about it. Forgive me?''

''Damn, you sure know how to get around me, lady,'' he murmured. ''I'm all set to be mad at you and in a few short words, you take all the wind out of my sails, and set me to thinking about being nice instead of being ornery as the dickens.''

''I was thinking hard thoughts about giving you a bad time,'' she admitted. ''And then I realized I need you too much to waste time arguing.''

''You need me? Honey, you don't know the meaning of the word. I'm horny as hell right now. I've been without your arms around me for too long, and all I had to hold me over was snugglin' behind your back the last couple of nights.''

''You *snuggled* me?'' she asked. ''I thought you slept way over there on your side of the bed.''

''After you went to sleep, I just kinda took advantage,'' he admitted. ''Couldn't stand having all that mattress between us.''

''And what do you call this?'' she asked. ''I'd say you're taking advantage in a big way, Flannery.''

''Big?'' he asked, moving his hips against her.

He was cocky all right. Arrogant as the dickens and cocky, to boot. And in spite of it, she loved him more than she'd ever thought she could love a man. A swell of emotion took her breath as he looked down at her and she saw a tenderness apparent on his face that filled her with joy.

''You know I love you, don't you?'' she asked, inviting his kiss as she touched his face again with her fingertips, holding him in place and lifting her head a bit to press her mouth against his throat. ''I don't give two shakes for any other man in the world, Flannery. You've got me right where you want me.''

''Yeah, I'll go along with that,'' he said, holding his breath as her fingers again slid to his chest, seeking the tiny, firm buttons that hid in the curls. ''Right there, sweetheart,'' he whispered, his breath catching as he spoke the name he was wont to call her.

And then, as if his patience was at an end, he rolled to his back, and with an ease that took her breath, he lifted her to sit astride him. ''The lamp's still lit,'' she said quickly, and I don't have anything on.''

''We can fix that. Lean over and blow it out.'' His grin teased her and she glanced toward the window. It faced the front of the house and the probability of anyone being within seeing distance was next to nothing, but she could not chance it. She leaned toward the small bedside table and in so doing exposed her breast to his close scrutiny.

He was still and silent, waiting for her to extinguish the light, and at the sound of the lamp chimney touching the base, he moved. Long fingers lifted the tender weight as his hand guided her breast closer, and she found herself imprisoned by his mouth, his hands forming her, his teeth and tongue drawing at the sensitive flesh. She tilted her head back, relishing the hot, tugging sensations, each movement firing currents within her. Deep within her body, a small set of muscles twitched in response to the teasing play of lips and teeth, and she groaned beneath her breath.

''Like that, do you?'' he murmured against her damp flesh, and before she could form a reply, he searched in the darkness, nuzzling her, seeking the mate to the puckered crest he had suckled with such skill. She rocked against him, in time with the movement of his mouth, and warmth swept through her as if she had been too close to the fire, making her skin hot and prickly, yet covering her with chill bumps at the same time.

"Jay!" It was a whimper of delight and he lifted her, shifting her to settle again atop his hips, where the hard ridge of his arousal pressed against her open legs. She wiggled against it and he moaned aloud. Lifting, she attempted to capture it inside her body, but it eluded her movements and a soft whispered word escaped her lips.

"You shouldn't be usin' language like that," he muttered, lifting his hips, the better to make himself accessible to her maneuverings.

"I don't usually," she said beneath her breath, aware of his hands plying her breasts, then sliding down her belly, his fingers moving in an intricate dance against the flesh that she'd exposed to his touch. "I only cuss when I'm frustrated," she told him in a harsh whisper.

"Well, never let it be said that I'd let my wife be frustrated," he purred, his fingers working to ease the fullness of his arousal into her narrow channel. "Ahh…" His goal accomplished, he sought the depths of her, and then lifted her a few inches, only to slide her back down his length. "My, that's nice," he said quietly, repeating the movement.

She was beyond words, caught up in the rhythm he set, only able to hold her own with his hands on her hips, moving her as he would. And then she bent forward over him, sobbing his name.

"Jay, I can't do this." She clung, wrapping her arms around him, her fingers scrambling beneath his back to better grip his body. Breathless, she inhaled deeply, shivering from the pounding of her heart, the trembling of her limbs. He turned with her, rolling her again to lie beneath him, and she curled her legs around his. Lifting to his thrust, her hands pressed against his back, and she was wrapped in the heat of his embrace.

It was good. It was more than good, she thought, as sensations of fullness and completion surrounded her. She tingled, her breasts taut and full against his chest. Trembling

ching with the need for his whispers of praise, she clung
o him. And then she felt the song of triumph burst within
er as he called to her, his mouth seeking and finding hers,
pilling the sound of her name over and over against her
ips, then against the strong lines of her throat.

"I love you, Clo." He spoke it aloud, as if he wanted
here to be no doubt of her hearing his declaration. And as
hough he wanted her to be certain of it, he repeated it.

"You're my wife, Clo," he murmured as though he
eeded to lay claim to the woman beneath him. And then
e lifted his head. "Did you hear me?"

She nodded, and her eyes filled with tears of joy. They
whispered the words in unison, as if neither could contain
he syllables of promise that begged to be spoken. As if
heir wedding vows were renewed once more, they mur-
nured their love aloud, and she smiled in the darkness,
olding him close as the sound of their voices blended in
he night.

They rode to town the next day at Micah's command.
Ie'd have been satisfied with only J.T.'s presence, but
hloe would not be deterred from going along. The small
ourtroom was filled to the brim with ranchers who had felt
he sting of losing cattle to the rustlers. In sorting out the
erd, several brands had been found altered, and the cattle
wners had made partial recovery of their losses.

Now they gathered to see justice done, and if they'd
ather have had a quick hanging, they were disappointed.
he men were all sentenced to more years in the territorial
rison at Laramie than they had a chance of surviving. All
ut Gus, who had a shorter sentence imposed and was to
e held in Colorado.

"Should have shot them where they stood," one man said
itterly, after Cleary spoke his piece on the witness stand.

"A few years back, they'd have strung them up instead o hauling them off to Laramie."

"Things have changed," J.T. said to Chloe as they lis tened to the undertones of violence that rippled through th courtroom. The judge banged his gavel on the desk, an frowned at the ranchers.

A representative of the Wyoming Cattle Owner's Asso ciation was present and he gave a glowing report of Cleary' record. "Bottom line is that the gang was broken up an the men responsible will spend long years in prison," th gentleman told the listening men. "There's still some vigi lante justice going on hereabouts, but in this case our rep resentative held to the line. We're satisfied with the result.

"And you?" J.T. asked, bending to whisper agains Chloe's ear. "Are you satisfied with the sentence they gav Gus?"

The man in question had shot a look at Chloe as Clear gave details of Gus's part in Chloe's rescue. And when th shorter term of his sentence was read, he bowed his hea and then looked over to where she sat and nodded.

"He's still a rustler," she said quietly. "But if for n other reason than that he spoke to me about Pete, I'm thank ful to him. I knew he'd go to prison, but I'm glad the judg was lenient with him."

They walked out into the sunlight, J.T. shaking hand with several ranchers he'd never met before, receiving the well wishes as they eyed Chloe and recognized J.T. as he husband. "Always liked old man Biddleton," one said, re moving his hat as he nodded to Chloe. "He'd be glad yo found yourself a good husband, ma'am."

"I'm not sure who found who," Chloe said with a gri at J.T., "but, I'm glad, too."

Cleary walked from the courtroom with the judge an halted as he caught sight of J.T.'s tall form. The two me turned to face each other, and Chloe felt a tingle of appre

ension touch her spine. With a final nod at the judge,
Cleary stepped closer and offered his hand. J.T.'s gaze narrowed as Cleary made the gesture and then he met it with
a barely imperceptible pause.

"I don't expect we'll meet again," the lawman said, "but
I wish you all the best."

J.T.'s free arm reached to circle Chloe's waist and he
tugged her closely to his side. "I've got the best," he said
firmly. "No matter what else happens in my life, I managed
to win the whole kit and caboodle when I married Chloe."

"Can't argue with you there," Cleary said with a smile.
"You don't have a sister, by any chance, do you, ma'am?"
His eyes twinkled as he looked at Chloe, and then he shook
his head. "No, I'm afraid you're one of a kind." He re-
leased J.T.'s hand and shoved his fingers into his pocket.
"I'll be riding out today. It was good knowing you both.
And you, too, Micah," he added glancing aside at the law-
man.

"Sorry you can't stay for the wedding," Micah said. And
then they watched as Cleary mounted his horse and rode
toward the outskirts of town.

Chapter Seventeen

"I'm not much help when it comes to sewing," Chloe told Tilly. "If you had to depend on me to make that wedding dress, you'd be getting married next spring."

"I think you're going to have other fish to fry by then," Tilly told her, lifting her needle toward the light, the better to thread it anew. She tied a knot deftly and bent her head to ply the needle through the seam she sewed.

Chloe watched her, her mind working in rhythm with her hands as she shucked peas into the bowl in her lap. "What fish you talking about?" she asked after a long moment of reflection.

"I thought you'd have figured it out for yourself by now," Tilly told her. "You've been plinzing around here for the past few weeks, girl. And unless I miss my guess, you haven't had your monthly since you got married."

Chloe's hands stilled their movement and she looked out across the yard toward the corral where J.T. leaned against the fence with Hogan, their heads together as they watched Lowery put a horse through his paces. The buyer from Montana was due today, and she noted that J.T. had taken extra care with his appearance, wearing a freshly ironed shirt and seeking out his best pair of trousers from the drawer.

And now Tilly was thrusting a new and disturbing thought into her mind, with her reference to the changes Chloe had only just begun to notice in her body. She looked at Tilly, frowning as she considered her aunt's observation. ''Probably just got my system all in an uproar, getting married and all.'' Her chin lifted. ''Besides I've got other things to think about today, with the buyer coming and us making some money for a change.''

''Yeah, well you'll be needing a few dollars extra in the next little while, the way I see it.'' Tilly spoke with an air of assurance that made Chloe bristle.

''I don't know what you're talking about,'' she said stubbornly.

Tilly placed her sewing in her lap and her gaze was level. ''I think you do, honey. If your mama was still alive, she'd be saying all this to you, but it seems like I'm fated to take her place, don't it?''

''What if…'' Chloe's hands flew to touch her cheeks, and her head spun for a moment as she considered the idea beginning to take shape in her mind. ''I don't know if I'm ready for such a thing to happen,'' she said quietly. ''I don't know how J.T. will feel about it.''

''Go ahead and spit it out,'' Tilly told her. ''Say the word, honey. It's not so hard, once you get your mind used to the idea.'' She leaned closer. ''I think you're gonna have a baby. I can't figure out why it's so hard for you to get it through your head.''

''I don't feel like it,'' Chloe said firmly, looking down at her belly. ''And I sure don't look like it.''

''It's early days yet,'' Tilly said with a laugh. ''Give you a few months and you'll be round as a pumpkin in the patch.''

''How am I going to tend to things then?'' Chloe asked in a whisper.

''Same way women been taking care of things for centuries,'' Tilly said. ''You just get used to it, one day at a time, and before you know it, you've got yourself a baby in the house, and a family to look after.''

''I never planned on having babies. At least I never thought much about it.''

''Well, you'd better be thinking about it now, honey.'' Tilly picked up her sewing and frowned at the stitches she'd made. ''We'll be sewing little gowns and hemming diapers and maybe making a quilt for that old cradle up in the attic.''

Her eyes had a faraway look, Chloe thought, as the words fell from her lips. And then Tilly shook her head. ''I'll never get this dress done, just sittin' here talkin'. You better run in the house and see how that roast is doing in the oven. Unless I miss my guess, we'll be having company for dinner.''

She nodded toward the lane. ''See that cloud of dust up by the town road? I suspect that big-shot buyer from Montana's about to arrive.''

Chloe stood, the bowl of peas forgotten on the floor by her feet, as she saw the figure of a man on horseback take form in the distance. Her gaze flew to where J.T. stood at the corral, and as she watched, he spoke to Hogan and then headed toward the house.

''I think our man's here,'' he said, grinning widely as he climbed the porch steps. His hands circled Chloe's waist and he lifted her easily, bending his head to kiss her with a brief, hard blending of lips.

''You'd better take a last look at those horses, sweetheart. They're about to put a nice chunk of money in the bank for us. And then we can be thinking ahead to the next crop of foals to fill that pasture.''

''And that's not all you better be planning on,'' Tilly said beneath her breath, earning a piercing look from J.T.

''What's that supposed to mean?'' he asked bluntly.

"You'll find out," she said blithely. "Now you better get on out there and parade those horses in front of the fella and earn your salt, son. Your wife and I have a meal to put together."

J.T. lowered Chloe to the porch, and she felt her heart skip a beat as she thought of the words she would speak to him later on tonight, when the house was still and they were alone in their bedroom. He might be ready to think about a pasture full of new foals next spring. But would he be prepared for the idea of a baby in his arms?

J.T. was elated, his feet feeling like they barely touched the ground as he spoke his farewells to Clive Stewart. The rancher represented a group of cattlemen in Montana, and by their authority he'd purchased every horse Lowery had paraded before him. Their coats gleaming in the sunlight, the mixture of three- and four-year-olds had tossed their manes and tails as if they knew they were on display.

"I'll be interested in seeing the results of your breeding program," Stewart said, reaching from his horse to shake J.T.'s hand. "And I'll be sending a wire back home when I get to town. There'll be six men here to pick up the horses within a week. Once they get them to Cheyenne, they can load them on a train there to ship up to Butte."

"We'll have them ready," J.T. told him, and then stuffed his hands in his back pockets as he watched the rancher ride away.

"Happy?" Chloe asked him, stepping down from the porch to take his arm.

"Yeah, does it show?" His grin was wide as he held out the contract for her appraisal. "Signed, sealed and almost delivered. Money in the bank for us, sweetheart."

"Thanks to you," she said, looking up into his smile, even as she wondered how long he would wear it, once she sprang her news in his direction.

"No, I can't take the credit for this batch," he told her "You and Lowery did most of the work, and the horses were here before I arrived. Now, a few years down the road when we put up the first of the paints for sale, I'll be willing to take some of the credit."

"You're the one who set things in motion," she reminded him. "I wouldn't have thought of contacting the Montana people."

"That's what you've got me for," he told her, turning her toward the house. Bending his head closer to her, he tightened his grip on her waist and spoke against her ear "That and a couple of other things."

Her steps faltered and he spoke her name, concern making itself apparent. "Chloe? Is something wrong?" He turned her to face him at the foot of the porch steps. "Are you all right?" His gaze swept her, hesitating only a moment on the fullness of her breasts. And then he grinned "You look all right, like maybe you're puttin' on a little weight."

"I'm not getting fat," she said defiantly.

"That's not what I said. I like the way you look, sweetheart. I sure wasn't being critical." And then he towed her up the steps and into the kitchen where Tilly was wiping the tabletop. "Don't you think Chloe's looking good these days?" he asked Tilly.

"You noticed?" she asked, and then turned to the sink where she wrung out her dishcloth. "Looks like all's right with the world, I'd say." And behind her, Chloe could only smile and bide her time.

"All right, what's the problem?" He'd cuddled her kissed her, been generally as nice and understanding of her mood as she'd let him for almost half an hour, and still the woman hadn't said two words to him. J.T. rolled to his back and drew Chloe to lie with her head on his shoulder. He fingers trailed through the mat of hair on his chest and she inhaled deeply as though something weighed heavily on her mind.

"Jay, what would you think about having a family?"

"A family? Like having babies, you mean?"

Her fingers stilled their movement and she nodded her head. "Yeah, like having babies. One at a time. Starting next spring."

"Next spring?" His heart jolted in his chest as he repeated her words. "Chloe? Are you telling me we're gonna have a baby in the spring?" And then held his breath for her reply.

"Tilly thinks so."

He rolled over, capturing her beneath him. "And what do you think?"

"I don't know," she said, the words a whisper of sound. "I've never had a baby before, never even thought about it. And now, if Tilly's right, I'd better do some hard thinking on the matter."

"A baby." He said the words as if the concept was one he'd never considered. And then repeated them, his voice as reverent as if he were being presented with a gift beyond comprehension.

"A baby?" He held himself above her, scanning her features in the lamplight. "You and me? A baby?" Her eyes were dark, the blue almost absorbed by the darkness of her pupils, and he thought she looked worried. "You want it, don't you?" he asked, suddenly wary of her silence.

"Of course I do," she said quickly. "I just don't know what it'll do to me, as far as working on the ranch and—"

"You'll do whatever you want to, Chloe. Taking care of yourself and the baby will come first, but you can still do whatever seems right to you. Tilly will help. You know she will. And if we need someone to take up the slack, we'll find more help. As long as you're all right, that's all that matters. And having a baby will just be part of us being married and together, only now there'll be three of us.''

He felt a foolish grin curve his lips as he thought about the tiny life within her body. "Can I feel him?" he asked, lifting far enough to peer down at her belly.

"Not yet, silly," she said. "She's barely big enough to make a difference yet, I suspect. But in a few months, Tilly said, I'll look like a pumpkin."

"What do you mean, *she?*" he asked. "We're gonna have a boy, aren't we?"

By the time Micah made all the arrangements and Tilly finished her new dress, the whole town was in on the wedding preparations. Micah was a popular man in Ripsaw Creek, and the small church was full as the couple spoke their vows. A wedding reception was held at the community center where anything of importance took place, and the tables were heavily laden with food from all the ladies who'd joined in to celebrate.

Unwilling to take the spotlight from Tilly and Micah's big day, J.T. and Chloe had determined not to allow the news of their coming parenthood be spoken aloud before hand, but Micah could not resist being the one to spill the beans. He stood with a glass in his hand, the punch generously spiked with a jug held by Hale Winters, and made a toast to the crowd.

"To my bride, and my new family. Especially to Tilly who's made me the happiest man in the world." And then as the onlookers laughed and clapped their approval, he turned to J.T. and Chloe.

"And to these two, who are gonna make me an uncle come next spring." A concerted gasp and a moment of silence followed his words and then bedlam broke out, with the ladies surrounding Chloe, pushing J.T. aside in their hurry to offer words of congratulations.

"Might's well stand back and lift a glass with me," Micah said, handing J.T. a portion of the punch. "You'll be playin' second fiddle to a baby for the next few months, son. You and me both, I'll be willing to bet." His grin was contagious, J.T. decided, as they watched the womenfolk, their voices rising as they gathered around Chloe and Tilly. He'd almost guarantee he was wearing the same silly look.

He reached up to loosen his string tie and accepted the glass of punch. "Here's to the future," he told Micah. And then met Chloe's eyes as she searched him out. His glass lifted in her direction. "To Chloe," he said quietly.

Epilogue

The winter was harsh, in J.T.'s memory the coldest he'd ever endured. And yet there was an edge to it, a challenge he'd never found in life before, and he gloried in the battle against the elements. They fought to keep the stock fed, working in snowstorms and hauling hay to the pastures and breaking the ice on the watering holes where the herd gathered.

The winds howled at night and the bedroom became a place of refuge to the pair who shared the big bed and slept in its center. Whispering their hopes and dreams, they forged new bonds during the night hours, and Chloe blossomed under the tender care of the man she'd married. All was not paradise, for they were too much alike to spend every day in peaceable agreement. But the making up was a delight to her heart, and J.T. was learning to stifle his tendency to give orders.

Snow piled up along the fence lines and the horses in the near pasture huddled beneath the shelter the men had constructed for their protection. The mares were rounding nicely, J.T. said, and excitement rose as the months progressed and it seemed that spring would finally be breaking through. And as far as Chloe was concerned, it could not come soon enough. The babe she carried made her cumbersome, and she yearned for its birth, amazed at her own maternal instincts as she struggled with sewing tiny garments and hemming diapers.

March found them walking in mud, as the ground alternately thawed and froze and then by late April, the foals began to arrive. The first was a surprise, Lowery bursting into the kitchen before breakfast on a sunny morning. "We got us a colt. Prettiest thing you ever saw," he said, excitement glowing from his expressive face.

"Where?" J.T. asked, reaching for his jacket.

"In the pasture," Lowery said. "Found him first thing when I checked out there. He was standin' all spraddle-legged, lookin' underneath his mama for his breakfast."

"Wait for me," Chloe said, rising with difficulty from the table, aware of a nagging backache that had kept her awake much of the night.

J.T. hesitated by the door, and then, as if he didn't have the heart to deny her, snatched her light jacket from the hook and held it ready for her to slide her arms into the sleeves. His fingers fumbled with the buttons, and she watched him, aware that her own would work more rapidly at the task, but willing to let him tend her in this small way.

They stepped down from the porch, and J.T. slowed his steps, offering his arm. "Hold tight, honey," he said. "I don't want you taking a tumble."

They walked through the barn and out the back door, heading for the pasture fence. Just beyond the barrier, a dark mare stood, head to the ground as a gangly colt nursed beneath her belly. White coat glistening in the morning light, the newborn was true to his sire's heritage, with large, dark spots scattered over his slender form.

"How about that?" J.T. said beneath his breath. "He bred true." His tone was reverent as they leaned on the top rail of the fence, and Chloe leaned her head on his shoulder.

"I suspect we'll be busy for the next couple of weeks," he said. "We bred late, but that's all right. They'll do better with the weather a little warmer."

He looked down at her, and his eyes narrowed. "Are you all right? You're lookin' kinda peaked this morning."

"I didn't sleep real well," she admitted and then winced as the pain in her back moved to settle beneath the heavy load of her pregnancy. It throbbed in a slow rhythm, drawing up the rounding of her belly into a hard, pulsing ball, and she drew in a sharp breath. "I think maybe…" Her voice trailed off as the spasm passed, but J.T. would not be deterred.

"Maybe what?" he asked sharply. "Are you starting in with labor pains?"

Her mouth thinned at his query. "How would I know? I've never done this before." She straightened and tugged at his sleeve. "Let's go back to the house. I left my breakfast on the table, and I'm hungry."

He did as she asked, holding her hand in place on his forearm as they walked. "Now listen here, Clo. I'm not riding out today if you're about to have this baby. You need to let me know what's going on."

Her glance in his direction was measuring. "Are you sure you want to be in on it? Tilly says it might get pretty sticky before it's over with." And then she paused in the middle of the yard as another spasm tightened her muscles and drew her belly taut. "You know," she said after a few moments, "I'm thinking you might want to go to town and see if the doctor's handy." And even as she spoke the words, she felt a warm rush of fluid leave her body.

Looking down in dismay, she muttered beneath her breath, and J.T. called out Tilly's name, his voice loud in the early-morning quiet. And then he bent, sliding his arms beneath Chloe's knees and under her shoulders, lifting her in his arms as he headed for the back porch.

Tilly opened the door as they moved up the steps and held the door open for their entry into the warm kitchen. "Gonna have us a baby, are we?" she asked. And watched as Chloe slid her feet to the floor.

"I'm fine now," she said. "Just need to change my clothes."

"What you need to do is get washed up good and put on your nightgown," Tilly told her firmly. "You can parade around the house for a while. Walking's good for bringing on the baby quicker. And you—" she turned to J.T. "—you need to haul buggy to town and get the doctor out here."

It was a relief to have Tilly in charge, Chloe decided as she stripped from her clothing moments later. J.T.'s farewell had been swift, a kiss brushed across her mouth and a cautious hug. She'd warrant he was busy saddling a horse even now. And then her thoughts were taken up with the tension that enveloped her as another pain swept from her back to circle the child within her body.

"I didn't know it would happen this fast," she told Tilly as she donned her nightgown. "Do you think the doctor will be here in time?"

"He'll make it," Tilly assured her. "But I don't think you're gonna mess around all day having this baby. Seems to me like it's in a hurry to arrive."

And so it was. Before dinner was ready, before the sun was directly overhead in the noonday sky, Chloe was deep in the throes of hard labor. And by the time J.T. had about worn himself to a frazzle, alternately pacing the floor and rubbing her back, she cried out for the first time, the pain seizing her almost beyond her endurance.

"Can't you do something?" J.T. roared at the doctor, whose attention was solely on the woman who labored in the big bed.

"She's doing it all by herself," Dr. Whitaker said with a grin in J.T.'s direction. And as Chloe strained with another pain, he leaned closer to her, his voice soft, his words encouraging. His hands worked briefly, and J.T. bent low over his wife, as if he would take the pain from her and make it his own, his whispers almost desperate in her ear.

"Take a look here, Mr. Flannery," Dr. Whitaker said, just moments after Chloe had strained and groaned with the final pain. "You've got yourself a baby boy." Tilly at his side, he tied, then cut the cord that joined mother with child, and the baby sounded his disapproval of the whole process.

J.T. looked up as Chloe laughed aloud, looking weary, but delighted with the doctor's pronouncement. "Well, dog-gone," she said. "Guess we'll have to try again if I'm going to have a girl." Her voice was trembling, but her spirits were high as she reached for the infant. Tilly wrapped a flannel square around the squirming, red body, and his cries filled the air as he was nestled against his mother's breast. "Aren't you a pretty one?" Chloe crooned, lifting her head a bit, the better to peer into the tiny face.

J.T. sat on the side of the bed, lifting one hand to touch the downy head, where dark hair grew in abundance. The pulse beneath his fingertips alerted him to the vulnerability inherent in such a tiny creature, and he felt a surge of emotion such as he'd never experienced in his life. He loved Chloe, deeply and with the fullest measure he felt himself capable of. Yet, for this helpless infant, this fruit of his loins, there bloomed within him a surge of protective, possessive, aching emotion that was almost frightening in its intensity.

"What'll we call him?' he asked her, his voice gruff as he cupped the miniature head with his palm.

"I thought maybe John," she said slowly. "For my father. And if you like, his middle name could be after you…Thomas."

"You're sure you don't mind that it's a boy?" he asked.

She shook her head. "He's beautiful, and he sure looks healthy. What more could I ask?" And then she lifted the baby from her breast, offering him as she would a gift for his approval. "Do you want to hold him?"

"Me?" His recoil was spontaneous, and she laughed aloud.

"You're his father. He needs to get to know you, right off the bat. You'll be spending a lot of time together."

"Come on out to the kitchen, J.T.," Tilly told him. "You can get your first lesson in giving him a bath."

"I'll just watch, I think," J.T. said, cradling his son in his arm as he rose to do as he was bid.

The doctor watched patiently as the tall man walked from the room, the tiny bundle in his arms taking his full attention. "Now let's get you cleaned up, Chloe," he said. "And then you can take a nap. I think you've earned it."

His name was indeed John Thomas. The baptismal certificate stated it in bold, black letters, and J.T. offered it for all to view as friends gathered in the ranch house to celebrate the day. "Another J.T.," Micah announced. "Thought one of you was enough to put up with around here."

"This one will be called John," Chloe said firmly. "One J.T. is all I can handle."

The sun was warm, the early summer day filled with the promise of good things to come, as the male guests trooped out to view the crop of colts and fillies in the pasture. Spotted foals romped in the warmth of the afternoon sun and J.T. proudly accepted the congratulations of neighboring ranchers and friends from town.

And yet, it was good to see the last of the guests leave, he decided later on, when the buggies pulled from the yard, and horses were ridden down the lane. Tilly served a cold meal of leftovers from the big dinner she'd prepared earlier, and before the sky darkened with nightfall, Chloe was weary and ready for their bed.

She nursed the baby one last time, and tucked him into

the cradle J.T. had hauled down from the attic. It was resplendent with the quilt Tilly had fashioned, and as baby John was tucked in, he nuzzled his hand, seeking and finding the thumb he was wont to suckle on.

"Sleepy?" J.T. asked, as Chloe turned to him and rested her head against his chest.

She looked up and her smile was warm. "I could probably manage to hold my eyes open for a little while."

"Long enough to let your husband do some huggin' and kissin'?" J.T. asked. "Will it be all right?"

Chloe nodded. "It's been well over a month. Tilly said I should be all healed up and ready for most anything. I thought maybe tomorrow I'd take a ride around the pasture and give my mare a little exercise."

"I'll get on her first," J.T. said. "Make sure she's not too feisty."

"I think I can manage," Chloe told him sharply. "I haven't lost my touch, just because I'm a mother now."

He bent to her, his mouth seeking hers, taking advantage quickly as she responded to his kiss. J.T. lifted his head and his smile was tender, his body taut with anticipation. "No, you haven't lost your touch, sweetheart. Not one little bit."

In the darkness of the night, he held her close in the middle of the big bed, his hands gentle, his mouth urgent. Quietly, he told her how he'd yearned for her, and as she responded to his touch, he moved to hover over her, bridling his passion as he carefully brought her to shattering release. And then he took her to himself, and in the sanctuary of their marriage bed they realized anew the joyous pleasure of becoming one flesh.

He whispered softly in her ear, and moments later called her name in the throes of passion. She was content, wrapped in his embrace, filled with the assurance of his love.

"I love you," she told him, and then smiled as he bent to bless her with his kiss.

''Thank you, Chloe.''

''For loving you?''

''Yeah, that, too. And for John Thomas. For giving me a family.''

It was not by chance, she decided, that J.T. had come to her. And her prayer wafted upward as she sent thanksgiving toward heaven. And then her eyes closed, her breathing slowed and she slept, aware that she loved and was loved in return.

*   *   *   *   *

Please turn the page for
an exciting preview of
Carolyn Davidson's next Historical,
which will be part of the

WILD WEST BRIDES

collection

Cathy Maxwell and Ruth Langan
will also be writing for this
exciting anthology.

Chapter One

Bender's Mill, Colorado

Jebediah Marshall stood apart from the crowd. Not just in his physical appearance, which was enough to make him stand out in any company, but in actuality this morning. He couldn't bring himself to join the group, just watched the hubbub on the train platform from a distance. Not that he wouldn't soon be involved in the ruckus going on.

He needed a few moments to think, to cogitate on what he had set into motion with his letter. It was too late to change his mind. He was only too aware of that. But marriage was a big step to take, and he was about half an hour from leaping headlong into that state.

The train could be seen and heard. Whistle blowing, smoke puffing from the engine, it approached from the east, vying with the rising sun to make an appearance in the town of Bender's Mill, Colorado. And aboard that train were seventeen women. Women who had come from various cities and towns in the east to make their homes in this harsh land.

And one of those women was Louisa Winifred Applegate Palmer. His bride.

He pulled the paper from his pocket, reading it in the

glow of the rising sun. She was a widow woman, which wa
fine with him. He wouldn't be expected to pamper and cod
dle her, since she would already be well used to marrie
life. "Efficient in the home," the letter said. Hard to sa
what that meant. So long as she could put a meal on th
table and keep his house and clothes clean, he wouldn'
quibble.

The advertisement had been simple. "Women available."
It didn't get any more basic than that. A woman was avail
able, and he needed a wife.

The folded paper slid into his pocket and he straightene
from his stance against the side of the train station. The me
on the platform huddled beside the tracks, peering at th
slowing engine, and he sauntered in their direction, satisfie
with lingering on the edge of the crowd. Seventeen wer
expected, according to the wire sent by the agent handlin
the transaction. The original number was twenty, but thre
of them had changed their minds at the last moment.

Jeb felt a twinge of apprehension at that thought, bu
shook it off. Just her name, *Louisa Winifred Applegate Pa.
mer* was enough to project an aura of dependability. Hi
bride would be among the number soon to depart the trai
He'd spent long moments trying to visualize her, havin
only the briefest of descriptions offered in the letter. Dar
hair, blue eyes, healthy constitution and of an age to hav
been married.

Now, as the train came to a halt, spewing cinders fro
beneath its wheels, he watched the conductor make an ex
from the passenger car, his step stool in hand. Behind hin
a golden-haired creature peered past the man's considerabl
bulk and Jeb could not help but wish his bride had the pink
and-white coloring of the first woman to make an appea
ance. She offered her hand to the jowly conductor an
moved down the platform as if she adhered to a script.

And so it seemed she had, for the rest of the wome

followed her lead, lining up three feet from the side of the train, their small valises and portmanteaus in hand. From the baggage car, down the platform twenty feet or so, a veritable stream of luggage spewed onto the platform, two men tossing trunks and suitcases to the waiting stationmaster. He stacked them haphazardly, already sweating profusely, his face glowing, grumbling loudly at the work inherent with so many passengers departing the train at one time.

Jeb counted, an almost unconscious activity, as the women assembled. An assortment of females, ranging from small to large, several of them downright plump, he noticed with a grin. They wore decent clothing, hats perched atop hair in various styles, curled, braided or in buns. Some were comely, easy on the eyes. Others were homely, but to the men who waited, that was a small matter.

They were *women*. Here for a purpose. And the men hovered in a semicircle in front of them, like so many turkey buzzards closing in on their prey.

Sixteen. He'd counted sixteen, and the wire from the marriage agent had promised one more than that. The ladies themselves checked their number, then turned as one to the steps where the conductor handed down the last of their group. Dark hair, Jeb noted. Somewhat on the rotund side, but with a pleasing face to balance out that fact. She stepped on the stool, then down to the platform, and a small murmur swept the waiting crowd of men. A hushed whisper met her appearance as a heavy shoe touched the stool, its sole built up three inches higher than its mate.

The woman was a cripple, and Jeb felt a moment's sympathy for the man who had spoken for this creature. Not for her the hard life to be expected on a farm. She would require a bit of pampering, he'd warrant. No wonder she was somewhat on the plump side. Probably didn't get much chance to work it off, with a handicap that would prevent her get ting around easily.

The women glanced at each other, and as if it were pre arranged, they lifted pieces of paperboard from inside thei outer clothing, the carefully printed signs appearing lik magic from cloaks and coats to be displayed in front of thei bodies. Sue Ellen McPherson read the nearest one, she c the golden hair and pert features. The next was Isobel Jack son, and beyond her the letters blurred as men moved for ward, reaching nicely for their brides, their eagerness almos overcoming their gentlemanly behavior.

Voices rose as couples formed, and Jeb circled the crowd looking over several heads in search of the name he sough Only three women remained unclaimed, separated by sev eral feet, as their companions were towed away by the me who had paid their fare. A cluster of buggies and wagor awaited, and young boys who'd gathered early to view th happenings this morning were pressed into service to hel with baggage.

It was a hubbub of movement and Jeb felt his heart be heavily as he waited for the crowd before him to part. Lik the movement of the Red Sea at Moses' command, it flowe to either side and he was faced with his future.

Hands trembling, she stood before him. Even from th distance of four yards he noted the wobbling of her pape board sign. The sign that read Louisa Winifred Applega Palmer. There was no mistake. Not only was she the last be claimed, she was his bride. Dark hair, blue eyes th possessed a calm detachment, no matter the trembling long fingers against the identifying sign she held.

And on her feet were black, sturdy shoes, one lookir normal to his eyes, the other proclaiming her problem, three-inch sole allowing her to walk in a manner that mig be considered normal. Whatever that word meant. And if that were not enough, on closer inspection he could n help but note she was more than plump, her outer clothing obviously covering a figure that promised to take its full share of the wagon seat.

Her face was narrow, her nose straight, her eyes wide-set, and her hands were slender. Yet, she was certainly a fleshy woman. And unless he missed his guess, the other men were all more than thankful that they had not drawn the short straw. He stepped forward and met blue eyes that were shiny. Surely not with tears, he hoped. She was presentable enough, but he could not abide a woman crying.

And the fact remained that she was not equipped to run a house and do all the chores expected of a farm woman. Still, he'd made a bargain, and he'd stick to it.

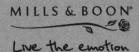

MILLS & BOON

PASSIONATE
PROTECTORS

Lori Foster
Donna Kauffman
Jill Shalvis

Three brand-new novellas
– packed full of danger and desire!

On sale 2nd April 2004

*Available at most branches of WHSmith, Tesco, Martins, Borders,
Eason, Sainsbury's and all good paperback bookshops.*